Spider & Turtle

Also by Adam Thaxton
Ten Ghost

Spider & Turtle

Adam Thaxton

Opabinia Press
Florida

PUBLISHED BY OPABINIA PRESS
218 Williams Road, Winter Springs, FL 32708

Cover design, cover art, and illustrations: Adam Thaxton
Cover stamps: dusteramaranth.deviantart.com

Opabinia Press 2017

Printed and bound in the United States.

Typeset in Bookman Old Style

ISBN 978-0-9832250-2-7

CONTENTS

Spider & Turtle

Spider & the Sun

A long time ago, everything was dark. There was no light, and everybody had to blunder around and eat raw food, and they constantly wondered how anything was even made in the first place. A dark world has nothing and no one really living a good sort of life in it, and a lot of ways to fall and hurt oneself, so it was very much like being inside a hungry cave all the time. Eventually, everybody got tired of this and held a big sing to talk about how they might be able to see things, though getting everyone together was a big task on its own, needing Firefly and Foxfire Mushroom to go around and collect folks.

Once everyone was together, they discussed what to do. Cicada said that he had seen a bright light to the east, and suggested bringing it back to everybody else, so as to take care of the problem. Spider raised one of her arms and offered to go and see what the light was before trying to get it. Brumtumbler said he could go and hide the light in his big feathery tail. Everyone agreed that because he had a big feathery tail, he should go and steal the light.

Brumtumbler ran off to the east and came upon a giant golden city covered with little fires. He carefully stole a little bit of the bright fires and hid them in his tail. This was a mistake, for the fire immediately caught his tail feathers on fire and burned them right off. Then a man came out of the big pyramid in the middle, claiming to be the ruler of the city, and he shouted at Brumtumbler and chased him all the way back into the darkness. Brumtumbler shouted and screamed and waved his little naked tail. When he finally settled back down, he climbed up in a tree and wouldn't

9

come back down.

Again Spider raised her spindly limb to ask if she could go. Before she could finish, Kuhdjoojoo bird called out that he would go, and carry back the light in his beak, so that they could all see it from the air. He went down there and saw the city, all beautiful and resplendent, and filled with so much light and heat the land was baked. He took a stick and caught up some of the fire, but very quickly discovered that his crown of fur was very flammable, and he burned it all off.

Annoyed, Rootscraper stood up and said that she would try next, and sauntered off to the city. Of course, by this point, the people of the city and their king had gotten wise to the little thieves, even though they were starving because of all the scorched land. They made the city fly up into the air, and Rootscraper kept stretching and stretching her neck to reach them, but could not. Sullen, she gave up and trundled back home, watching the city come back down and land again just to mock her.

Hearing this, Spider slipped quietly off into the darkness. Spider went up to the golden city and called out to the man inside. He came out, and his arms and head were made of such bright plumes she could barely see, and he was clearly the source of the fires. She explained to him about the darkness that existed to the west, and he laughed and said that nothing could grew where he lived, because they had nothing but light and fire, which has the sort of tendency to burn everything away. She listened to his story and laughed herself, as was customary, asking if the man would like to take care of both problems at once; he said that if she could do so, he would marry her immediately.

Nodding, Spider quickly spun a great web and crawled up into the sky, shouting back down at the man that he'd have to catch her first. The man went back into his city and made it rise off after her; he was going to catch her very quickly, and she realized this was because her back glistened in the darkness, so she spread millions of dewdrops across her web so that she would become lost in the tiny points of light. They chased each other all across the sky for many years this way, though eventually, Spider found herself caught, busy spinning another section of web. When the man asked why she had run away, and she pointed to the earth, which now sprouted with all manner of plants, and all the animals could be seen clearly by the light of the new day.

He wondered at all this, and she explained that he would

have to keep flying through the sky as if searching for her, and in that way, food could be grown in the earth and the land wouldn't burn up. He agreed, but only if she honored their marriage, which she did, and they had eight beautiful children, who, to this day, crawl about on the web that holds up the stars, checking it for torn bits. If you look up carefully, you may just see them, still spinning.

Ikasa Spider

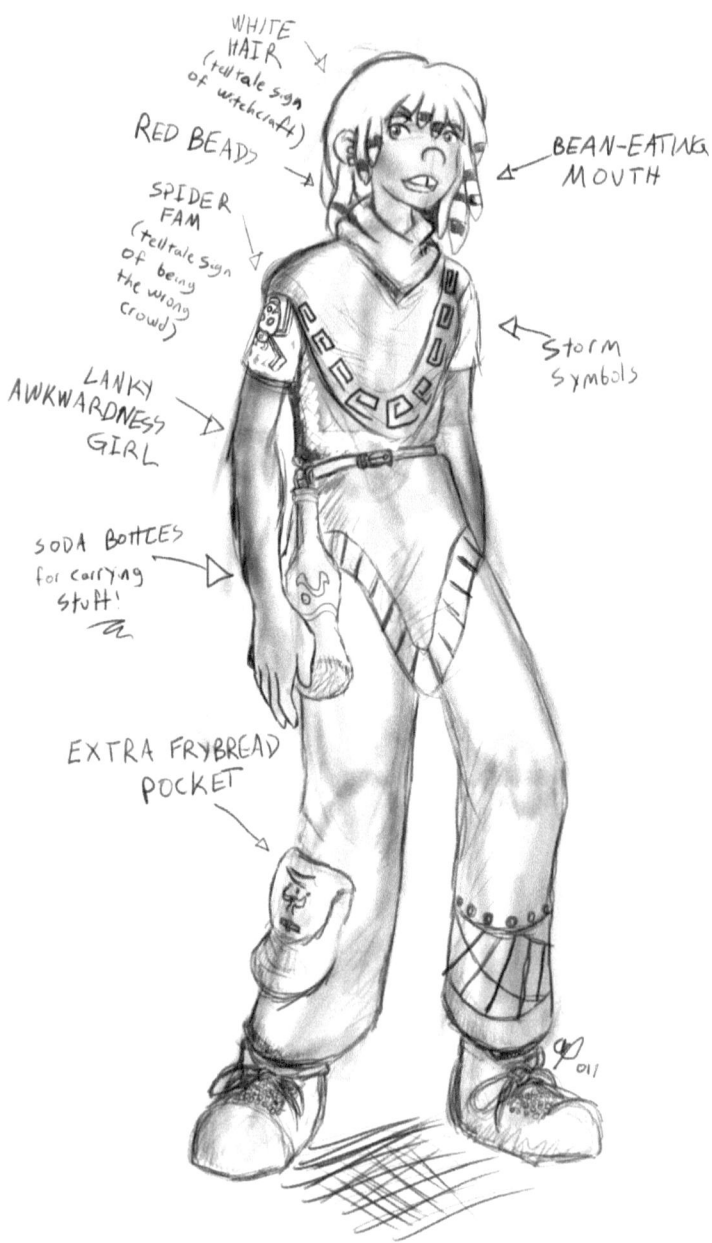

Chapter 1

The Drive

Ikasa Spider lay back in the remains of her pop's blessing store and listened to the cicadas cry out a mocking dirge. The city oaks cast veils of moss to the wind. The late afternoon sun bore down onto the concrete, and turned the long necks and broad carcasses of backhoes into stoves. She watched a pair of storks fly by overhead, their gurgles echoing down into the street. Their leather-winged bodies twisted into snakelike forms through her end of the soda bottle, right up before they disappeared at the edge of her vision. She felt the last bits of dried hibiscus flavor turn bitter on her lips as the water in them was washed away by Sun's caresses. She fought for a few more drops.

Twisted lumps of metal, piles of multicolored sand, and exposed piping grew along the street now like mildew over a gutted carcass. She rose up with a heavy stagger on gigantic feet to chicken-skinny legs, stooping like a vulture in her oversized smock. She wished the store was fixed up again, with all new freezers and fresh, sweet-smelling paint around the wonder-working circles. She recalled behind closed eyes the cozy stairs that went right up to the snug, warm rooms of the house on top. She thought back to cool nights spent at the window of the tiny room she shared with her brothers that gazed up at three or so persistent stars that fought the city's light like pinholes punched in the drywall.

She brushed off her jacket smock, the dark one with the long golden sleeves that she sewed together because she liked being wrapped in a sheet. She hid the buttons under a flap on the left side and stitched the Spider family patch on the right shoulder, the tight white flecks that dominated the shoulders ran in splotches down to her wrists. She had her jeans and moccashoes, the beaded sneakers that her little brother would get when she outgrew them. Her hair grew long and white for a girl her age, right down the middle of her back like a boy's hair, and wrapped in little red beads pinching off little finger lengths. She raised her arms and planted her feet hard into the dirt, asserting herself until her hands went cold and her clay-colored knuckles wore out.

Nothing happened. Not even recalling the house and store had brought either of them back, and she assumed the Princess of Trash must have come and taken what remained to her court. The mana weaving it down among the spirits of the dead and misbegotten tools and materials, taken away from her family, never to be a part of theirs in the eyes of others again. The truth, as she saw it, was that the family wouldn't be moving if that wasn't true. She decided that's why the magic wouldn't work. She sighed and kicked over a board, revealing enraged and rusted nails. It was a tantrum ritual. She offered up her tears and shouts to whatever spirits would listen as she broke old supports. The black and grey towers of the city, cloaks about them dancing with white and yellow paint, leaned in with curiosity.

"I thought they chased all the spiders out when they tore down that old cobweb!" Jeremy Potter Wasp yelled from the other side of the chain link fence. "Quick, squish it! Crying like a squonk that's been caught."

Leveling her gaze at him, she locked onto his dark hair and loose red and white striped shirt. He had his family patch on his shoulder, all skittering and greyish-brown. She sneered and swept a heavy sleeve in his direction.

"Shut up, Jerry, you're a squonk!" she said, brandishing the empty bottle over her head.

"You know what this fence is for, right?" he laughed. Jerry crawled under the metal fingers, wiping his pants free of dirt. "It's to keep people like you out. What're you doing here, anyway? I thought you guys were leaving today."

She pointed at him and hissed.

"I don't got to leave until I want to," she whined, holding out the empty bottle. She held one thumb rested on top of the lip like

14

she was readying a hose as it threatened to escape her grasp. "Besides, I thought maybe I could at least find my *Sunhawk Rocket Brigades* books if I came by."

Settling down on the curb, she tapped the bottle on the ground.

"But it's all gone! My fucking stupid shit of a pop didn't tell me about the whole house getting torn down!" she said, throwing the bottle as hard as she could. It shattered. Cold droplets brushed her cheeks.

Jeremy dropped down next to her and leaned back into the remains of the wall.

"They didn't tell me, either. My folks said you just had to get out. I thought you took all your stuff out when you went to the motel two days ago?" he asked.

She felt the blood rise into her cheeks.

"You writing a fucking book?" she said, but didn't let the moment of anger last very long. She kicked the dust instead. "Momma Spider told me in no uncertain terms to leave my fucking funny books behind. I wasn't gonna be no nerd and I wasn't gonna act like no boy on her watch, no, it's all managing my brothers' finances and wearing dresses on the sing-floors I got to look forward to. I was hoping I could at least sneak some of them out. Pop ain't no better, really. Both're stubborn sacks of piss. Not unhappy about taking money, but they don't want to give out no Spider mana to nobody."

"Nah, the construction crews came and looted everything," he replied while sweeping his hand over the block. "Not just your place, either. They tore up all three joints. They were like maggots on shit."

She popped him in the shoulder.

"Fine, funny books aren't shit, but still," he said, giving up his hands. "It stands."

"Them workers took my mana, Jimmy."

She buried her cheeks in her palms and felt her skin turn hot, her fingers shaking, and her eyes turning to mush. She wanted to go back to Carson next year too, even though middle school was over, and dreaded the prospect of a new school and new stories to learn all over again. She was irritated to when Pop had mentioned the store ran out of money just after she finished middle school. She felt worse for her older brother, Eddie, he'd have more to purge from his memory than she ever would. That was the part that really got her, anyway.

"It's not just the funny books, you know?" she said, jumping up and raising her arms. "I thought maybe I could, I don't know, I thought if the building was still here I could call it up and beg it not to go away. Maybe I could get to live here just four more years, you know? I could be out of high school and then the store could run out. That way I could stay here with you and Frog and we could go to high school and graduate together."

She slumped.

"But that's it," she said, rubbing her face. "That's the end of it, right?"

"Yeah, well. That's what Spiders do, don't they?" he said. "Run from the sun? That's why they're always skittering away from the light, right? So the sun doesn't find them?"

Sniffing, she cleaned herself a bit and laughed.

"Eh, I guess so," she answered with a flat tone.

"Anyway, speaking of Poppa Spider," Jimmy said. "He sent me to find you. He's trying to get the last bit of shit tied up and didn't want to run off trying to chase you down."

"That's how he always is," she grumbled. "He needs a Frog's lesson more than I do about sending people to do his dirty work. Don't do nothing you'd be better served doing yourself."

Knocking a pebble around and crouching down into the dust, she found the edges of the shop sign, and lifted it up with a grunt. It was metal and heavy, and she guessed it had been knocked down when the building was plowed under.

"Where is that fucker, anyway?" she asked.

"Frog? He's doing band stuff. Missed you at school today. What's that?" Jimmy said, pointing.

She wiped off the outward side and turned the lettering so he could see it. "Wonder Worker Services: $5." The words were stenciled onto the side with military white spray paint letters, over the top of a scavenged street sign painted dark yellow. She picked it up, despite the awkward square size of it, and shoved it under her arm.

"Pop made it," she answered. "For the shop. Fifty comic books for curses cast, rain called, spirits summoned, and thunderbolts thrown."

"Wow, he made that sign all by himself?" he asked.

"Fuck no," she said with a giggle. "He made my brother and me do it."

"There we go!" he shouted, lacing his fingers behind his head. "Ikasa the Spider's back!"

She swung the sign at him mockingly, as he dodged away and laughed. He dashed up to the north end of the block and unlocked the gate of the demolition site for her. Ikasa took a final inventory of the torn-up road, the shops knocked over and dried out like shriveled cicada skins, and tried to overlay what it all had looked like before the bulldozers, and found nothing any more. The mana she thought she felt earlier had all either trickled away down storm drained or was hiding in the sign she carried. The end and rubble was all she could see. She felt her cheeks starting to burn once again as her eyes went bleary. She huffed and stomped off down the sidewalk.

"Man, you're all depressed again," Potter Wasp said with an air of false annoyance.

The other blocks in Talequah district weren't very well off either. As the city grew, it had burst outward from downtown like spattered jelly, and the home businesses lost out to larger and richer stores. Other districts had tall and gray buildings covered in concrete and glass, with sharp grotesques carved like storks or hornheads and figures of people cast in bronze holding up the sky. Talequah had seemed almost rural in comparison, located on the other side of the lifted highway among scattered trees like mold on bread.

Talequah waited southeast of the 500-story structures that dominated the downtown area, a brazen hillock that cast shadows like a sundial across the urban landscape, choked by the high income districts. Her home used to be far enough out to get sunlight for the full day, where scattered oaks draped in long haired-moss could grow. Still, they were rare, and used as aesthetic cream on slowly drowning factories and shops, long arcades covered with tarps, and stores that packed up at the end of the day.

To Ikasa, tent shopping had seen its time, as had independent general stores and wonder-workers. They all worked for some bigger family or company now, or else they died, and her father's refusal to sell the business had resulted in its utter collapse. There were still a few places in the dead hallways of the market buildings. A diner that was only open for breakfast, a health food store that belonged to some large chain that had crept in, and an after-market appliance dealer sat as the remnants amid makeshift stalls built into abandoned stores.

She dug through a few book boxes in the stalls when they passed them. Ikasa couldn't come up with anything interesting. They were all mostly knock-off toys, hand-bound empty journals, and silk flowers. When they emerged from the redevelopment area, the sky to the east had already turned dark purple and the west was deep red and orange, cut through with streaks of golden clouds like dry waves of maize. Letting the air out of her lungs, she made her way to the motel where her mom's dim red station wagon waited. The front passenger door was a faded primer and the car was missing a rear bumper. The swollen lump sat laden with the family in a depressed crumple, all personal clothes and blankets, with only a few pots and talisman parts from the store.

Seeing her pop with the last few bags, trying to find a place for them in the back seat, she jogged up and held the sign up over her head. He ran his hands over his dark hair, adjusted his glasses, and sighed when Ikasa started lashing the sign to a spot in the rear bags.

"What are you doing?" he asked, dry and tired. She pulled the ropes around the edges so that it stood up a bit proudly, if rickety, on the roof by the passenger side.

"Being a Spider," she said. "We're Spiders, right? You're not allowed to stop this."

He laughed and patted her shoulder.

"Thanks," he said.

"Everyone ready?" Janet, her mother, shouted, kicking open the door to the motel room with a final pack over her shoulder. She nodded to Ikasa. "Good to see you, sweetie. Glad you decided not to walk over the wasteland. And Jeremy."

"Hello, ma'am," Potter Wasp said, saluting with half his effort.

"Ikasa, in the car now," Janet said.

Nodding, Ikasa climbed into the open door and saw her two brothers, Eddie the older one, and Butch the twerp, both patient, their objections worn out. They were squashed between bags, and her mom threw another one in, telling her to hold it while they drove. She leaned against the door and huffed out one side of her mouth. Potter Wasp knocked on the window, and she rolled it down.

"Here," he said, holding up one of Frog's reeds and one of the switches from his home computator, a signal dial adjuster. She took them. He dug in his jacket for a small stack of comics and tossed them at her, as well.

"What's this?" she asked, flipping through issues of *Amazing Wonder Fantasies* and *Daring Rocket Tales*.

"Some of our mana. For your bag," he answered. "And the books you lent me last week."

She pulled two of the patches off her smock jacket - angular, boxy spirals that represented clouds in the sky, and passed them out the window. Her pop gave her a long glare, but said nothing and settled for climbing into the passenger seat while her mom started up the car. She knew what her pop wanted to say, and so just gave him a petulant glare of her own while stuffing the reed and switch into the leather bag she kept around her neck beneath her jacket. Watching until she couldn't see her friend anymore, Ikasa settled down on the window and got as many tears out as she could until they passed through the progressively smaller walls and even the city faded into the forest night.

The signs of the dead littered the roadway. The abandoned houses and farms far outside of the big city scuffled quietly behind street lamps that had long since burned out on the lonely highway. As the roads stretched farther from civilization, the cracks in the highway became unmanageable at any great speed. The car crawled among them, shuddering when they crossed over into dirt here and there. They drove for two days. Ikasa read her comics all over again with a flashlight as many times as she could until she was forced to give them up to her little brother.

After that, she ended up with her bag in-hand, and then rubbed the leather and bead surface, looking over the spider symbol. There were two sets of limbs up, two sets down and she remembered the package it came in from her grandmother, which had a few letters and three dollars. She clutched the bag in her palm and curled her fingers to feel the collection inside. She felt the meaning turn her arm to sleep, erupting into a cold prickle. The two new items were easy to pick out, bad high school oboe practice and scrabbling notes down in a code switch book. She held the bag up to her face and drifted on a haze of intention that assaulted her face with a numbing burn.

There was a great void with it, like the space amid the bowl of the night sky, and she caught her memories as glittering points of light among the material of the heavens. A fossil seashell from a bad birthday found her crying under a tree while everyone else was off at the playground. The tab from the first can of soda she'd ever had told her about her uncle's visit when she was six, beach glass from her visit to her aunt, and the little plastic bobber from her first trip fishing. There were other things, too, an ancestor's armor bead, the fish bone tattoo needle that first inked her shoulder, and a bit of her white hair from her first haircut. She'd tied it off with some brumtumbler head feathers, brown and black, and kept it on a leather thong that she stole from one of mom's liquor bags. She remained motionless, holding her mana like an ice pack to her forehead, watching the forests and swamps go by until she could no longer really stay awake.

She was the first the sun reached when it took a testing peek over the mountains to the east; she squinted back to consciousness and saw that Pop had taken over driving at some point and Mom was asleep in the passenger side. The other two were out as well. Her little brother was pitched forward in the seat with his arms hanging from the seatbelt as he breathed. She watched trees whip along outside, cypress trapped in green nets of wild grapes just on the other side of the chain link fences by the road.

There were far fewer cracks in the highway, and - along with a viable radio station belting out weather reports between sock hop - a lack of sandy pits and rain-gouged ribbing in the road gave rise to the idea their car was approaching civilization. She was briefly sorry that she hadn't been awake to see the lonely jungle. She wondered if those things meant they were getting close to town, or if it was just someplace where the government actually threw money at the highway. Pop adjusted the rear view mirror over the dash and glanced back in her direction.

"When you were born," her father said. "Your great-grandma on my side, Maize, was the first to see you. You had a full head of white hair then, and she claimed you were a witch and that we should drown you in the river. Your grandma on your mom's side told her that we don't do that anymore, and in a Spider family, a witch wasn't a bad thing at all. We named you Ikasa, for the Xiuteotl daughter of the sun who comes back to wander around the earth during the winter."

He adjusted his own glasses before shifting gears.

"She's supposed to be quiet and respectful," he said, laughing. "Man, did we botch the shit out of that one. Not sorry."

She snickered a bit and smiled, turning her mana over in her hands while listening to the soft trumpet on the radio and the wind outside. The shadow of a sign raced past the car.

"Oh, hey!" he shouted, putting all his attention back to the road. "Bridge on the 47, coming up!"

Her world turned brilliant. The foliage took a quick break and showed off thick limestone pillars rising out of the shining turquoise river below, allowing the road to proudly bear the signs of human hands upon the world. At least until they dove back down into the forest shadow, racing by dappled ferns and catching momentary glimpses of railroad tracks. Hoppers ran in a small pack out there, wild ones mixed with feral domestic breeds, feathers dingy and covered in dirt, their long tails slender and bobbing stiff while they ran. She suddenly felt vulnerable, despite their distance, and cranked up the window.

The town began with abruptness; she could see no buildings greater than a single story from the road, and if they existed, they were obscured behind the others. The scattered trees that made up thin lines blocked her view from the back seat. A sign by the first stop light welcomed them to Shimookooah. She lapsed into a soft fugue as the car rolled through unfamiliar plaster and brick boxes out into another forest, through another, even smaller town, Fort Hammock, to the northwest, where another blue river passed under the road. Her father turned south, the bridge bereft of the train tracks.

They pulled up to a house set in a sandy clearing, a few trailers lashed together with a makeshift second story and a smattering of sheds, chicken wire, and logs piled far from the mailbox, hidden behind a line of oaks, pine trees, and vines. The second floor was just part of a cabin with holes cut in the sides for windows. The whole thing had been painted a bottle blue punctuated with bright, reflective aluminum. She couldn't shake the feeling that Grandma's web hadn't been built to house five other spiders, though it looked like a mansion of natural wood supports. Pop stopped the car and got out, stretching, and Ikasa took her comics back from Butch. She stuffed them into her jacket before climbing out of the car.

"I'm going to wake everyone up," he said to her. "Go get Gramma Spider; tell her we're here."

She nodded and began a slow march up to the front door. Still waking up, she felt sweaty from the night and her hair felt stringy; the clay she put in it yesterday had clumped up and dried into crumbles. It occurred to her that she hadn't seen Gramma Spider since she was very young and didn't know what to expect at all. She'd vaguely recalled having her puffy Tsiwegi cheeks made fun of, and her mom yelled at for marrying a northerner, and she stopped at the door. Ikasa held her hand in a fist, knuckles touching the wood.

She drew her hand back. The morning sun put another notch in the sky. She felt the heat rising not just in her chest and cheeks. The cicadas kicked into gear and tore the forest in half. She laughed, listening to their familiar cry, and knocked three times. Just like every good Spider.

Chapter 2

Settling In

There is a very old joke that goes around the Ootsooduh land.

A long time ago, the swamps and everything used to belong to the Nakoodah, and there's a story that says it wasn't ever a swamp. Anyway, they had this thing where they would show themselves to travelers. To see if the wanderer had anything harmful in him, they'd say "Chuh-hee-chuck, give me a present!" We still do. Most of the time this is a small amount of liquor, bead, spirit money, or other small gift, just so long as the traveler laughed and gave out something. However, in the places like that land, near the Moon's Road, there is such a thing as "southern hospitality." Gifts may be as strong there as dinner with the family, old clothes, or a stay overnight in the home.

Now, it so goes that big old Deathwalker, angry as he was about losing his land when the Tsiwegi people were formed (that's a whole other story entirely, mind), saw Thunder walking about in the forest with his cane and suit on, Deathwalker went and hid behind a stump way ahead of him. When he saw old man Thunder come around the bend, jumped out and shouted "Chuh-hee-chuck, give me a present!" Thunder, not to be outdone, calmly said "you can have the whole southwest, with all the swamps all the way up to the mountains!" and carried on his happy way, singing and stepping high, singing, "You keep my storms coming and we gots a deal!"

Anyway, that's why there's so many poisonous plants and animals over there and why Ootsooduh land gets lashed with so

*many storms coming in from the western sea. Deathwalker has his
way with the whole place.*

The door opened to the smell of fish and burning palmetto
hearts. Gramma Spider wore an angry glare and a yellow pull-
over shirt. She had a mess of necklaces and bracelets, and her
hair hung loose and stringy. Her skull had grown eminently
visible in age. Her skin came wrapped so tight, sun-whipped, and
dark as the earth that she gave the impression of a sick cocoon.
She pressed arms like willow charcoal into the door frame as
though a stiff breeze might send her tumbling into the clouds as a
spray of hateful dust. Grimacing at Ikasa, the old woman looked
past her to the car with narrow, clouded eyes.

"Ain't this fucking backwards?" Ikasa's grandmother said,
lighting a cigarette with the cherry of her previous one. "Ain't I
supposed to run out of money and come live with your ass?"

Ikasa waved with a small, exasperated huff.

"Hey, Gramma," she said.

Gramma walked by her with a lazy gait all the way down to
the car to watch Daniel and Janet unload. She lavished a pat on
Butch's smiling head and yelled something incomprehensible at
Eddie in Xiuteotl before slinging a few bags over her own shoulder
and stomping back up the concrete stairs leading into the trailer.

"I suppose you want to see your fucking room," the old
woman said, walking up the stairs.

The gutted innards of the trailer had long ago been replaced
with wooden floors and hand-made support beams turned black
with age and smoke. Gramma took Ikasa up the new,
unblemished stairs that thumped and creaked with every footfall
like straining bone into a hallway lined with feather cloaks and
winter solstice lights. She opened a door to a bare room with a
mattress slumped sadly in the corner and a pair of windows that
looked out over the backyard into an empty, overgrown chicken
coop. Mashed blue carpet, faded and stained despite how new it
was, ruled over the floor. The walls kept a slightly stained, gray
look to them, with faded green flower-print wallpaper. The whole
thing smelled of musty acrylic.

"I get my own room?" Ikasa smiled.

Gramma nodded and dropped the bag on the floor. Having to
share a room with her brothers her entire life, Ikasa couldn't get
over the idea of her own room. To her, it seemed as though it were

an impossibly huge vaulted cavern that trailed off into eternal corners rife with the bodies of dead insects like a museum collection. She rocked her feet on the carpet and stifled a smile, wondering if there was a lock on the door to keep her brothers out.

"I know you'll complain," the old woman shouted as she headed back down the stairs. "And girls don't carry things, anyway, so you don't got to lift no fucking finger to help out your family. Just sit tight."

Ikasa frowned at and felt a need to do something. The early day had laid out a hot blanket, creating a thickness in the air, so she took off her jacket and jogged back to the car. The room could wait for now, all gray and barren, and even unpacked, she wouldn't have anything to stock it with other than piles of clothes. She skittered out among her family and did her best carrying lighter things. Tiring out quickly from the heat, she ended up raiding Gramma's icebox for a bottle of mango soda. Her icebox now, she thought, pressing cold glass against her cheek and stepping out into the side yard.

She took a long moment to smile at the joyfully dangerous scrap hidden in the tall grass before rocking to get a look around the tree trunks that clustered in the hammock, coming across a dip in the forest at the far edge of her vision. She remembered something from a year ago about springs and a river out there. She blinked, let her jaw drop, and dashed around to the front of the house.

"The balcony supports are all driftwood," Gramma said to Mom, pointing up to the second floor. "Took most of this shit from the river and Black Ant's junkyard. All got thrown up between me and the Armadillo, the neighbor cross the way, when I heard you was coming. My husband is good looking, but you give him a hammer and all he'll do is crack acorns."

"Woda! Gramma! I'm gonna look for the river!" Ikasa shouted, and started to jog off.

"You watch your fucking head!" Gramma yelled back. "There's deathwalkers out there. Centipedes, hodags, squonks, alligators. Poison-breath snakes that steal dreams. This ain't like Makatuweh, it's not exactly the heart of civilization."

Ikasa stopped in mid-jog and pumped her legs, suddenly a bit worried, even as a heavy cloud passed over the sky, not sure if the old woman was serious or not. She decided on the latter and kept going.

"Not this close to town!" she laughed over her shoulder.

"Ain't just critters! Storms come fast out here!" the old woman cried out. Her voice was nearly drowned out by the palmettos.

Leaves and thick brown vines went by, and Ikasa scrabbled over limestone jutting out from the forest floor like boiling waves. The river came up all at once, a long gouge in the earth carved out from the sand and stone with a mess of jagged pillars all along it. The water was clear, and gentle green weeds floated freely like hair in the very deepest parts of the river, stocked with bream. Down on the bottom, amid the mud and grazing on the plants below crawled some oversized salamander with a wide, boomerang-shaped head. She halfway wanted to jump into the deeps after it, but resisted and instead shimmied down the bank into the shallows, feeling the cold water fill up her bead-work sneakers, and she stomped along with the flow.

Ikasa brimmed with furious anticipation, forgetting the stress of moving for a time and listening to the soft chatter of the breeze amid the hammock coupled with the satisfying metallic ring of the creek. Bird tracks and the long, scraped furrows that storks left behind littered the mud on the banks. Clouds of midges hung in the open, bombed by wasps seeking little packets of clay to fill their nests. She smiled at the cloudy sky.

Around the bend, she ran into other children: a boy and a girl about her age and a smaller boy, probably six or seven. Their skin the deep red of country folk. The creek remained shallow, and a broad spit of limestone and gravel made a good spot to congregate. The youngest, dressed in blue with a black and white headband that trained down past his waist, was crouched and watching minnows trapped in a hole far from the river flow while the girl, in deep reddish-browns, waded about in waist-deep water. The other boy wore a button-up shirt and dungarees, with bare feet. Ikasa caught glimpses of their family knives in sheaths before she realized she hadn't brought her own. The older boy with the bird patch had a pair of pants over his shoulder, probably the girl's. Ikasa froze, an animal in headlights, before taking note of the patches on their shoulders.

"Hey, Crawfish!" she shouted to the girl. "What's biting?"

The girl gave Ikasa a cold stare and nodded to the boy on the shore.

"What're you doing out here, Spider?" the boy asked with a laugh, smiling with his lips pulled back.

"I just moved in down the way," she replied, pointing up the direction she'd come.

"She means the old lady's place, across from Armadillo." The girl waved and slogged back to shore. "I'm Mary Crawfish, that's Ehano Limpkin, and that's little Ronnie Blue Crab over there."

"Ehano?" Ikasa said with a laugh, and shook the boy's hand. "Like the bringer of rain Ehano? I'm Ikasa."

"No shit? Big cousin! So why'd you move in with the old lady?" he asked.

"We used to have a wonder-worker store down in Talequah, but it went under because of the Andersonville Bill, you know? Redevelopment sucked up most of the business and my folks're stubborn as hodags," she answered.

"Can't find it, guess the turtle got away," Crawfish said with a sort of grim finality, and pulled herself up out of the water, throwing her pants back on and shaking her head at Limpkin and shrugging before pulling up a wad of mud and weeds. "I found a shoe, though."

"So, is school out right now, or something?" Ikasa asked.

"It's Saturday, we don't have school on Saturday way out here. Talequah must be up by a big city or something," Crawfish said. "Summer vacation starts next week."

"Yeah, I used to hang with a Frog and a Potter Wasp," she answered. "I need new friends."

"There's three of us, too!" Blue Crab nodded sharply. "Three big fishes!"

Limpkin patted him on the shoulder and smiled.

"You're bad luck, Spider, on top of a group of three fish, you've got to be feeling extra magical if you want to join us. Else go find friends elsewhere."

Three fish was a sacred sort of number, three fish, two poison snakes, and five rivers, all hearkening back to the creation story told by the Hornheads. If they considered themselves three fish, adding a fourth person was asking for trouble. Especially if it was a Spider. She was starting to like Limpkin; he reminded her of her older brother, except far less likely to stuff her head in a cabinet and repeatedly slam the door.

"Alright," she said, knocking her own chin in the air. "Fine then, I'll invoke a challenge. That'll clear up the trouble it'd cause, right?"

Their jaws dropped. She grinned wickedly, having caught their attention. She wasn't sure they used them out here, and sure as Death's Country had no sun in the sky they didn't have challenges in the city, either, but it was worth a shot.

"That's some serious old school," Limpkin finally answered.

He seemed to think on it a moment. Thunder bowled in the distance like a passing stone.

"You're gonna catch that," he said, pointing up.

"I'm the girl!" Crawfish stomped on Limpkin's foot, making him wobble like a bird. "I get to choose the test!"

She pointed up.

"You're gonna catch that," she said, nodding firmly.

"The raincloud?"

"No, not the raincloud, dummy!" she shouted.

A bright light flashed high above them, snaking into the clouds like a long, crinkled garden house made of neon.

"That. The lightning bolt. Catch one and you can join up."

Ikasa felt the slow beam crawling across her face; she pulled her lips back and tightened her fists as her shoulders and ankles tingled. There were a hundred things to do with lightning. Most of them could get her grounded or beaten. She did a quick mental check. All of them were worth it. She laughed, throwing her head back and whooping before scrabbling up the limestone nearby. She needed to get to high ground.

"I think she's going to try it," Blue Crab belted out behind her.

"Should we stop her?" Crawfish answered.

"No way!" she heard Limpkin answer.

She heard them chase off after her. Eyes ahead with determination, she ran until the trees broke, the wind barreling strong and hard down the paved road she crossed. Grassland stretched out for a good forty feet between it, and she spread out her skinny arms and spun.

"Oh, hey! Are you guys Ootsooduh?" Ikasa asked. "I have to know."

"They are. I'm all Kaweekyooh, except for that bit of Nuwep and Turmek everyone has. What about you?" Limpkin said, and jumped down the shoulder of the road. He slipped a little.

"Okay, my great-grandma on my mom's side was Xiuteotl, that's where I get my name, her husband was Kaweekyooh, and so was my grandpa. On my pop's side, my grandparents are Nuwep and Tsiwegi," Ikasa said, patting her cheeks. "They say I have Tsiwegi cheeks."

"You've got the Xiuteotl nose," he said.

He laughed and put his hands up over his head.

"Do you have a green headdress?" Mary asked.

She grabbed her face.

"Aw, I do?" Ikasa whined. "I heard they used to smash babies on river rocks."

"White-haired ones, way back in the day," he said, and pointed at her. She grinned and handed him her soda before she started climbing up the nearest power pole.

"Is that dangerous?" Crawfish asked, as Ikasa started to pass the point where they had to yell at each other.

"Very," Ikasa replied. "But, you know, spider? Climb? Get it? Oh, for the press record, I do have a green headdress."

She faced the growing wind, and her face stung a bit from the strength of it. Gramma wasn't lying, the storm came fast. The dim clouds had transformed into a black and furious boil in less than half an hour, and they threatened with strong, bellowing roars. She got to the top of the pole, small splinters in her hands, and stood up on the very top, catching purchase amid the more dangerous bits of the transformer. She imagined she must look either very cool or very stupid, and glancing all the way back down to the ground, she decided it was likely some combination of both. Stretching out her arms again, she hollered at the sky.

"Hey, Thunder! What have you got?"

No answer was forthcoming. She glared at the sky. The clouds roiled and bubbled overhead, moving swiftly into their places. They couldn't hear her in the slightest, and she could tell. Why Thunder hadn't called back was a little strange, but she recalled a story Gramma told one year during a summer festival she couldn't name, but from that memory, dredged up the real name of the one who managed the storms here in Ootsooduh.

"Hey!" she screamed. "Big footed deathwalker bird!"

There was the sound of a mountain crumbling in the distance, louder and sharper than she'd expected. She clenched her teeth and tried not to flinch. Deathwalker was anger, a big bundle of thoughtless, petty rage. He'd respond better to childish mana. She took a long breath and called up her annoyance at having to move, her mother's initial refusal to sell the old store, and her pop's agreement. She called up the loss of her comic books and all that was truly important, trying to build a lead of short anger, stacking it high like piles of dry sticks.

"You heard me!" she shouted back. "I'm calling you out! You got high ground, you got big strong wind and black clouds, yeah, but you still don't know how to work that shit! I'm from Makatuweh, where Thunder still makes a bigger, better storm than you!"

The wind picked up; warm droplets of rain fell on her face, running down like sweat through her white hair, tied off with red bands into shoulder-length braids. She wobbled a bit before planting her feet more firmly atop the pole by wrapping her ankles around each other. The air was charged, and the hot breath of the land was on her neck. She licked her lips and spat, wiggling her fingers at her sides, loosening them up like she was facing one of those kids at school that used to take her lunch money.

"That ain't nothing!" she howled. "Come on, then! Show me what you got! Big old Gariax making a drizzle out of her piss over Maple White Land is scarier than you! What have you got? I bet it's nothing! You got-"

There was a brief moment where her body tingled before her entire field of vision went white. She threw up her hands, and they burned hot with fire. She closed her fingers and felt the searing rage of the lightning. She couldn't tell the difference between the sound of her scream and the grating hiss of the air as the white light lashed about like a snake in a grinder. For a few terrifying seconds, she felt no weight. The ground came up under her with a heavy jolt, air escaping her lungs in one big burst out her nose. She swore she tasted blood and took a heavy gasp before she was able to roll up. Her ears still rang and eyes still saw nothing but a sea of light. Her clothes felt restrictive, choking her stomach. The metal in her earrings stung like needles driven into her flesh, and she resisted the urge to let go and rip them out.

Sight came back even as she wrestled the angry lightning, flopping like a garfish on the deck of a boat. It raced up a tree, leaving black veins and a smell like bumper cars and broken batteries. It jerked her forward, feeling like it weighed a thousand pounds, and threatened to fling her back up into the sky. Where it slammed into the earth, it dug furrows and set small fires, trying to wrench itself free of her hands and back off into the sky or deep under the ground. She started looping it over her elbows, trying to wrap it up like a rope, though it was wriggling like a siren hauled up out of the river, and resisted her.

That was it. She ran one free hand up the bolt, loosely, and gripped the far end between her thumb and forefinger like it was a snake, It immediately went still in her hands, shuddering with a soft and lithe dance while she clutched it. For a brief moment, she considered trapping it in her soda bottle, but the bottle was so far away up over in Limpkin's hand that she couldn't reach it. Instead, she clenched her teeth and strained herself to call up other memories, happy things like her uncle's visit the year before, her tenth birthday, laughing at the radio with her family, and even the time she was sick and got to eat breakfast in bed. If the bolt was sent by Deathwalker, it wouldn't be able to stand up to that.

The memory came out of her eyes, nose, and mouth like fishhooks dragged through her throat, and mana came with it, her mana and her name. She poured herself into the lightning, feeling her flesh bubble and pop where the lightning touched, even as she felt filled with a momentary cascade of energy. Her life was instigated and ended in less than a second, created to strike back at some stupid girl standing on a power pole, but she was stronger than that, so much stronger, with her humanity to beat back the urge to scatter herself up across the sky again. She had mana: friends, prestige, power, a family name, and the lightning had nothing but its way to mark the world before passing into nothing. Ikasa won, and she devoured it into her arms. She was left coughing, palms in the dirt and the three kids from the country staring, shoulders fallen and hands loose to their sides.

She stood up and tried to slow her breathing down. Her body still quaked and heart pounded loud enough that it sounded like a river of lava in her ears.

"Do I get in?" she asked.

Crawfish nodded with a sort of amazed stutter as the other two simply blinked and looked at each other.

"Can I get my soda back?" Ikasa asked.

She took a drink. The rain had started to water it down, turning it into something with a lightly sweet recollection of soda, rather than what she expected. Limpkin shook his head clear and raised a hand.

"It's really coming down, split up and meet again tomorrow morning around ten? Same place, down by the creek bend, unless it stops raining later on," he said, grabbing Blue Crab's hand. "I'm gonna get Ronnie home!"

They nodded, splitting apart like cockroaches in the light, and Ikasa was left alone to the rain. She jogged down the road, back up to where it met the dirt road that led down to Gramma's, that shock-blue house waiting in the trees. Pop already had the wonder-working sign up and leaning against the outside porch. She jogged up to the car port and into the dry air above the dirt, crisp and with the smell of tamales pouring out of the kitchen. Gramma must be cooking; mom always burned them inside the corn husk. She raised her hands and let out a howling whoop like an old-time warrior. Moving didn't seem like such a bad thing anymore.

Chapter 3

Sunday Morning

Spider and the Sun have many children. They're easily seen in the sky most nights, and they move quietly among the web. They hide among the stars, but can be seen if you look carefully. The trick is that Spider's daughters don't twinkle. Among them are Tunana, the quick one, Tleyah, the sister to the earth, and Ikasa, quiet and respectful, yet clever. There are others, but they live far out on the fringes of the web, and do not often come so close as to visit.

Ikasa is a name spoken many times and used in many ways, at least in the old days. Ikasa the planet, Ikasa the magician, Ikasa the daughter. There's a story the Achtakatoh tell about the last age, Norwago's age, and in its five thousand years. We sailed the sea of stars, skittered along Spider's webs in a world of light and knowledge, and touched with metal fingers the bottoms of the oceans. They knew their world was short, and as they reached for the sky they forgot how to use their feet. Their heads swelled and their arms and legs turned into sticks like spiders themselves. They no longer needed S'keah, and it was not good, and not bad. As they did, and their world approached its end, there was another Ikasa.

She was the daughter of a simple sailor, but she became a powerful magician in her day. The Star-Bringing Witch, they called her, and she stood as a giant, her head up by the moon, she was so tall. So skinny, they said, that if she stood up straight against the stars you could still miss her. She was an ever so powerful and dangerous magician. She defied every taboo she heard of, and she conducted many strange rituals and experiments out of the sight of those who would question her motives. She practiced such black magic as shapeshifting, burning organs into charcoal to make her guide marks, and held congress with monsters from the outside. There are rumors that she even ate cheese and drank milk!

So it came to be that the age was ending, and this Ikasa was told that ages end and nothing is permanent. For previously, all her life, she had lived in perfect eternity, and this moment of reflection threw her into a rage. She shouted blasphemies at laws and eternities who had no faces to blame, no evils to recount, or answers to give. She demanded an answer from Death, who shrugged and told her that everything ends, and that she should be grateful she even received a warning, and Ikasa's power was such that she spat in Death's eye.

And Death allowed it, saying, "no matter if you seal away all that is you from my sight, we will still meet one another, by and by. I am a kind sort of death. I can wait."

Ikasa's bed was a grubby brown and gray mattress with bent springs just tossed into a corner, but it was also piled with blankets filled soft downy feathers. When the first cutting sliver of the summer sun pushed into the window, it didn't slap her in the face. Rather, the thing beam of light would slowly expand until it washed over her eyes after she'd already been awake for a few minutes. She struggled with consciousness until she had to cover her burning cheeks with a pillow and then sat up, squinting at her ruffled cotton fuzzball hair in the mirror quickly before realizing that she still had a few months before school started. She threw on some pants and followed the smell of frying cake into the kitchen. Her feet thumped on the hollow floors past unpainted doorways and tarp-covered windows.

The breakfast table was screaming; plates were stacked haphazardly on reams of paper that smelled of old syrup, blood, and ink, scattered among wood, animal bones, and feathers. Pop rubbed the creases on his face while he ate and wrapped sing-sticks for sale to tourists while her older brother, Eddie, bickered with mom about being allowed to wear what he wanted around town because of whatever girls he wanted to see him. She took a seat next to Butch, quietly filled a plate with corn paste and stuffed sweet potatoes, and picked up a piece of hornhead bone to wrap while she ate.

Life was returning to normal; around the time she had gotten to sleep, pretty much everything had been unpacked, and she had managed to steal two dollars from Eddie without him noticing during the whole business. The score meant comics, maybe a movie, lunch, and enough candy that she'd probably be sick by the time dinner rolled around.

"Hey, Gramma," she said. "Fort Hammock's north, right?"

"That's ten miles," Gramma Spider answered. "You gonna walk it?"

"What, seriously? That's like two hours or some shit!"

"You let her talk like that?" the old woman croaked.

"We let 'em all talk like that," Janet shrugged. "Kid's gonna do it whether we're around our not. If we don't give the words any mana, they don't have mana."

Gramma muttered something about logic and pointed her lips at Daniel.

"You gonna go look for a job today?" she asked him.

"Figure I got to," her father answered, tossing another stick wrapped in leather and feathers on the table. "I'll see if we can't get a wonder-worker list put in the directory. We all got to pitch in."

"Government pension says I ain't got to do shit, and I'm the homeowner," Gramma said. "Maybe what you ought to do is go into town with Armadillo today and see what they got at the mound for us. Alligator family has been on me to go dancing up at the mound sings, and I'm too old for that. Maybe we dress up Ikasa as her namesake, she can shut her mouth for five minutes, and maybe earn a few bucks during the summer holiday season."

Eddie laughed with this, mouth full, and shoved Ikasa with his elbow.

"She's saying you don't shut up," he said.

Ikasa pushed away from the table.

"Gonna walk!" she said.

"Two miles down the road there's a little square with a general store and a couple diners. I think there's a bit of a garage and a grocer, too," Gramma said. "It's less than an hour walk if that's all you're going to do."

"Is there a bus?" she asked, slipping on her moccashoes and tying them off. Gramma just laughed and pointed.

This time Ikasa made sure to strap her family knife to her left pant leg, were she'd sewn in seals of her grandparents' lines. She took up her .22 pistol and holster and a defense knife and strapped them to her belt. Lightning fought for release out of her fingers, which made her put a little more assurance in her step than usual. She did a quick hike out to the dusty coquina and chalk road before turning back through the woods to try and find the river again. She needed awahakah, strong family and friend connections, if she was ever going to have any hope of being a wonder-working magician.

The other three weren't at the river, and she squinted in annoyance at and the muggy heat. The water had turned into dark tea overnight and risen up over the embankment where they had met yesterday. There was a woman with a beer bottle and a cigarette maintaining a set of fishing poles beneath a coiled oak tree. The long lines waved gently in the flow, and the woman breathed in tune. She looked like she was from points north, a little lighter-skinned than the people she expected to see this far south, but still dark as wet clay, with her hair done in shoulder-length braids, and her tired face recklessness with age. She had several strings of beads in her hair: big, heavy ones that clattered among themselves as the breeze teased at them. Ikasa felt the woman's mana hit her like a heady wave, stronger than her smell. She turned her head to look at Ikasa, and the woman's gaze flocked with power and prestige.

She went back to her poles and took a drink. Palmetto trees clapped their hands and laughed.

"If you're looking for the other kids, they done went up across the river to Fort Hammock," the woman said, her voice burnt onions. "They said a witch'd be by. Didn't expect them to be right."

"But Fort Hammock is ten miles away! I need a bike."

"No, the mound is ten miles away. Fort Hammock is just on the other side of the Calabokee, and that's just two miles north," the woman said. "You want a beer?"

"No thanks, that shit's poison," Ikasa answered. "So are the smokes, you know. They'll kill you."

"That's good to hear. There's things in me I want dead," the woman said, putting the bottle to her lips.

Ikasa sat down like a listener at a fire and smiled, teeth out, like she was greeting someone for the first time. She grinned at the woman's mana, and went fishing for her own water at her belt, taking a quick drink from her canteen with a wide parody. The woman went back to her poles, most likely expecting Ikasa to scurry off. After a few moments, she ever so slowly turned back around.

"There a reason you're still here?" she asked. "Good kids don't hang out with drifters."

Ikasa laughed and patted her right shoulder, circling her fingers like a picture frame right over where the image of a Spider was sewn on to her shirt, holding the stars in its arms, and smiled as cutely as she was able. The woman seemed confused for a moment, screwing up her eyebrows and peeling back her lip, but then went wide-eyed and let out one quick laugh. Ikasa grinned like a shark and snatched at that, opening up her right hand to catch the mana in a pool.

"Gotcha!" Ikasa shouted and whooped, clenching the hand closed and waving it around over her head. The woman leaned back against the tree and let out one quick, astonished breath.

"Wow. You are one ballsy little kid. Opened me up, did you?" she replied. "You're trying to build awahaka connections with me?"

Nodding, Ikasa pumped the air. The woman was strong; building a connection with her would be sure to send both good fortune and trials her way. It all made for better wonder-working. She caught the first bit of it falling into her like milk striking water, and she soaked it up happily.

"I guess now I gotta introduce myself," the woman grumbled.

She stretched and stood, cracking her back and knees. Letting out a groan, she moved like she hadn't been up on her feet in hours. She picked up her hat, which had a broad brim and every few inches there was a hole punched in it for a string of beads to dangle, and dropped it on her head, which matched her loose jacket and heavy trail pants well. Putting one hand on the short handled corn-scythe she had stuck on her belt, she took in the air.

"I am Sadie Kaw," she said. "I invented squash blossoms and reap corn fields in one go! The wind blows where I say! I grew a blueberry the size of a deathwalker heart, once baked a Johnny cake the size of your house, took the tops off cyclones to make cotton candy, and dug the whole Wookahnee valley with a swipe of my corn-scythe! That's who I am, and where I'm going, only the trails know!"

The woman fell back down and landed on the seat of her pants. She laughed, then pointed at Ikasa.

"Your turn, kiddo!"

"I'm Ikasa the Spider!" she replied, slapping her knee. "I'm from Cahokia, and I caught a lightning bolt. My folks lost their shop to the Bureau for Integration of Andersonville. My pop says the BIA gots to come to a house fire because they put a wet blanket on everything!"

Sadie Kaw sniffed once and downed a heavy drink of her beer before going back to her fishing lines.

"It's a start," she said. "You best move on to your friends, little witch. I think they said something about going to Wilmer's."

"What's Wilmer's?"

"It's a general store," Sadie Kaw said, fixing Ikasa with a long stare. "Get moving afore I tell a late night story. Not them fun ones. The other ones. You know them."

There were stories that story keepers told when the fire's near dead and they're tired. They don't want to tell them anymore, and you don't know if it's a story or a joke. The stories had no real ending, either. Just a cut-off right at the good parts. They'd get up to leave, and nobody would them because they're not going to get anything but a backhand, because the storyteller is old. So everyone just sits around until the fire dies and they go to bed.

That wasn't what Sadie Kaw meant, though. It really meant that Ikasa'd catch a fist if she stuck around any longer, so she bowed out, skittering away to the east. She spent her time working over the mana she just got, forging the basic tines of the awahaka connection and looking for the road. She found only a paved trail with no clear markers other than absence of grass, with its cracked pavement already hot and littered in great cracks that went all the way down into the dirt. She wished she'd brought more water and turned left, heading north. The walk wasn't as far as Gramma had led her to believe. She crossed a long, low bridge over a wide, shallow river with an unearthly pure blue sheen to it, dragging itself like thick wool over limestone. There was an artificial furrow along the center, dark blue with black-hair weeds crawling along the bottom, clearly for boats passing by. Fish armored and many-legged swam visibly in the shallows.

Buildings waited just across the concrete bridge as squat boxes, resplendent in cracks and plaster with marvelous decorations in painted advertisement and chalk. More than one sat abandoned, the plate glass in front broken in like wide mouths with jagged teeth screaming frustration at the clouds. The buildings huddled in loneliness and despondently drew in their own dust, fringed cloaks wrapped around them like rain shrouds. A group of them mingled in and out of their walls to take spots at the remains of a fire that had claimed one of their own. She spotted some graffiti on the shadowed interior walls, prayers mixed with childish images and crushed glass just beyond view.

She came across the Wilmer's easily, a cinder block monument with two huge windows taking up the front, though barely any glass could be seen at all through bright signs and stacks of empty bottles piled in artful pyramids out front. It sat between a small dessert shop and an accounting office, looking very much like any black and white film she'd seen of a small town. She stifled a laugh at the audacity of it. Four grackles sat along the facade, with a fifth white one in the center. They heckled her and flew off as she approached; she watched them go with her teeth set back.

The three kids from yesterday were already inside, down among the wood and metal racks stacked with household cleaners and signs for appliance catalogs. They were engrossed in a wooden pinball machine Ronnie was winning at, even though he had to stand on an orange crate to reach the buttons for the flippers. She leaned against the machine and waved, causing Ehano to smile and wave back, nudging Crawfish. She smiled, too. Ronnie kept staring down at the machine while electronic hums stung the air and the bells cackled. Spider checked around, looking at the grease speckles on the glass top of the machine for anything resembling a pattern.

"I saw an omen outside," she said. "Four black birds and one white one."

"You think it means something?" Ehano asked.

"Of course she thinks it means something, she's a magician, and a Spider, too," Crawfish waved him off.

The statement reminded Ikasa of where she was, and she shuffled off into the store to grab a few drinks and a bag of chocolate, all wrapped up in brown paper that had seen more than one customer. She dumped a few extra things into her pockets when the overweight clerk wasn't watching and then returned to the other three, dropping snacks off on the orange crate.

"Oh, shit, thanks," Crawfish said.

"Courtesy of my big brother," Ikasa said, and leaned on the cabinet again, still searching for patterns. "Black and white birds are from Death. What does it mean?"

She put her hand on the wall.

"What are you doing?" Ehano asked.

"Looking for the fucking hook," she hissed back. "Four birds, one white one, mysterious woman in the woods. Maybe I can force it?"

Mary fixed her with a rapt gaze, knuckles tightening on the machine. Ehano popped the cap on a root beer. Ikasa leaned into the wall and hummed, replaying the morning in her head. She felt a cold prickle in her fingers. Ronnie lost his ball and kicked one of the pinball machine's legs. The machine wobbled, sending a wave of nearly imperceptible shudders among rows of local preserves and leading Ikasa's eyes to the front of the store, where the news rack toppled over, sending papers scattering. One of the comics slid down the borax aisle right up to the wooden crate.

She grinned and knocked it under the box with her heel before Wilmer in his apron could get to the rack and set it back up. He shot a glance back at the four kids, as if weighing the effort of telling Ronnie to cool it, but he settled for flicking his hand and collecting papers and comic books off the floor, then checking for any that might have gone out of his reach. Ikasa dropped a dime into the pinball machine for Ronnie. He started it back up again without a word.

"He doesn't talk much, does he?" she asked Mary, who shook her head in response.

Wilmer disappeared back around the corner, and Ikasa transferred the book from the crate into her shirt.

"Mostly it's because of his folks," Crawfish answered. "His uncle Andy is taking care of him since his parents died two years ago, something about a car wreck, I don't remember. How old are you?"

He let go of the pinball machine with his right hand long enough to tap his middle finger and his thumb together, the symbol for eight. Ikasa nodded and leaned back against the wall.

"Is this what you guys usually do?" Ikasa asked.

"I don't know how it is in the city, I heard they have video arcades there and real soda shops, like up in Shimookooah proper. Around here, we usually hang out until Alligator shows up and hogs this corner," Ehano answered. "Then we go out to the river and throw things in the water. The list of things to do around here runs to fishing, swimming, watching Blue Crab win at pinball, shooting glass jars, and waiting for a festival. And now, watching you catch lightning bolts."

"Last night's rain made the river flood," Ikasa added.

"That was just a little creek," Mary said. "The Calabokee's still good to swim in, if you're not afraid of what might be in it. We could show you the other ponds, another bridge, or I live next to the Stetson, it's a big tract of forest out west out past my house. The Crawfish own all that land out to the main fence."

"Fence?"

She made a box with her hands.

"Big fence sections out in the woods to keep the bigger animals off the roads or discourage them from coming near a town. They can't come into the town proper because of the town's mana, but they sure can get too close," Mary said.

"Gramma warned me about hodags and deathwalkers."

"Well, you did kinda invite his wrath down on you," Ehano said, shrugging.

He knocked his head back up to the front door and pointed with his lips.

"Alligator's here. Brought her brother, too."

Ikasa caught sight of a bigger kid, probably three or four years older, covered in scars and with a dead grin on his face. His hair fell down in thick clumps, and his tan skin was an ever deeper olive than the others. One particularly jagged scar traced from his eye back around his ear. The girl with him had a similar look, wearing a feather and turquoise bead headband that Ikasa usually only saw during festival time, making the girl either deliberately old fashioned or wealthy enough to be an idiot, though her smile showed no teeth. Ikasa didn't trust people who didn't show their teeth when they smiled. They came with hangers-on, three of them, a Catfish and a pair of Palmettos who wore the symbols of their families proudly on the back of their jackets rather than on their shoulders.

Mary nodded to the others and they snatched up what remained of the items Ikasa had bought. They scurried down the side aisles as the Alligators languidly pushed their way to the back of the store, moving with a grace barely constrained by some palpable anger. Ikasa felt their mana wash over her like ripples in a lake. She refused to meet their eyes, though she took note of their steps and avoided them like she might a king's, only breathing easy once they were out of the store.

"You said the nearby river was the Calabokee, right?" Ikasa panted.

Ehano nodded.

"Calabokee is the Queen of Alligators," she groaned. "This town lives and dies with the Calabokee, doesn't it? Palmettos are everywhere, too. No wonder they're so confident. They have all the mana."

They took a quick break to catch their breath before Ikasa stretched and slammed her awkward sized feet into the gravel.

"What was that about in there?" Ehano asked, lilting his head a bit.

"It was about setting the hooks. Part of why I hated leaving was that I needed to have power here like I did back there, and the powers I used back in Cahokia won't work here in Shimookooah. I need new ones. New awahaka, like you guys. And now there's four of us, and a powerful old woman in the forest, I was looking for hooks to sink into, places I could set an anchor line and build a web. Maybe we're the four crows? The white one is the old lady in the woods?"

Ikasa slapped her palm.

"That's it," she said, and laughed. "I'm gonna steal some of them alligator's mana."

The others looked at her like she'd just kicked a hatchling. Mana theft may have been taboo, but among Spiders, well, the family had a mandate to act just like Spider, and that meant sacred theft, especially from those who felt their position was unassailable. She was pretty sure the others knew it, since they'd been okay with the magazine stealing, and tried to remember if those were secret stories or not. She shrugged and pulled the pulp out from under her shirt with a broad smile.

It was a copy of *Eerie Shock Stories* and the cover had a woman in a white dress made almost entirely of fringe pointing down from between a pair of dark mountains at a man in a brown uniform carrying a ray gun rifle, running at the viewer through a dark forest, his features drawn into a shocked frown. Red lettering on the cover happily declared "Death Makes No Judgements – But One!"

She rolled it up and stuck it in her side pocket, calling out to the other three.

"If you ever want to see me catch a lightning bolt again, I'll do it," she shouted back. "Can we go swimming?"

Ehano clapped and whooped in turn, resulting in a cry from Mary and nothing from Ronnie, who just jogged along to follow them.

"And remember," Mary said, holding up her hand. "If you should encounter wildlife!"

"Put your gun in your hand. Always run first, shoot second!" all four chanted.

Chapter 4
The Neighbors

Winter is death and silence. I am capable of toiling alone in those times, without the harangues of would-be hands begging for work and suddenly trotting off after any young thing that passes them by, and I can work in silence without hearing their startled or annoyed cries. My broad hands always felt better after the day's work without them. So I was working, as I say, alone, the farm a restful lady in the snow, surrounded on all sides by white that billows around her like a dress. She laid silently with her gentle lips half-parted while I massaged the land for the coming spring, when a man arrived in tatters.

He had a wild look, and his clothing was like that of a soldier with pockets torn open and the bits of it held together with whatever straps he could have scrounged up, a collar of thick stork hair from a bomber's jacket wrapped around his throat, and leathery wings tied up in a bundle around his neck. He was followed by a smell, a dry and mummy-like rot lacking the sickly sweet scent of wet flesh, and I realized he had an actual stork tied to his back like a survival pack. I thought it odd, but he waved me down in a near-panic, and I felt that I must oblige him.

"Buddy, can I have a smoke?" he said.

I nodded, and passed him the one I had tucked behind my ear. He smoked like an artilleryman or sharpshooter, hand covering the cherry so that even the smoke melded with the falling snow. I asked him why he was so far up in these mountains, and he cast his glance about the dead silence of the day, eyes hungry, darting back and forth.

"You avos?" I asked him, fingering the revolver in the back of my pants.

"My men," he moaned. "I was the one that slew them all, not the enemy."

"Excuse me?"

"I killed them all," he said, calmer. "It feels good to admit it, right?"

He took a long drag, and I tightened my grip on the pistol.

"We were, listen. We were supposed to watch the border zones, keep an eye out for those Imperialist bastards to the east. Everything was fine for a while, just some short skirmishes at most, nothing spectacular, but we got orders to cut off a supply line to a camp further north. That was when we got deep, down into a long and cold valley full of mist, see?" he said, and let out a heavy breath, hands still up by his face. "Let me tell it. We got lost down there, a valley that winded every which way, forever in every direction. We had no stars, only mist where the snow line met the hot jungle."

We found a trail, a long and winding one that passed by glowing spirals marked in the stone, dancing figures, and this, this seal. Like a bird with wings open, or a pair of corn sickles. Something. We could barely tell under the fog. Thick mushrooms and giant mold everywhere. We came up into some ruins where we camped, still utterly lost. We were running low on food and water. Some of the others begged to drink blood or cut their own gums to fool their thirst."

He laughed heartily and flicked away the remains of the cigarette.

"Then, wouldn't you know," he said. "We begged and pleaded, and right out of the fog came a stork, tall as a man's chest, walking on all fours, and the Captain said its fur was too thick to be down here among the wet jungle, and so he spooked it, telling us to follow it right up out of the valley, and so we did, never giving it the room to vault up and away into the air. We watched where it ran up to the rim of the valley, deep through long and ancient hallways beyond stairs and finally emerging out of the hole, and it went to hurl itself into the air. And I shot it."

He laughed again.

"I shot it dead! Bang!" he cried. "The Captain and the others turned to howl at me, but the fog disappeared the instant I did, and *they smiled and laughed and they all fell upon it and ate it. I was terrified that it might be an omen, so I, you know, I didn't eat any of it. It didn't seem like a crime, no sir. No, sir, no crime at all."*

But then, the hunger came again for them, again as their lips blackened and their teeth became bare and their skin shriveled all up along their bones. They stumbled for me and I took up the stork and ran, I belted away through the dead snow and they came like shambling trees, skin like broken bark and eyes cold and dead. They blamed and howled and I ran ahead of them. All the way until I found a campsite where there sat a man with a bowl, nearly naked and wearing smears of paint and mud, five lines crossing his body, wearing a dead white crow about his neck. With him was a woman in a white corn cloak with a white crow whispering in her ear. They were playing poker."

The pair of them looked up at me, and the man pointed at me with his bones, and he shouted 'you won the others! Now let me play for him!' He started to shuffle, and when he did, she snatched up the cards and said to him, 'don't roll, you win him, see how he carries the stork? He's already took the mana of his crime, I keep my chips!' and the man laughed at me again."

He pointed at me with those rib bones again and bound the stork to my back, and the lady told the squad to hound me still, and not to ever let me cross back into my homeland. I can never go west, either, the old man owns my soul, not the woman. The woman was Death, and she took up the pack of cards, the chips with the faces of my squad, and walked away. The man grinned and disappeared into the snow, so now I walk here, in the snow, unable to descend anywhere other than that cursed valley and carrying this dead stork on my back, its guts empty and its skin sewn into mine."

I looked him up and down, and he let out a heavy sigh.

"Why are you telling me this?" I asked, and he fixed me with worried eyes.

"My squad, they are still hungry," he said. "They come to eat one of your animals. They would have eaten you, if I had not stood here."

I stared at him as he went, straining my ears to listen in the distance, hearing the pained cries of some animal, unidentifiable by its wet gurgles. It had already struck the snow, so I could make no measure of its size, but I could certainly tell that it was being eaten alive. Letting out one long, slow, breath, I caught sight of his image leaving me in the exact opposite direction he had come, slowing fading into a gray silhouette, and I muttered a prayer under my breath that I should never see him again, thinking I might move my farm a little closer to the border.

He was as he always will be – cursed by Death.

Something Ikasa found out quickly about Gramma's house was that it got unbearably hot during the day. Gramma also did not believe in ice trays. She ended up lying around in shorts or an oversized loose shirt, letting her gangly limps drape over the couch or the blankets in her room while she read her new *Eerie Shock Stories*. Eddie once tried to take the magazine, for which she rebuffed his efforts by attempting to nail one of his more expensive jackets to the outside wall of the chicken hutch in a sling-type setup. He quickly acquiesced, of course, but not before spitting between two of the pages. She let it slide for the time being, and almost shoved Butch while blaming the older one, but didn't feel like starting a fight in the summer heat.

She had read all seven stories in it by now, which consisted of the usual list of four short stories, two novelettes, and the novel serial, and had winnowed down the relevant hooks to three that spoke of Spiders or of Death, "In the Web of the Hungry Queen," "The Farmer in the Snow," "The Man from Ikasa," and "Korthrag's Marvelous Longhouse." Each of them dealt, respectively, with a Spider family story, a story of Death and White Bird, a stranger come to move to a new town (who had turned out to be from Ikasa, the fourth planet), and another historical story about moving to a new town. She'd wondered which among them might mirror her situation the closest, but insisted to keep them all with her for the time being. The main line was the four and one birds, she knew, but any of the others could be what they wished for her to find.

At least a week had passed since her arrival in town, and she'd quickly discovered that Okola, south of the wide Calabokee river, was nothing but a single paved trail with no shoulder and a whole set of unpaved roads that cut through scrub and hammock, and living there meant that one was really taking their life into their own hands, among the beasts and the storms and mocking fields of sandy pines and yucca.

She stood up once the cicadas got too annoying and padded down to the kitchen sink to get some water and to wash her sticky, sweaty hands. When that didn't work, the faucet dead as a frog mummy in the corner, she made a plan to use the hose out back. She could hear the soft murmurs of the television in the flower festival room, a tile-floor room surrounded by glass windows set a full foot below the rest of the house, looking out over the yard and its waist-high grass.

"Hey!" Gramma's voice cranked out from the back of the house.

Ikasa slipped into the door there.

"Yes'm?" she asked. Gramma Spider was sitting with her husband, Kapu, a slender, sculpted young man scarcely out of his mid-twenties who had no business being with the wrinkled bundle of sticks. He leaned against her as they watched day time variety shows. Gramma knocked her head once and gave Ikasa the stink eye.

"You ready for a quest?" she asked.

"What's that?" Ikasa said, furrowing her brow in confusion.

"A quest. Here's a dollar, go get Gramma some smokes and a twelve-pack of Sharp."

"A dollar isn't enough to get both-"

"That's why it's a quest!" Gramma snarled.

"Did I do something to you?" Ikasa whined. "It was Butch! I swear!"

Gramma took a moment to breathe in and compose herself, slipping into her more familiar nature.

"I am not upset because I have been through happenstance and calamity forced to deal with you while the rest of your folks are out. You are the least of my concerns, oh variegated offspring. Thou crass mutt."

She gestured with her broom handle cane.

"I am upset because my own fucking stomach is trying to turn what remains of my shriveled black fucking uterus into the battered subject of a fucking taffy machine in order to promote the inconvenience involved in furthering youths like yourself!" Gramma Spider gurgled. "Now, if you would please, I would like to bleed in silence! If you won't get the smokes, at least go to Armadillo's place across the road an' pick me up one block of ice and eleven grams in a bag. There's more money on the counter. Take your fucking time."

Ikasa couldn't clear up which was worse in her head, that Gramma Spider spoke so directly, or that it meant that Gramma

Spider could potentially still have children. She pushed it out of her mind and snagged the two dollars on the counter and added that to the silver dollar she'd already been handed, as well as the big black ice tongs. She still had money from the other day, and felt like the richest fucking kid in the world. The tongs made her feel like a real spider with fangs ready. She headed out the side door into the tick-riddled yard and jogged across crushed coquina and lime out into the dusty road, right over to where Armadillo's place was waiting.

The neighbor's house mostly kept the tree line back by looking ornery as a porcupine after a rainstorm. Random wooden slats kept the whole thing together and bent, arthritic nails threatened to lash out at childish flesh that got too close. It had, at one point, been a pre-fab trailer of the sort they were using in the Bureau for Implementation of Andersonville to make sure everyone out in the storms had a home to call their own so that the government, more specifically, the tribal confederacy, didn't have to come out and actually assess the reality of the situation. Instead, they could pretend the whole thing about low-income families in places like Okola and its environs had already been solved.

Bradshaw Armadillo was the sort of man who rooted around in dirt and trash to find hidden gems. He was swollen with age and wisdom, though mostly with the wisdom you could buy at the store for twenty-five cents and came with two slices of processed cheese. During the day, he sat in his car. His gentle, worn-out rusted hulk covered with peeling leaves of rust that called itself The Hunting Lady that loved him, and he loved her right back. He had married her when he got back from the war, and they'd been that way for twenty years, or so Gramma said. His trailer home didn't have air conditioning, which made it excellent as a greenhouse for growing pot, but The Hunting Lady still did, and she fawned over Armadillo like a happy lover, helping him wind up asleep during those hot summer days.

When Ikasa came up, two hoppers emerged from the sawgrass, one with a misaligned jaw dotted with a sparse growth of teeth and the other with a milky eye and an uncertain wobble. They slithered up like two hideous murder-turkeys with a single minded purpose to slobber happily all over every newcomer while coming back for more. She scratched them on their stubby little bird necks and they made little gurgling, warbling inbred bird noises. They tried to gnaw and preen her clothes and she swatted them and laughed until they went back to shitting on things they weren't allowed to shit on.

By this time, Mister Armadillo had dug his way out from under his girlie magazines and empty cigarette and candy boxes and dried half-eaten bread to wash himself lightly in the air. He smelled like the specter of Death herself was gonna come rising up out of the west wind just to check and see if he was fit to go. He let out a shallow and chattering laughter and shook the trees and made The Hunting Lady shudder with a non-family-friendly sort of glee.

"Well, you're real new," he said, teeth golden as the dawning sun. "Spider's kin, huh. Did they tell you I was an Armadillo?"

"I ain't no Scorpion or Beetle," Ikasa said, laughing back, throwing out mana like a cast net. "Should I be worried?"

He had half-opened his mouth to say something, lips tilted in a half point back out to the road, but she seemed to catch him off guard, so he sat back down, shaking his head.

"Gramma wants fifteen grams and a block of ice," Ikasa said.

"Get a block of ice at the store up on the Nokaha for seventy-five cents," he said, tossing her a small paper bag. "A dollar for that."

A stack of dried buds in rested in the bottom of the back, about seven in all, drawn from a small pile of them that had been drying on the dashboard of The Hunting Lady. They smelled delicious and sweet. Ikasa nodded her head and stuffed in it her pocket, wondering if she'd get any, half thinking she might steal it, but remembering that Gramma, like her mother, believed that if Ikasa could still move after getting caught, she hadn't been hit hard enough.

"Just your looks enough made me laugh. I owe you for opening me!" He said. "You need a ride to town, up to Shimookooah, Leeseenoo, maybe even Bryson, you let me know."

"What's in Bryson?" she asked.

"There's Yellow Garden Spider's dreaming stone down there," Bradshaw said. "It's a Chukto village, though. They moved in, let me think. I think way back when Mokwepet and the Wokadonah joined up. They came in when the Kaweekyooh took the land from them."

"I thought the Ootsooduh ran this land?"

"They do! That don't mean they have any claim on it that the

Confederacy didn't give 'em!" He waved his hand. "The Wakwahnoo tribe technically should have this land, being that they're made of both the tribes of owners, and so own it by blood spilled, but the Kaweekyooh, who are now the what, the Ootsooduh? They got some members from those other two tribes, too, just not anywhere near as many. Then, so do the Akneeqa and the Xiucuscu."

"That's," Ikasa wondered for a moment. "I know that woman's story."

"Who? Xiucuscu?" he asked. "Know of the story, the birthing one, but not the story itself."

"It's a Spider secret story and just a girl's story, too, so I don't think I can tell it to you," she said. Her brothers didn't know it, that was for certain.

"So, I didn't get to meet you folks when you moved in, had to wait until just a couple minutes ago, and I'm selling you pot," he slapped his right shoulder. "So this is proper, I'm Bradshaw Armadillo! This here chariot is my wife, how skilled are you at seeing the metaphors?"

"I'm Ikasa Spider," she answered. "And not very much."

"No fooling. Your grandma said your parents were old fashioned types. Said a few other choice things, too, not ones I'll repeat here," he laughed. He seemed to think for a moment, looking back at the inside of The Hunting Lady, and pushed a stack of questionably photographed magazines off the passenger seat. "You know what? Get in over there, I'll drive you up to the rotter shop and tell you how the Calabokee river got to be where it is!"

She was half worried that the door would fall right off when she pulled it open; it wasn't the original door, and still the color of primer. When it opened, it made a noise like a small toddler being pulled across a linoleum floor. The seat was hot, the cover cracked and stiff, and there was an old bead blanket pulled over the back that dug rather comfortably into her shoulder blades. The car's mana was a cool confidence in the heat.

"This story is about the Ntonaka. See, there was this warrior among them named Kohsonohka the Great-Song Man," he began, starting up the The Hunting Lady by simply tapping the driver's wheel, who rumbled like a sleeping mountain. "He wasn't a killer, and had a reputation for not killing his enemies. It was a bit of a mean thing to do in those days, to take the mana of a fallen enemy without killing them, but he was the sort of man we'd want around today, with good, strong singing and dancing. In fact, he loved dancing and singing so much that it was all he did, even on the battlefield. He had a wife, as well, Wohona the Drawn Razor, whose voice was like a whisper but whose insults cut deeply. He loved her as much as any man might love a woman, like rain pounding on dry stone.

In his dreams one night, he saw a woman that put his wife's beauty to shame, and he felt monstrous for thinking so, but when he brushed the hair away from her face and pulled the headband that covered her eyes up over her forehead, he discovered she had no eyes at all. She smiled at him in his horror, and she brushed his cheeks with her hands. She told him that she was Calabokee, the Queen of Alligators, the Crooked Water. She told him that he'd be her husband before too long."

Bradshaw put up his hand over the windshield, dramatically waving at the trees, which whipped by and waved moss like a cheer line.

"He said back to her that he already had a wife, and he was sure that she wouldn't be the type to accept a co-wife position. Oh, the Queen of Gators just laughed at him and left his dreams in peace," he said. "So, he went out and told all the wonder-workers he knew, and they tried to help him with songs and thrown sand, and he even went out and fished for clams all day, but when he returned home, he found that the wash hadn't been done and there was only a small bird for dinner, no fish or arrow reeds. Wohona, in her anger, told him that all day whenever she came down to the lakes or the thin, dark rivers, alligators chased her away or tried to eat her."

Wohona wasn't the type to let that sort of thing rest, you know, especially after she had the situation fully explained to her. She went all the way out into the limestone hills to look for Calabokee, and when they found each other, oh, they argued for some time, Wohona staying calm, and Calabokee becoming angrier with every passing moment. Eventually, Kosonoka ran up and picked up his wife, escaping into the forest. Calabokee followed them, and caught them in a big basin; to hide his wife, Kosonoka quickly dug a hole and put her down in it, and faced the Queen of Alligators alone."

"Wohona agreed to that?" Ikasa asked.

"Oh, of course not!" Armadillo answered. "She moaned and

screeched at him, but he was taking a woman's job into his own hands, so it was perfectly acceptable for her to do so. Now, Kosonoka asked Calabokee why she was trying to kill his wife, and she said the prospect of killing his wife and giving him such great despair had filled her with so much joy that she had got a little ahead of herself. She said to him, she'd been listening to his songs and she said that if he could sing a song that made her cry, he and his wife both could take her mana and she'd have no more to do with either of them."

"She had no eyes," Ikasa said, knowing full well what she was supposed to say at that point.

"I know! That's the whole point of the thing, you see. Spirits aren't fair, they just are. Anyway, he agreed, and so sang a song about longing for home and family, as well as a long, beautiful river made of crystal clear water, about wishing he was on a gentle raft flowing down through cool waters. He sang about playing with his brother, and about how he wished to be by his mother's side so that he could die, and the Queen of Alligators listened quietly, rolling her coils around until, at last, well, they say six eyes opened on her head and began to weep!" He said.

"Suddenly, her brother, Oehtkohtokun the Angry Thousand Eyes, came around, and he didn't see what had actually happened. All he saw was his sister crying and a man filled with joy. He lunged in to attack Kosonoka, and all at once Calabokee attacked her brother, shouting in rage at him. The two of them rolled right into that big basin where Kosonoka had dug the pit to help his wife, and he was too late to save her from being crushed."

"Where they landed in their fight, they bled. Water spilled out from their guts, and Kosonoka cried tears that mixed with them, and where his tears fell, the limestone burned away, digging a deeper and deeper pit. Eventually, brother and sister broke away, and Calabokee hauled herself into the deep caverns in shame, where she still bleeds even now. Kosonoka drowned himself in the headwaters, and they say that she would not let him pass on to Death's Country, and he lives in her underwater court to this day."

"So, the Calabokee is the dragon's blood?" Ikasa asked.

"Depends who you ask. Up where the two rivers meet, there's a Blue Crab singing stone, where you can make blue crabs if you know the right song, and they'll tell you that the Calabokee is crying still, and that it's her tears, not her blood, and over by the headspring at the Alligator's stone? They say it's her blood," he shrugged. "What do you think?"

"You'd have to ask the Calabokee, wouldn't you?" Ikasa said.

"And that's the rub, you're a wonder-worker's daughter and a Spider. What do you think Calabokee would say if you asked her?"

Ikasa thought about it for a moment, and remembered once when her father called up a spirit of a couple's house to adjudicate a divorce, and how difficult it had been to explain to the house exactly what was going on, and the entire concept of division of property. She recalled the couple's frustration with the whole deal, and how the pair had simply decided to walk out without paying.

"'I am bleeding,' the river would say, and 'I am crying.' She wouldn't say which is the water," Ikasa answered.

"You're a smart kid," Bradshaw laughed. "This is the place. Go get your ice."

She nodded quickly. The parking lot was gravel, and the general store was made mostly out of an even older building and a lot of corrugated steel. Some ancient, googie-star sign rose up out of the curb, covered with smatterings of rust and chipped red paint, broadcasting the prices for guano ethanol, offering water, and cornahol. Bradshaw had parked where he could fill up The Hunting Lady, and she whispered filthy things to him while he ratcheted the gas pump. Ikasa went inside and tossed up seventy five cents for a block of ice and went back outside.

She wondered if Gramma would be mad that she didn't walk.

Chapter 5

Television

Xiucuscu was the Woman Made of Blood who fell to the earth from the moon. She hatched from a silver egg and she would wash ashes and grow kumquat trees with her shouts. One day, she came upon White Bird sitting up in a tree and waved happily at him.

"Do you not know who I am?" he asked her.

"No!" she replied.

"I am the White Crow! I tell Death where souls are at!" he said. "You should be frightened of me!"

"I see no holes to the country where Death rules," Xiucuscu said back. "And should I die, why would I not want Death to know where my soul is? Do you not do a service to the dead in this way?"

White Bird nodded, knowing this was a wise thing to say, but he was still a very egotistical bird, and so he directed her to the tree upon which he was sitting.

"Why do you not take a fruit here?" he asked.

She looked into the branches of the tree, seeing that the fruit were, indeed, very curious looking, and when she did, White Bird spat right down onto her arms and cawed with a dark laugh. He flew in a big circle around her head. Suddenly her arms became heavy and pulled her down like great weights, and she gave in to horrible pain, screaming so loud that it shook the ground below her.

In six months' time, it became obvious that she bore an infant *inside each arm, and was exiled by her mother to the wilderness, where she was taunted for three more months by White Bird, who came by to revel in her pain. Eventually, she became so distraught, she set a trap for White Bird to catch him in a big net. When she finally caught something, it was a bright green squirrel-bird she had caught instead, who begged her to stop.*

"Let me take away the pain!" the little squirrel-bird said. "There are so many of me, but only one of him! I will take the death you mean for the White Bird in his place."

"Why should I, when White Bird has caused me this distress? I do not want children now!" said Xiucuscu, readying to cut the squirrel-bird free.

"If you kill White Bird, then Death will have no eyes. The dead will wander the world! I ask this in return. When a warrior kills an honorable sacrifice, the soul of the sacrifice goes with them when they die, and they are served by the warrior until they move on. Do this for me and my descendants, and I will eat all the White Bird's sins forever."

Xiucuscu was impressed by the squirrel-bird, and so agreed.

"If you take the place of my hatred for White Bird and my children will bear your feathers for mana in this world, you will travel with me into the next, and we will be friends and partners there," Xiucuscu said.

She cut the two infants from her arms and found a boy and a girl. The girl was made of stone with the ocean for blood, and the boy was made of wind with fire in his veins. Seeing they were not made of blood and corn, she wondered at them and made a headdress for the girl out of squirrel-bird's feathers and a necklace for the boy out of squirrel-bird's bones. The girl was the first queen of the Xiuteotl people, and she and her brother had many adventures, though that is for a different night.

But for the time being, that is why Xiuteotl girls all have a squirrel-bird headdress.

Television was the great distraction; it was far more effective than the radio and when Ikasa was getting bored with it, there would be a swap to a commercial like a stage performer snapping his fingers. Their television was a black and white cabinet number with a gigantic, four button clicker the size of Ikasa's entire hand with the words "Mission: Control" written in flowing cursive on the front side. The rest of the room was Gramma's monument to boredom, decorated with a number of cozies and sing-sticks of every shape and size, including some too big to ever be used in any kind of ceremony.

Ikasa had her legs looped over the back of the couch and dangled her head off the cushions such that she was effectively seated upside-down, watching three women sitting on a couch argue amongst themselves as to the best way to host a dinner party in the home. She had briefly imagined a monster breaking in and menacing or even eating them, but the television steadfastly refused change the direction of the programming, no matter how much she clenched her teeth or claimed her family was Spiders and patrons of electronic technology.

Pop came in to the room, button-up undershirt ragged with color and with quick-sewn striations down the arms and back. He sat down on the couch and watched for a few minutes, silent, with one of Gramma's beers in his hands and his pomade-rich hair starting to stick every which way. Every so often, he stole glances at Ikasa and sips from his beer.

"This show can't be that interesting," he said.

"It's not," she answered. "I wish it was Captain Science."

"Well you know, there are things you could do around here," he offered.

"I picked up the side yards so they're ready for mowing," she replied.

He nodded slowly and turned to say something again.

"I primer painted the backside of the second floor," she said. "I patched two holes in the chicken coop. I made lunch. I shoveled dino guano off the back yard into the separator. I tried calling Limpkin's house, but nobody picked up. The Crawfish man said Mary was busy, and I ain't walking all the way over to the Blue Crab's house without the other two."

He laughed and elbowed her in the leg.

"And here I was told big city life spoils girls and makes them not want to do any house work."

"Who said that?"

"Your gramma."

"Well, Gramma's mean. Way meaner than I remember her being."

"You were younger and dumber last year," he said.

"Pop!" Ikasa shouted, and mock slapped him.

"I'm serious," he chuckled. "Think about all the shit you

didn't know last year that you know now. I mean, shit, the reason we chose to move out here now is because Butch is at the verge of knowing what's happening to him a bit better and if we tried it last year you'd have thrown an even worse fit."

"You what?"

"If we'd tried to pull this last year. We had a couple projects going, but it was your last year of primary. We'd have had to pull you out during the last year of school. You'd have thrown a worse tantrum than you did."

She looked away from him and frowned.

"You were gonna sell the store and you didn't?"

"No. We've gone into debt to keep it open. We owe Nihpej-Wodara company around seven thousand dollars. Shit, that's part of why we moved down here. State laws basically let us hide from the company indefinitely."

Ikasa righted herself and watched a woman on the television start to dress a brushrunner for roasting. It was naked of feathers and its legs and claws were stuck up in the air while the tail draped, dead and languid, over the edge of the counter. Ikasa screwed up her brow. She couldn't nail down why po's words made her angry, between a self-loathing for throwing a tantrum in the first place and someplace deep in irony where her parents gave mana to a big company in order to hold off giving mana to a big company. She was not happy about the lying, either, or the refusal to give up mana and money so strongly owed.

"You could have sold the store, but you just let the property run out? You took out a loan to let the property run out? Why the fuck did you do that?"

"Your mother already went over this with me."

"This is why men aren't allowed to make financial decisions!" she shouted and pushed herself up from the couch. "Why did you do that? Why did you lie to me?"

"We gained more mana from having you in that same primary than we'd lose otherwise. You can't just look at the family's awahakah connections, sweetie. You've got to look at all the other mana."

"You lied to me!" she screamed. "Can't you see how much mana we've lost now?"

She shoved her way out the side door and stomped off into the woods. Pop was shouting something about Spider mana, but she didn't quite hear it. She wasn't sure she wanted to hear what he was on about, either. A year ago, he had taken the sign down from the front of the shop. He'd said it was to stop the bank from harassing them. Her world then fell into context. Late-night meetings, foreigners in solid colored suits, and the near-constant rituals to Spider that seemed apologetic and prostrated. She punched an oak and she wrung her hand out. She watched her knuckles turn purple and felt them heat up.

She dragged herself much slower through the trees, feeling her whole body tense and release with undefined rage. She tried to even out her breathing, as rage wasn't a Spider thing, and thus something she felt the need to work through, even if it'd catch her later. One of the small limestone boils emerged by her feet, running in a tiny trickle down the hill. She took it as a sign and washed her hands and mouth before running droplets over her ears and down her hair so they beaded up like stars.

Leaning against a tree, she spat. She had even gone the last few days working hard in an effort to make the best of the situation. Now she wasn't sure what she wanted to do about anything. The family was under Nihpej-Wodara's power now, and she wondered if she should ask Gramma to look for curses. Wodara was a banking company that was an arm of a department store chain, but she really couldn't nail down why her mother would be willing to create debts that Ikasa might inherit. She sat down and rubbed her closed eyes until she saw spirals of light and strange landscapes.

"Hey, witch," she heard Sadie Kaw's voice say. "You're out here? Are you casting a wonder?"

She looked up. The woman was smirking, a day's pack slung over her shoulder, and she was with two others. One was a great boulder of a man with thick hair and a sandpaper beard, his skin as dark as the mud from a swollen river, and hands gnarled as mangled cauliflower. The other was younger, slim, wearing suspenders and a light shirt only gently stained in the day's sweat. She gave a weak wave to the both of them.

"These're my buddies, Ol' Pete and The Natural," Sadie Kaw said, pointing to the two men. "We was just gonna go up to this field I found and get an early summer harvest."

"It's not harvest time," Ikasa said, as Sadie Kaw helped her up.

"Yeah, well, I know some tricks," she said, slapping her shoulder. "You've seen the White Bird's blood I carry with me.

He's a spirit of the harvest. Come with us! You can have some sweet corn and you can tell me all about who you were casting curses on."

Ikasa nodded. She followed along, eyes a bit blurry and legs still unsure of what was happening, as they trundled through the forest. Sadie Kaw yammered on about something pertaining to animal movements in the nearby woods, asking The Natural if he'd mind terribly much about scaring up some meat for the lot of them as soon as they were able. Ikasa had long ago realized these folk were adventurers, with their patchwork clothing, the stink of the road about them, and the evidence of blood stain all along their hair. The Natural's talk of hunting with a knife and a complaint about the expense of bullets certainly confirmed it.

"I'd be shooting dollars right off our pockets," he had said.

The field the woman had been talking about was old, with a weathered and decayed farm house back up against trees that threatened to swallow it up, reaching around to block windows like parental hands in front of a child's eyes. She could see the river some distance beyond - the Calabokee - wide and shallow, and held herself back from running to it to check for turtles or fish.

"You can't grow corn here," she said. "Can you?"

The Natural stretched and clapped his hands in dust. He pointed his lips at Ol' Pete, who then tossed him a small bag.

"Sure can," said The Natural as he chucked seed grains out into the field, small handfuls at a time. "We checked with the house. Some fellas set it up so that the corn grows every year in this field. House didn't know how long they been gone, it just says that every year the field tries to grow up, and every year it can't."

"Pete! Toss me here that rainstorm we picked up!" Sadie Kaw shouted.

He threw a mason jar swirling with blackness at Sadie Kaw; she wrestled off the lid and shielded her face as lightning and rain leapt out every which way, the black turning gray and very quickly soaking the field before turning into a white puff and drifting away. She laughed.

"So, what's the deal?" Sadie Kaw said. "Who was you casting a curse on?"

Ikasa had to snap her head out of the momentary awe welling up in her chest like a thick balloon. Recovering herself, she looked away back at the river.

"Nobody," Ikasa huffed and sat down.

"It ain't nobody," Sadie Kaw grumbled. "It's your pa."

"How did you know?"

"You're just a hair under it bein' boy troubles, so it's either you got brothers or it's your pa. An' a little birdie is tellin' me you know how to handle your brothers," Sadie Kaw's answered.

"Avos," Spider sighed. "It's my pop. It's complicated, okay? My folks lied to me."

"Folks lie to kids all the time, that's how they do. Parents especially."

Ikasa punched the ground.

"That's not what I meant! Besides, that's stupid!"

"Is it now?" Sadie Kaw asked. "Here's a secret. Grown-ups only lie when they think they have to, and really, parents don't like to lie to their kids. It's not fun for 'em."

"They don't?" Ikasa rubbed one of her eyes. She refused to cry. Crying was for boys.

"You know all them stories about monsters? Them movies and campfire stories and comics they say is for kids all about the monsters that come and drag you off?"

Sadie Kaw checked the edge of the corn field and measured her height against it. The stalks grew taller. She smirked.

"That crud's really for grownups. See, they know they got to lie to you, and that scares them. So does telling the truth, because the world don't make no lick of sense, even to one of us grownups. They got this hazy recollection of their own childhoods and want to make yours better because they got guilt. But they hear stories like that, and it tears off all the nostalgia like claws ripping open a feather pillow. It makes them remember all the garbage their parents did to them, all the garbage that made them scared, isolated, and living in the world where nobody listens, and they feel guilty," Sadie Kaw said. "But, then, you know? They suddenly think about what they might have missed, and about all the things they didn't listen to you about, and they think about all the bad things that may have found their kids - all the monsters and wild men and women out there in the brush, and them kids take an interest in monsters because the monsters listen."

"Why's that?"

"Because the monsters love children," Sadie Kaw shrugged. "Like a miser loves gold."

Ikasa tightened up her jaw. Sadie Kaw had a mana Ikasa hadn't seen or felt until it hissed between them like freshly gutted entrails. The woman smiled with her lips pulled back, and was immediately friendly again.

"So, your pop lied to you, and you went and ran off?" Sadie Kaw asked.

Ikasa nodded as Sadie Kaw crossed her corn sickles and ducked, snapping forward into the fields, almost flying as her legs pumped. Ikasa watched as the woman left a coiling trail in the field, tall stalks waving as she passed, closing in like a rushing stream. A whirlwind burst out from the center of the corn, picking up speed and size as the cataract rolled to the edge as an ever-widening circle in the crop, sending shredded leaves, stalks, and harvested ears tumbling skyward. They all fell inside the funnel, drawn up into the whirlwind, and the mulch calmed, drifting slowly down as Sadie Kaw stood in front of a stack of the field's corn, sickles held straight out to her sides. She laughed once.

"Nailed it!" she shouted, pointing one her sickles at Ol' Pete, who scarcely gave up a glance from his flask. "You owe me a fiver!"

Ol' Pete grunted and took a drink.

"In the future, this is how they'll grow it all!" Sadie Kaw said, laughing. "With some big machine that does it just like that, all trapped thunderstorms and rain, and little slicing blades that dig it up and put it up in nice neat stacks!"

She looked back at Ikasa.

"You're still a kid, right? What exactly has you riled up about all that business, then?"

"I told you! My pop lied!"

"So you said, but what'd he lie to you about?"

Ikasa leaned back in the dirt.

"My pop runs a wonder-work business. Calling family spirits, talking to the trees and the ground, he said we just ran out of business this last couple of months, but really they didn't have the money for a year. They took out a loan with a big company just so they could keep the place."

"I haven't heard a lie yet."

"He didn't tell me they took out that loan! It was all just so I could finish middle school in the same school!"

Sadie Kaw gave her a flat, unimpressed grimace. She looked back at Ol' Pete, who just shrugged and mouthed something

Ikasa couldn't hear.

"You're serious?" the woman finally said. "What's your problem with that?"

"Because it costs me money when I grow up!" Ikasa said.

"You let your ma worry about that," Sadie Kaw answered, walking over to Ikasa and then dropping down onto her toes. "I think I see the deal."

"What's that?"

"You," Sadie Kaw started up. "Well, you don't want to be a kid. That's what I bet. I bet you want to march right down to the mound right now and take your adulthood trial."

Ikasa crossed her arms.

"So what if I do? What if I want to and run all the way back to Cahokia?"

Sadie Kaw flashed her lips-sealed, no-tooth grin again and Ikasa felt like she was drowning in muck. Ikasa grit her teeth and crunched up her cheeks. She shot back with her own bit of lightning, and the woman rocked on her feet a little, eyes wide and showing her teeth again.

"Ok," the woman said, and slapped her knee. "You don't got to go all the way to the mound to take that test."

"I don't?"

"Naw, I'm a wonder-worker, you just seen us do it!" she said. "How about this, witch-girl. I test you. If you win, I will name you an adult. If you fail, you come work for me whenever I say so, and I teach you how to do wonder-working my way, too?"

Ikasa was suddenly on edge. Something didn't seem entirely right about Sadie Kaw. It was something to do with her shoulder patch and the mana she carried. There was so much pain and bile in it that it seemed visceral, literally so, and such things were warned against in the stories she had been told. An image danced in her head of a backwards sing and charcoal made of scorched bones.

"Even if you lose, you can still do it Spider's way. Anything I teach you is just extra."

Ikasa bit her tongue.

"I'll win your stupid contest," Ikasa said. "You'll see."

Sadie Kaw laughed. It was a biting, sharp laughter with short tilts scattered here and there. She really did look like a crouching bird for a second.

"Here's how the test goes," Sadie Kaw said. "You can decide

after I tell you this."

She sniffed and pointed at Ikasa.

"Go to the mound when your folks mind you to do so. You have to dance in Ikasa's dance."

"That's it?"

"I ain't done," Sadie Kaw snapped. "Right after you get done here, today or tomorrow, you got to get down to Mary Crawfish's house and get her. That's real important. You got to actually go to her house to get her."

"So, what's my task, then?" Ikasa asked.

"That's it. You'll know when you're done. Just talk to the White Bird about it when you think you're finished," Sadie Kaw said. "He's up in the springs area. You best find him first so you know who to report back to."

Ikasa nodded.

"I'll do it," she said.

Sadie Kaw laughed again, a friendly one this time, patting Ikasa on the shoulder and sending her on the way with a little push. Ikasa scrabbled back out to the tree line and gave a wave.

"Here!" Sadie Kaw shouted, throwing her arm in the air and letting loose a small bag with a white raven stitched in cowrie beads on the side. Ikasa caught it, feeling it heavy in her hands, filled with something loose and gentle. "It's the seeds from just now. Don't plant them unless you want harvest-ready corn stalks sometime in the next ten seconds."

"Yes'm," Ikasa headed off into the trees.

She was still a bit angry at her father, but she decided to head back, anyway. If there was a test involved, she could stand to be in the house. Even if Sadie Kaw was full of crap, she was still incredibly powerful and her words required respect. She still felt the hot prickle of the mana that woman possessed, boring out at Ikasa through Sadie Kaw's eyes and palms. Ikasa fingered the White Bird bag and frowned. Something wasn't clicking right. She recalled the omen she saw at the store the other day.

Tossing the in the air once and catching it, she hooked it to her belt and walked home. She had to go to Mary Crawfish's place tomorrow to play. This test was going to be easy. She laughed.

Chapter 6
Mary Crawfish's House

One day, the chief of the people was hunting in the forest. He was hunting for a symbol to give life to his people, and eventually came upon the tracks of a great hornhead. This made him excited, for the hornhead had breathed its dreams on the world and slept itself into the past, had invented great songs, and witnessed the creation of life.

"Grandfather Hornhead!" the chief said. "Surely you will show yourself to me, and become the symbol of my people. We will share our blood and be together as family."

He followed the tracks through the forest, letting his eyes rest on nothing else, even as the sun went down and darkness swallowed the forest. He ran faster and faster, barely able to contain his excitement. Suddenly, he ran into a spider web and fell to the ground, becoming wrapped up in it and unable to move. He was very angry, and lashed out at the spider that was there between the trees, but it jumped out of his reach.

"Grandson," the spider croaked at him. "Why do you run through the woods, not watching where you are going?"

"I was watching!" the chief shouted back.

"No, you were watching your feet, only looking down, never seeing where you are going. What was so interesting on the ground?"

The chief felt foolish, and sat up while the spider began to unwrap him.

"I am following the tracks of a great hornhead. I seek a symbol

of strength for my people, to share my blood and gain power."

"I can be a symbol," said the spider, standing up and wrapping the web into a pillow for the chief to sit. She cast her wickiup over the two of them and gathered up sticks for a fire.

"You? How can you be a symbol of strength? Hornhead breathed life into the earth, and can sing himself across the songlines beneath the stars. He can sleep himself into the past, and the greatest of trees parts for him."

"Who makes the songlines?" the spider asked, grinning ear to ear.

"The great web in the sky can show us where the songlines are woven by the wife of Sun."

"Ah, so Sun's wife, who is Spider," she said, nodding. "What a fantastic person, to make the roads the hornhead must follow, who hangs the stars on the sky, and whose daughter upon which you live. Who is patient with those who accidentally destroy her home, who hunts nothing, but to who her food comes. I weave a web and look for wisdom in it, and is that not strength? The power to sit and wait and be polite when your world is on fire around you?"

The chief nodded in the presence of this knowledge, and pressed his lips together.

"Will you be that symbol for my people?" he asked.

"I have already said so," Spider replied. "Sing the yellow-garden spider song, and we will share a bowl of our blood, I will adopt your wife as my daughter, and all your descendants will be magicians."

Ikasa picked along the Nokaha where it crossed the river into Fort Hammock, glass bottles on her belt filled with water, clinking against each other, and most of a sandwich in her hands. Armadillo's hoppers had picked up on her when she'd stopped by the old man's place for snacks and a drink. They were still following her, trotting ahead and skipping along behind, poking their long noses into logs or piles of shit, eating what they could and begging with croaks and ruffled feathers for whatever scraps Ikasa would toss at them. One of them ran up down the road and flashed its wings.

She took the bridge across into Fort Hammock and stared down the road from Wilmer's up to the mound, almost out of sight by the blur of the daytime sun. She took another bite of her sandwich and rolled salted meat and mustard around on her tongue. Squinting at the mound's mana, she turned her head away to face the river. The bright blue-green water squabbled with space among the limestone, thudding softly in her ears with power, her eyes felt bruised and raw just from the act of looking. She took a left, going off the road onto a little sandy path among the mosses and ferns.

The north Nokaha had the sweet stink of rotting flowers with a sticky miasma that clung to her neck like thick hands. She followed the shade of the plants and the Calabokee around behind the stores, picking through dense rubble crawling with growth. Chunks of concrete and even older brick formed little hollows and loose piles carpeted in greenery. It gave way to limestone and she got a clear look at the thick forest on the south bank, knowing that Gramma's house was someplace over there. She unhooked a bottle from her belt and took a drink of lukewarm water, watching the tree line for a few moments before moving on across the limestone until it turned to white sand.

The Crawfish lived down at the end of a rough street almost the same color as a bloated fish and gave up into broken slabs down at the end facing the river. A stack of cracking brown metal belied the shape of an ancient car in the middle of the road. Ikasa could make out part of a fence assembly just poking through the edge of the forest southwest, a barrier to keep big animals from poking around the verges of civilization for snacks. She thought she could see more fence support beams around the streets, but saw mostly houses made of trailers, sheet metal, and scrap wood, like at Gramma's neighborhood.

Mary's house was the nice one, a single airstream set in an open field and surrounded by short, harsh-looking pines of a young age that nobody wanted to touch because they'd get sticky gunk all over their hands. When she knocked on the door, it rattled on loose bearings, and the slender, shirtless man who answered gave her a bleary stare that smelled of a thick, penetrating gasoline stench. He scowled and shut the door; Ikasa heard indistinct shouting before the door opened and Mary stepped out.

Ikasa caught quick glimpses of the interior. Whereas Gramma's house was gray, yellow, and blue pastels, faded by the harsh light of the sun, Mary's trailer was all deep rust-colored reds painted over dark brown. There was a cracked radio case in the corner and the dining room table was piled high with glass pitchers and mugs. Mary Crawfish shut the door and stepped down, quiet.

"Hey, Spider," she mumbled, and grabbed Ikasa's spare wrist to lead her back to the road.

"Your dad smells like piss and gasoline," Ikasa said.

"He makes white junk for tweakers," Mary answered.

"Ah," Ikasa said, not really understanding, and fed one of the hoppers again.

The door opened on the trailer and that man threw a bundle of trash out into the yard before knocking his head at the two of them.

"I thought I told you to take your fucking friend and get the shit out of here!" he howled.

"Yeah, okay, daddy," Mary nodded, and tugged on Ikasa's wrist, dragging her forcibly back out into the street.

They walked a bit until the airstream was out of sight and Mary turned Ikasa around.

"I thought if I didn't pick up the phone you wouldn't come down here," Mary huffed.

"I came down because a weird lady I met in the woods told me to," Ikasa said. "You thirsty?"

She offered one of her water bottles, and Mary nodded. They kept walking back up the road to the sound of the cypress strand's conversation with itself in the slow breeze.

"Mary? You still out here?" came the voice of Crawfish's father. "You two come back here, now, come in and get something to drink!"

Mary closed her eyes.

"Let's go up to Ronnie's," she said, picking up her pace.

"Shouldn't you mind your pop?" Ikasa asked.

"Ain't no use minding him," Mary said, starting to jog as the shouts grew in volume. "We can cross around at Barpost, that way we don't have to go into town, come on."

Down at the end of the road on the north end, Ikasa caught sight of a fence line that ended some distance up into the limestone and pines. The signs on the facing side warned that it was non-powered and that leaving the road put her at wildlife risk.

"Won't this put us outside the fences?" she asked.

Mary pointed at Armadillo's hoppers.

"We got them, they'll go ballistic if there's something we need to run from."

She had a decent point, so Ikasa just nodded and carried along until Mr. Crawfish's shouts choked in the screech of cicadas and calls of birds. They followed dirt trails and narrow paths among scrub oak until they ran up into another tall section of fence humming with the sound of live electricity. The great arching pillars curled like fingers, forming a protective hand reaching to push away the jungle beyond. Ikasa squinted when she saw watch towers in the distance, trying to figure out if anyone was up in them with guns or radios, but couldn't make out any movement.

"I'm sorry," Mary said, kicking a loose piece of rubble.

"What bout?"

"Pop's got more crazy since mom died. 'You're the last Crawfish girl in Ootsooduh,' he's always saying."

"Is it true?"

Mary stopped and crouched at the side of the road. Ikasa crunched her way over to the shoulder and sat down. Mary was staring down the hole on top of a little clay chimney in the ditch there, biting her own lip.

"Crawfish hole, they dig these burrows and pile all the mud up top," she said. "And, I guess so. I don't know any others."

Mary listened at the end of the chimney and stood up to brush her knees.

"Hey! You want to go down to the sing-stone with me, lightning girl? Let's go get Ronnie and we can sing up some crawfish and cook them!"

"Isn't that a little irresponsible?"

"A Spider!" Mary shrieked, a smile on her face, and pointed. "A Spider's talking to me about responsibility!"

Ikasa laughed and stumbled about, arms straight out in front of her.

"Come and join the many!" she groaned.

"You have movies up in the big city?"

"We sure do. It cost fifty whole cents to get a ticket and so we sneaked in the back door instead, then watched everything that was up there. *A Scratch at the Door*, *The Fairest Young Man*, *Invasion of the Whispering Empire*, *Phantom Kingdom*, all that stuff."

"Well, tickets are twenty cents here, big city girl, but we don't pay for our movies, neither!" Mary said, starting up another jog.

Ikasa rocketed off after her with hands raised, hoppers barking along behind her, and they ran until the road ended and they stumbled among loose limestone and saw palmettos. Only sandy trails marked the presence of civilization, the rest buried in tall oak the stuck out against the cloudless sky. Ikasa stopped at the edge of clear waters in a deep limestone pit, choked by lazy weeds. She followed the shoreline with her eyes and pointed out over the water.

"Is that a boil under there?" Ikasa asked.

"This is Barpost Hole," Mary said. "There's big caves underground and sometimes when they get too dry the ground up top falls in and makes these big pits, then Calabokee breaks through the ground and fills with water. There's lots of holes here and there like this."

"They say places like this are where the Alligator tears splashed when the warrior who wouldn't fight played music for her, don't they?"

Mary nodded.

"That's what they say. But then they also say there's a black magician who owes his soul to evil spirits up around the ruins to Leeseenoo."

"They do, huh?"

"Yeah! He has a lantern and snoops around windows at night with a whole swarm of razor-tooth storks, they say he had a finger made of stone that he lent to help kill a poisoned rootscraper that thought it was a man, and that he's looking for the ones that owe him the finger back."

Ikasa laughed.

"What's so funny?" Mary snorted. "It's spooky. I've seen his light!"

"We got the same story up in Cahokia," Ikasa said. "Except he's an old jazz man, too! There's a song rhyme.

'Oh, mother come with her eyes of coal,
a fifth of rock gwine take my soul,
here I come to walk the earth,
gonna burn it all for the worl's rebirth,
when Death come to take my hand,
them evil ones gwine make 'em stand,
ol' whiskey rock's that evil's home,
gwine to deal myself right to the bone.'"

Mary grabbed herself by the shoulders and shuddered.

"I know you're supposed to be irreverent and all, Spider-girl, but there's lots of songlines and sing-stones around here, can you, like, not sing it?"

"Was it that bad?"

"No, it was that good. I know you know the story about the singing man and the alligators. We was just talking about it."

"Ok! Then I need Crawfish powers to cut through evil!" Ikasa shouted.

Ikasa shook her hair so the red wooden beads clacked. She clapped once and held her pinkies together, fists balled up.

"Evil spirit!" she said, whirling to face Mary.

"Go away!" Mary shouted, eyes narrowed in seriousness with lips drawn together, and snipped on both Ikasa's fingers with her own held up like a pair of claws.

Ikasa felt the pinch and clutched her hands, taking a step back.

"What's wrong?" Mary asked.

Ikasa giggled.

"You were really into it! You put so much mana up front that you hurt me with your river bug claws!" she said, throwing her hands into the air and breaking into a run again. "River bug! River bug!"

"Stick leg freak! Stick arms! Big dumb head! You look just like a spider!" Mary shouted, throwing bark at Ikasa and laughing.

The hoppers swirled around them and they chased one another across the shore of the hole until they were swallowed by the scrub again. Birds warbled and scattered, and two big ikehyookuh with brown feathery bodies, heads with proud crests, and long black legs jumped away into the bush when the girls passed. Mary stopped to follow them, pointing at the place where they'd been browsing.

"Look, poop!" she laughed, poking some white, berry-filled scat with a long stick.

"My pop says the super scientific term is shit," Ikasa answered.

"He does?"

"Well, the words 'shit' and 'guano' don't make me and my brothers laugh uncontrollably."

"And poop does?" Mary asked with a wicked grin across her face.

"Yes."

"Say it," Mary scowled.

"What?"

"Say 'poop!'"

Ikasa scrunched up her lip, doing her best not to break out laughing again, and just smiled and snickered. Mary cupped one of her ears and leaned over to Ikasa.

"Still not hearing it."

"Poop!" Ikasa blurted out, unable to really contain herself.

"It's like a spell, isn't it? It sounds like something is showering down and making a lot of noise!"

"Yes. Like poop," Ikasa giggled.

Mary fell over onto the blue hopper, knocking it down, and while it protested a bit, it quickly forgot why and started gnawing on her hair.

"How close is Ronnie's place?" Ikasa asked.

"Just around the nearest fence line," Mary answered, pulling a loose feather from the hopper. "Do you know their names?"

"Nope, just that Mr. Armadillo don't tie them up like he ought to," Ikasa answered, scanning the trees until she saw the gray coils of wildlife fencing high up in the trees to the northeast. "Let's go get Ronnie and then look for caves."

"Sure," Mary said, standing up. "I know a cool one."

"Avos!" Ikasa replied.

Mary gave her a flat, sarcastic glare and then threw up her arms.

"City girl," she said.

Chapter 7
Headsprings

There was once a very old people, older than even the people who live now, and they were nothing like human people. They could change from one thing to another like stone being carved, but they were more like the earth than even that; their bodies were brown and rough and made of clay and blood, rather than being made of blood and corn like all of us, and they thought in the same way the Everywhen spread out. They built great stone cities; their remains can be seen on the shores of the sea, where Uluguru the paddle-lizard swims. Their bodies would ripple like the surface of the water, and they could appear in any shape. They were among the creations of the Mother of All Things, and when the big hornhead went to sleep, they were one of the people he would dream about.

One of our people found out once that they're still alive, even after that old time's all turned into rocks. It was Raw-Meat-Girl, actually, but this was after she learned how to make her own fire, so she's Cooked-Meat-Girl now. Anyway, Cooked-Meat-Girl was looking around to find some rocks because she wanted to test out an idea, and when she picked one up, it was covering up a tiny hole in the ground, and she got on her hands and knees to look down inside.

Down in the hole were these big, broad, wide caverns that were all filled up with people milling around, many of whom she recognized from her village, and they were all laughing as they filled up the room. They took up the big bladders of palm wine *they'd managed to steal and shared them around.*

"Look at how much we have got from them this time!" one man said, and then he stepped out of his skin and became a tall creature, bald and with giant olive-colored eyes. "There is no blood in any of it, so we can all drink!"

The others laughed and did the same, and they punctured the bags with their little fingers, and as they drank, their arms slowly turned into leathery wings and their heads became long and gnarled like crocodile faces, and they squatted and hunched over, becoming ever more chattering. Cooked-Meat-Girl very quickly replaced the stone and ran away, and did not trust anyone in her village who wouldn't mix blood with their palm wine.

The Blue Crab family's house was a collection of sheet metals and tarps bound up into a box that smelled of burnt bread and liquor out in a field surrounded by the white sand of the scrub. The sun was bright enough that Ikasa had to squint and shade her eyes, and the yard was clear of thick clusters of oak that choked everywhere else. Scattered pine trees standing tall and alone stretched their toes to look over at the little house as it churned out smoke from its single stove pipe. Ronnie sat out front, about half his arm's length deep in a hole with a wooden bin full of hopper chicks next to him, which the big ones ran over to inspect and preen. Ikasa figured Ronnie's uncle Andy was the man dressed in an undershirt and sleeping shorts poking through empty bottles and casting them aside. He looked up at the girls when they approached.

"Any you girls got fifty cents?" he asked.

Ikasa shook her head.

"Mister Blue Crab, we're gonna take Ronnie and go up to the headspring!" Mary shouted, and the man did little else than to wave an empty bottle.

Mary turned to Ronnie.

"You wanna go?"

Ronnie nodded and wiped off his hands. He picked up the bin and moved it back into the house, coming back counting his dimes. He made a little flipper motion with his hands and furrowed his eyebrows.

"Nah," Mary said. "We're going up to Oksachee. Maybe we'll see maize cutters if we're sneaky."

Ronnie nodded and stuck his hands in his overall pockets.

Armadillo's hoppers checked his wrists and hair before going back to scattering themselves across the scrub again. Ikasa felt the back of her neck prickle with fear or excitement about the prospects Mary had mentioned; she'd heard of maize cutters but could never imagine seeing one. Like hoppers, but bigger and meaner with knives. The pulps painted them a sort of noble savagery that made grown men and women quake at their mention. She had thought that their designated territory was two states north, and that they'd be far away from such things.

"Hey!" Mary shouted. "You looked kinda spacey."

"Oh!" Ikasa said. "I'm fine. So, what's Oksachee?"

"There's these ruins up by the headsprings, up at the entrance to Wohona, these caves that the Ntonaka thought led to the underworld. You should see them, they have this big gate, and deeper in, a sealed door."

"Does it really go to the underworld?"

"Probably not."

"And where's the Crawfish sing-stone?" Ikasa asked.

Mary hopped up on a long stone furrow that looked like granite.

"It's a red swamp crawfish stone, so they're eatable, but not perfect. Not like fire-backs. It's up just east of the headspring on a little island, I'll show you."

Ikasa nodded and slapped her palms on a tree as they passed.

"Hey, Ronnie, where'd you get those hatchlings?" Ikasa asked.

"I found the eggs in a box by Wilmer's," he said.

"It speaks!" shouted Mary, waving her hands.

He promptly shut his mouth and picked up the hopper with the bad eye, looping his arms under its wings and wrapping his elbows around its front. It made gurgling baby bird noises and tried to gnaw on his hair, stiff tail flapping around in excitement.

"Should we go get Ehano?" Ikasa asked.

Mary scowled for a moment, but shook her head.

"Nah, today he's with his parents over in Shimookooah," she answered.

"What's down there?"

"School registration."

"Already? Ain't it the start of the summer?"

"My pop says Ehano's family's in the next rung up," Mary

said. "Means his bike gets a bell and he gets to register for school early is all. He's also on the storming team and they want his paperwork cleared so they can start practice before school starts."

"What an ass," Ikasa said.

"Yeah," Mary giggled.

Ikasa watched Mary scamper over a few other blocks and hop across a small gap where a cluster of scrub oak was growing.

"So, who built this stuff?" Ikasa asked.

"The Nakoodah, I think? They lived here after the Ntonaka. They're the ones who built Oksachee."

"Okay," Ikasa said. "What's it made of?"

"Coquina," Mary replied. "It's kind of like fossil seashell concrete. It's really soft though, our teacher last year brought in some pieces and showed us how easy it is to make crumble, but hard to make it shatter in huge chunks. It's like bread. She says people used to use it back in the days when cannons were the big deal."

Ikasa squinted, picking out little crushed shells and bugs all buried in the stone; the weight of ages pressed out from the rock, and it was warm where she touched it, but not from the sun.

"You caught lightning, you're like a magician, right? Can you tell how old it is?" Mary asked.

"Maybe," Ikasa said.

She put her hands flat against the stone, feeling out the bumps and crevices. Her skin prickled. Ikasa heard something like the cry of seagulls. Her body felt snug and tight, perhaps wrapped by a blanket in sand. Something delicious and wonderful rolled over her head and she reveled in long and delicate limbs and rainbow sheen.

"I'm by the seashore. There's birds I can hear. I don't know what kind they are, or even if they're birds. I can't see anything, but I can feel the waves pounding. Each wave brings me food," Ikasa said, dragging her fingers slowly across the rock. "I'm crawling on the sea floor now, something different. I can see fish, maybe, moving above me. The food is in the sand. I pull myself from the sand and cut into myself."

She let go of the rock and hissed at the odd dichotomy, shaking her hands to get sensation back; pins and needles crawled across her palm. She shook her head to try clearing out the vertigo.

"It's really old, like a million years at least. I can't feel things unless they're at least that old," Ikasa said, gnawing on the ball of her hand.

"What about who made it?"

Ikasa picked her hand closer to the coquina, but pulled away before actually touching it.

"I'm not that precise, I'd probably just puke," she said. "My mom's way better. She can tell exactly how old something is, I bet my gramma is even better."

"Okay," Mary said. "What about these, though?"

She pushed aside some saw palmettos fronds and stepped into the atrium of some ancient plaza; the scrub ended abruptly and gave way to thick-leaved plants and tall nut trees crowding in over the tops of coquina causeways and doors that once opened into grand halls, now tunnels to more greenery. Stairways rose up to collapsed bridges and aqueducts, and black mold carpeted a great alligator head sculpture dotted with six eyes that wept droplets of water into a cistern in the ground. The tiny jungle covered the ruins with a protective hand, and spirit lights drifted in the air like weightless snow. A thick wave of meaning fell over her like stepping from a summer day into a climate-controlled department store. Ikasa just about threw up and dropped to the ground, clutching at the dirt and moss.

Ikasa made a gurgling noise with the back of her nose and spat. The town had been pretty bad when she first got to it, but she hadn't felt weight pressed down so hard on her since living in Cahokia. Her shoulder blades felt like they might buckle and snap.

"It's already here. I heard sometimes they dig up ruins or build new stuff on top of them. I don't know why nobody built on this one," Mary said.

"I do," Ikasa coughed. "Holy shit."

Ronnie laughed and dropped the hopper. Ikasa rested her hands on her knees before standing up all the way.

"Is there someplace else here?" she asked Mary.

"No," Mary said.

Ronnie wordlessly stepped up to the big alligator feet all around the washing pool, filled with clear water and cushioned by gentle mats of green algae. Little minnows in the stone-lined trough gasped for air and snatched falling mosquitoes. Ikasa wondered if maybe there were some snakes or turtles in the fountain for a brief moment before Ronnie reached down into the leaves clumping at the bottom and drew out a small Spider cameo. It looked ancient and like any stone and gold key of some bygone era, barely recognizable and highly stylized.

He stepped up to Ikasa and handed it to her, directing her to the relief to the south, between two step pyramids. Ikasa looked at the cold, wet package in her hand and wiped away a whirligig beetle and some dead leaves. She looked where Ronnie had pointed, and saw the likeness Hiqillipll, the bird-squirrel, being presented as if dead to the woman Xiucuscu. It was a strange thing to see so far to the southeast, and she could imagine an artist or an archaeologist coming down here and roping the place off for weeks. However, she saw a place where the spider fit, just under the dead bird in the hands of Xiucuscu; Spider was presenting the bird to the maiden.

She steeled herself by pretending she was one of those rogue archaeologists in the pulps, two-fisted and ready for whatever might come. She slipped the relic into the cache in the wall and held her hands still. Xiucuscu leaned out over the Spider and bowed as was customary.

"Spider," she said. "You must tell no one of what you find here. Here is one half of a shame I can't understand. With you, must the other shame be hidden. Take both shames and bring them together, or keep them apart, as you wish. This is the gift I give to you for giving me aid in childbirth and teaching my boys to play ball."

Xiucuscu nodded with respect and was stone again. Everyone stood around and stared at the hole in the ground where the sacrificial bowl once rested. There was a chamber down below that Ikasa could see, maybe some four feet down. She was still holding the Spider idol.

"Ronnie, you knew about this?" Mary said.

Ronnie just nodded. He pointed up at the head of the Calabokee and trailed his hand down to the bas relief of the singing man beneath her and the woman hiding in a cave below.

"Oh," Mary said. "I feel kinda dumb now."

"How so?" Ikasa asked, trailing her legs into the hole. She stuffed the spider stone into her pocket.

"Wohona cavern is really near here, I bet this connects. The Nakooda must have built right over the top of it."

Ikasa lowered herself to the floor and fumbled around in the dark. Dropping down onto her knuckles, she loped around a moment before realizing she could nearly stand up in the actual chamber. She picked up a limestone rock and clutched it in both hands, squinting and pressing her lips together.

"Don't let me stay in the darkness," she said. "Please, don't make me stay in this place without your guidance."

"What are you doing?" Mary shouted down.

"It's too dark and I'm scared!" Ikasa shouted, trying to invest her voice with no small amount of real fear. She gripped the rock tighter, close to her chest, and sunk down into a corner of the cavern. Mary dropped down next to her, with Ronnie following quickly.

"Please," Ikasa said. "I'm so scared. So scared."

Turquoise light tried to fight its way out of her fingers, and she held up the stone, now bright enough to illuminate the whole of the cavern.

"So, you weren't really scared?" Mary asked. "You were trying to get a favor out of the rock."

"A little. Most rocks are different colors. Wonder why this one's turquoise?"

"Well, it's sure not limestone, that would be red. Maybe it's copper? We read in school that the Ntonaka used limestone to filter copper out of the water," Mary said.

"So you think this is an old water chamber?"

"Maybe."

The hoppers squeaked at them from above the hole, unwilling or unable to make the trip down. The three kids turned north and started taking steps down into the hole.

"It's funny, isn't it?" Spider asked.

"What do you mean?" Crawfish answered.

"Crawfish, Spider, and Blue Crab all go down into the underworld to find a mystery cave, and for what?" Spider said.

"To solve the mystery of the secret shame!" Crawfish shouted, making clack-clack noises with her mouth and hair beads, pinching her fingers.

"So you all saw that, too?" Ikasa looked up at the last beam of sunlight. Ronnie walked by and nodded at her before carefully descending the staircase.

"Yeah, heard Xiucuscu telling you to do something! Come on, then! Best go and do it!"

"She didn't seem that interested in whether or not I do anything at all," Ikasa said, taking a few more steps down.

There was a sealed door, and Ikasa stopped at it.

"Can you read this?" she asked Mary.

"Yeah, ok," Mary said, squinting, and she motioned for Ikasa to bring her a light. "It says 'We place this in a barrier of stone to remind us of some minds too unable of allow themselves absolute freedom,' or something like that, and then these over here are Ntonaka numbers, not Nakooda ones. See? This guy wearing the Hornhead skins is five."

The whole of the door was covered in reclining figures. Ikasa reached out to tap five. She'd always liked five. It lit up. Something seemed familiar about the door, a sequence of numbers she liked.

"Okay. Which one's three?" she asked.

Mary just pointed at the symbol of a folded net held by a merchant. Spider tapped out three-eleven-seven, and the door began to open.

"That was eleven, and seven. All primes?" Mary asked.

"Yeah. It's the combination I use on all my stuff."

"Maybe it's the thing you asked to keep from a previous life," Mary said.

The room was a thick and wide chamber ringed by strange metal pipes and even more strange writings that had no meaning, but in the center was a cot and spread out over it was a thick white blanket with red beads here and there. A few books sat on the ground near the bed, and the few pots nearby smelled of cinnamon bark, tannin, and other things - papers, metal boxes, and long, broad pieces of metal melded with the stone. She pushed over a stack of books and looked down. The room had the look of an office, a magician's lodge, and a prison to its dingy, natural corners.

"The line of confluence leads to this chamber," Ikasa said flatly.

"What?"

"It's the word pop uses. The threads I had followed to get that pulp in the store have been part of the line of confluence, important sites in the path of the webs."

"What does that mean?" Ronnie asked.

Ikasa frowned and looked at the cot in the center of the room. It beckoned her to lay down, to stare up at the crystalline growths on the ceiling. She checked for story threads reaching away but found none.

"It means, as of right now, if I do nothing, that cot-chair-table thing, that's the end."

"The end of what?" Mary asked.

Ikasa fretted her lip. She was certain there was movement in the darkness at the back of the chamber. She became so sure of it with each passing moment that she didn't notice Mary grabbing her arm and Ronnie turning around to leave.

"I don't think we're alone down here," Mary said.

Ikasa nodded quickly and started to back away from the room.

"Maybe Xiucuscu can close the door up top," she said.

"Yeah, let's go, this is seriously creepy. The Ntonaka sealed it up for some reason," Mary said.

They re-emerged to daylight and the rock stopped shining. Ikasa threw it back down into the hole with a hefty thanks and some of her day snacks. She shivered. She was going to sit in that cot, whether she liked it or not. Sitting in that little bed holding a turtle would be a shame. She wondered if, when the time came to sit in it, she wouldn't be so afraid of it. That part made her neck go cold and her teeth ache. The idea of welcoming whatever fate the cot held in it seemed monstrous.

Chapter 8
A Crawfish Stone

This is not the story of Spider and Sun's first daughter; there are stories before this one and ages beyond it, but those are far more secret, and neither men nor women know of them. This is the story of Hornhead's dream of the beginning of life on our planet before it had life of its own.

The Mother of All Things came to the wind-lashed stone in the heavens, aboard a screaming mote of light. She touched herself upon the ground and found she was not alone. A hornhead slept in the desolate land, and when she woke him, he expressed as much confusion as she, for when he went to sleep, there was a world, but it seemed the world had been unmade.

"So!" The Mother of All Things said. "Let us put the world you dream of here before us. Sing this song I will teach you!"

And they sang together, and from the great trumpets of Hornhead sprang mountains and algaes and little bubbling things and armored things and soft things that swam in the sea.

"Let us see what else we can sing!" the Mother of All Things shouted. And she sang, too, and she sang clay into stranger things and hid them away under rocks, pointing to them and saying "When it is their time, also sing at these rocks."

So Hornhead and the Mother of All Things sang and danced until they were tired and could dance no more. However, she saw that her creations did not change, so she looked about here and there until she discovered the shattered pieces of a great many things that came to this world before she had, and took each of the two thousand fragments and made every one of them into a maintainer or destroyer, to help her with the task of making a new world. Ymanu-Jela the Dreamer of Life was the name of one such being, and the Mother of All Things told him to dream of animals, and so he did. She took them from his head and put them around on the land. Another was named the Black-Haired Woman Who Mothers A Fiend in Her Breast, who was a destroyer being, and the Mother of All Things told her to dream of stones. She took those from her head and put them around, too. From there, she made the dragons and the angels of the earth and watched and waited.

That's how I remember it. My gramma used to tell a story where she made the creators and maintainers first, and another story without Hornhead at all. She was also pretty heavy in her bottles, though, so I can never really be sure the story is reliable to reality, but the touch of a story is immaterial to whether or not it is true.

Ikasa closed up the tunnel with the spider key and tried to pretend she wasn't worried about what she'd found down there. She stretched in the open air and let herself be swarmed by Armadillo's hoppers while they checked her hands for anything she might have found down there. Mary knocked dust out of her hair.

"I'd show you other things that are out here, but I don't know that if I do you won't make something scary pop out again," Mary said. "Spiders. Why did I agree to this crap?"

Holding up both her hands, Ikasa shook her head.

"No, I promise! I won't do anything else like this."

Mary gave her a fake scowl and stomped along the moss line before Ronnie shrugged and followed along.

"Maybe we'll find some woody grubs on the way to the Crawfish stone!" Mary said.

She climbed up an old staircase and stepped along the wall. Ikasa moved along the ground, watching the cracks in the road and looking at old alligator etchings scrawled over with new, stranger graffiti made of spattered ink and bright earth paints. Long serpents with horns and monsters usually found only in the deep wilderness were drawn with hunched figures carrying spears as they thundered through plains and jungle. She barely noticed the corner of the ruin when she arrived. She collided with coquina brick and her nose took on a sharp pain. She heard Mary laughing.

Down by her feet, Ikasa saw crumbles of what she thought might be black pebbles and crouched down to spread her fingers around in the remains.

"What did you find?" Mary asked.

Ronnie picked one up and crushed it between his fingers.

"Ash. Someone had a fire," Ikasa said.

"Was it campers or isolators?" Mary asked, looking for a place to jump down.

"I don't know," Ikasa said.

She moved loose bricks around and checked the wet soil by the ruins until she found two-toed footprints as big as her hand scattered about.

"Maize-cutters," she said, recognizing the pictures from schoolbooks. Seeing them in life was a bit of a frightening thrill, and she touched one, feeling the throb of inhuman mana in her fingertips.

"There's a clan that lives up here. Maybe they were taking shelter during the last couple of storms," Mary said. "What's it feel like?"

"Like an artist, but not like a human being at all. It seems angry, just because?"

Ikasa found half a splintered blade tucked under a rock, wrapped in gauze and attached to a wishbone of wood.

"Or maybe he's upset because he broke his knife," Mary said.

Ikasa flipped the knife around in her hands like it was gold, palm to palm. Where there should have been a handle, there was an arrow or wishbone shape, supported by a single splint between the branches. Ikasa tried to wrap her hands around the center bar, but it was a tight fit.

"How do you even hold it?" she asked.

Mary clacked her teeth.

"They bite it," Mary said.

Ikasa stuck the knife in her pocket.

"Show me the Crawfish stone!" she shouted. "No more distractions!"

Mary threw her arm out.

"The Alligator stone is east of here, but the Crawfish stone is more northeast. We'll go up there and you'll see where it's put up. My mom says there's a songline that goes twenty years west up behind it."

"Back or forward?" Ikasa asked.

"Both," Mary answered.

There were tiny creeks and muddy pits all along the path, bare of life save tiny minnows and brown muck. Mary stamped up to a tall piece of limestone with a giant inverted crawfish drawing, eyes downward and pincers open. Ikasa felt the strength radiating from it like a thick haze, and her skin prickled with the sensation of tiny, needle-like feet. She squinted and shielded her eyes.

"Maybe I should back up a little bit?" Ikasa said.

"Maybe," Mary said. "But then you wouldn't get to hear the Crawfish song, you know?"

Ikasa nodded and balled up her fists.

"Spider, Blue Crab, give me a backbeat," Mary said.

"Chala-hah, chalah-ha," Ikasa started, looking down at Ronnie.

Ronnie smiled fiercely and nodded.

"Boom-chepa, boom-chepa," he began.

"Not a sock beat!" Mary said.

Ikasa clapped and laughed.

"Crawfish's name is Tsa-tsima, should I use that instead?" Ikasa said.

Mary gave a thumbs-up, and Ikasa and Ronnie began again.

"Cha-cheema! Cha-chee-mah!" they shouted and clapped.

Ikasa declined to catch the words that came from Mary's mouth, using her own voice to drown out what Mary might say, so that she wouldn't steal the song by accident. The stone stayed as it was while Mary took to hopping from one leg to the other, holding her arms to her sides and favoring her left, waving around her hand in a figure-eight. She sang until Ikasa felt her own legs growing tired, and she took to pleading at the stone in her mind's eye, pressing onward through a familiar sensation not unlike vomiting from her arms and legs. Her head swam, and she stopped singing to grab her nose and cough. Mary was breathing hard and staggering away into a tree for support. Ronnie just let himself go and fell into leaves.

Crawfish burst from the earth. They came from leaves and behind bark, crawling out of mud and spilling up over bits of stone and one another. They swarmed around Ikasa's feet and she sank just a bit. The hoppers danced around and snatched up a few of them here and there for play or food, picking up crawdads with their jaws or hands.

"Catch some!" Mary shouted, and Ikasa stretched out her poncho to use as a basket. Ronnie stuffed his pockets and Mary used up the front of her dress. There were giggles and screams, and Ikasa ended up with stacks of tiny crawfish in her makeshift sack.

Mary motioned them up along the path to a sandy spot cleared among the trees, littered with broken quahog fossils and wide slabs of thin stone. Mary dropped her pile and set up a few rocks around the old fire pit, building a little fire with deer moss and dried sticks. She pulled up one of the stone slabs - some old seashell of enormous size - and put it up on the rocks, waiting for it to heat.

"You can twist off the heads and put the tails on the stone, or just throw the whole thing up there," Mary said.

Ikasa nodded and tossed a few up; the bodies seemed pretty gross once she twisted off the head. Their organs squelched out like little piles of toothpaste. Ronnie just tossed whole crawfish in. A pile of tails slowly grew, and Mary stoked them like coals while they hissed.

"This is like roasting, really. We should maybe be boiling them into a soup, but we don't have a pot."

Sneaking one out from the bottom, Ikasa sucked the tail out and chewed.

"They're pretty sweet," she said.

"They are, but these kind have a strong aftertaste. You're not eating the organs?" Mary asked.

"They seem gross," Ikasa said.

Ronnie picked one of his up and ate the whole thing right out through the back of the carapace. Ikasa grimaced.

"They're the best part," Mary said.

Somewhere in the distance, a deep scream echoed across the trees. Ikasa felt the air shudder. Mary looked up into the sky like she was expecting a storm.

"You remember we was talking about the stone finger of the black magician? They say he's still owed the finger, and until he gets it back, the poison rootscraper is never gonna find true death," Mary said. "See, what I heard was that a long time ago these three kids found out the rootscraper was going around killing people to take their skins. They chased it for a little while, but it almost killed and ate one of them. So they read that they needed a spear with a tip made of a stone finger, went up to the Leeseenoo ruins and met a man in the smoke who gave them his finger made of stone. They sharpened it up and next time that rootscraper came around, they stabbed it and it disappeared into mist."

Ronnie crunched down on another crawfish.

"But the magician told them kids they owed him a finger," Mary said. "He's never come back to get it, though."

"So the finger-spear is still out there?" Ikasa asked.

"You bet," Mary nodded. "So is spear-finger."

"Who?"

"That's another country story," Mary said. "Over in the mountains way to the east, base of the Moon's Road, there's two witches, and they argue all the time. One of them is Snakeface, she wears a wooden mask and has a face made entirely of rattlesnakes and water moccasins. She's in an argument with her sister the spear-finger witch, who has one really long finger and her skin is impossible to break. I don't know if she's dead or not, because I never heard a story where she died, but sometimes I hear they get into arguments up in the mountain and the arguments turn into storms and one or the other gets blown down into the Pahayohkee, that's the big marsh that takes up most of Ootsooduh that runs south out into the Central Sea, so we're right in the middle of them sometimes, right?"

"We read about that place before we moved here. The River of Grass shaped by rain and fire, child of the hurricanes," Ikasa said. "It's big, huh?"

"Yeah. They say it's the body of an old king," Mary said.

Ikasa dropped back into the sand with a crawfish tail in her mouth.

"Hey, Ronnie," she said. "How come you don't have a pistol yet?"

"His daddy's not allowed to have one after getting arrested," Mary said. "So he can't even step foot in a gun store until he's got the okay from the sheriff."

"Well, that's an easy thing," Ikasa said, standing up and brushing off her pants before unbuckling her holster.

"You're giving him your .22?" Mary said.

"If he wants. It's better than not having anything at all," Ikasa said. "I can just go get another one from my pop or when a trader comes by or have a new one made or whatever."

She held the belt out to Ronnie, who picked it up and turned it over in his hands.

"Go ahead and pull it out. Point it at the ground or at a tree or something. Just not anybody," Mary said.

"Yeah. It's a single action, so there's no safety, but you have to pull back the hammer before you do anything," Ikasa said. "Support with one arm while keeping the trigger arm loose but steady. Don't lock your arm by extending it all the way."

Ronnie pointed off into the bushes.

"It's not going to hurt most animals you shoot with it, but it's going to make a loud noise and that's what's important," Mary said.

"Yeah. Also if you have to shoot anything, just pull the trigger like it's a water gun, don't tap, just take one smooth action," Ikasa said.

He had to use both fingers to pull back the hammer, and he stumbled back when the weapon clicked. He pulled the trigger, and he winced. There was a rough snap from the hammer slamming down. Mary looked at Ikasa with a half frown.

"Don't worry. It's not loaded right now," Ikasa said. "I have some spare cylinders that are, I just thought maybe you should get used to pulling the trigger first."

Ronnie played around with it a bit more. Mary moved his fingers every so often. Ikasa and the hoppers ate more crawfish. Eventually she got out her spare pre-loaded cylinders and set up her water bottles on the crawfish cook stone so that Ronnie could take a few shots at them. He used up a good number of rounds before Ikasa gave up.

"It's fine for now," she said. "Not everybody is destined for the fast paced life of a professional bottle hunter. I guess it's just only important if it makes a loud noise."

Ronnie grinned and strapped the gun belt over his waist before sitting back down for more crawfish. Mary cooked and everybody ate until they were nearly full. Ikasa unpacked her kelly can to boil some water.

A stork flew overhead, croaking as it flapped leathery wings. Ikasa fell back onto the sand again.

"I haven't told my parents yet."

"About what?" Mary asked.

"The old lady, Sadie Kaw, she told me I got to go dancing up at the mound."

"Spider-girl, you are a pile of weird," Mary said. "Can't wait for Ehano to come back and put some normal back in here."

Ikasa laughed and watched a few clouds go by. The hoppers came by to lick her face and hands clean of grease.

"Hey, Ronnie, can I have one of them hoppers?"

He nodded and grinned. Ikasa stuck a hand in her pocket and felt the bag that Armadillo had given to her. She grinned wickedly and pulled out her knife.

"You got any paper with you?" she asked Mary.

"Maybe, why?"

"We got this one more thing before we do anything else," Ikasa said.

"What's that?"

Ikasa pulled the bag out of her pocket and pulled free two dried buds.

"Got this from Mr. Armadillo's garden," she said, and Mary sat up and crawled closer.

"All right!" Mary said.

Chapter 9

The Mound

The story is a lie, unless you are a Spider.

Spider loves all her children, and there is very little she wouldn't do in order to protect them. One day every animal was sitting around talking about their own families and how many virtues they have.

"My children are strong, and they can thrash their enemies about!" said Alligator. "Without strength, no one is anyone."

"My children are full of courage," shouted Green Lizard. "Without courage, no one is anyone. What use is strength without courage to apply it?"

"My children are resourceful," said Scrub Jay. "Without resourcefulness, what use is either of those? To smash a wall perhaps, but nothing more."

Spider skittered by.

"Loyalty," is all she said.

"What does Spider know about loyalties?" asked Alligator, burbling water.

"Without loyalty, any virtue you possess does nothing but serve your enemies," Spider replied. "My daughters circle around me and my husband in a perfect dance. Our friends and family may collide, but they all do so with loyal, unwavering precision. I am loyal to my magicians, and any bargains they make will be fulfilled as promised. Loyalty to a person is just the same as it is with a dropped stone. You expect the earth to make the stone fall, do you not? That is loyalty."

"If that is loyalty, then, each of my daughters is worth a

thousand Spiders!" Alligator snapped.

"Then we shall test this. I will call in my daughter Ikasa and give her a command. Then you must call in one of your daughters and give her the same command. If there is any hesitation in either of our daughters, then you lose," said Spider.

Alligator agreed, and so Ikasa was brought in.

"What is it, mother?" she asked.

"Kill me and offer me to your father," said Spider.

Ikasa did not blink or even shake, but instead she drew the family knife from her leg-sheath and drove it into her mother's chest. She cut out her mother's heart and held it up in both her hands to her father, Sun, and when she had done so, began cutting Spider's back skin to make a jacket.

Alligator, ashamed, sank under the swamp and boiled with rage.

Ikasa came downstairs with a greasy face and hands that still felt like grub skin. Eddie stood in the living room. He had his long hair pinned back in a ponytail and was adjusting his vest in the wall mirror. He tugged on the triangle patterned sleeves and looked at Ikasa as she came down. He flicked her in the forehead and she scowled at the sharp pain.

"Dude. You're not dressed, Mom's going to kick your ass," he said.

She huffed and looked him up and down; he was wearing pants with a wrapped cloth around the lower left leg that looked new, with a patch that had the family's car stitched in and among the clouds and storks. His shirt under the black vest was light yellow with white speckles all throughout, like a yellow garden spider. She opened her fist.

"You're just lucky you're wearing mound regalia," she said, and shoved him. "Are we going up there?"

He just smiled. She stepped past him and yelled.

"Mom, are we going to the mound today?" she shouted.

Her father brushed past her, straightening his hair band.

"Yes, we are, your mother told you last night," he said, snatching a beer off the living room table. "Go get in your Spider dress."

She grumbled and started up the stairs.

"And put on your squirrel-bird headdress!" he shouted back.

Ikasa stopped.

"I hate that thing, it makes me look like a TV tribal!" she screamed, stomping upstairs.

"Hey, shithead, you are a TV tribal!" Gramma Spider screamed back.

She kicked her door once and dug through her clothes briefcase until her mom appeared in the doorway holding a long dress with a single rattlesnake-designed sash.

"Put it on," her mother said.

"I want to take a bath!"

"No time for showering, you should have been up an hour ago when I came in."

Ikasa gave an angry look and quickly washed off her arms and stomach in the sink so at least she wouldn't feel like grime all day. She didn't even remember mom coming in at all, but that wasn't as important as snatching the dress away and grumbling about the whole issue. It wasn't even a real mound dress, considering she was so lanky she still fit into the one-piece training dress that had all the vests and proper layers already sewn in. She slipped it right over her head and adjusted it so the embroidered Spider patch was over her family tattoo and yanked out the oppressive neck collar a little before digging up her wicker hatbox.

Wiping off the top cover, she unlatched the little tarnished copper clasps to the sound of beads scattering everywhere; inside was a folded silk sheet and a wide headdress with long metallic green feather plumes. Embroidery reminiscent of flames made up of a pair of wings that would wrap down around her chin and a crest like an open beak filled with teeth up at the top. Her mother had taken her down to the breeder to look at squirrel-birds, little bright green skittering creatures with tiny scaly hands and red feathers along the rump. She had picked one out with a bright yellow plume on its tail and her mother had her choke it to death and cut and dress it. She fashioned wooden spools and painted them black to go out of the sides, and every feather and bone had gone somewhere in the piece. She ate the rest and drank the blood; it had sickened her at first, and it had taken her several days to finally choke it all down.

Assembling the piece and pulling it down over her beaded dreadlocks, she came downstairs to find everyone waiting at the door, all dressed for the mound visit. Gramma Spider was still in whatever house dress she felt like wearing and Kapu had a flower shirt on that made him look like a college student dressing up like an old man. Pop tapped his watch once and led everyone to the car; Ikasa and Eddie took turns shoving each other until they finally got into their seats, all reasonably separated.

The car was cramped with everyone in it. Ikasa was bunched up next to Gramma and Butch, Gramma's stick-arms folded over each other like a scarecrow. Kapu sat in the seat behind them and played with Gramma's hair. He and Eddie carried on some hushed conversation while the car pulled out.

"Up here's where they've been pulling concrete," Gramma said as they drove onto the Nokaha. "They pick up big chunks of the old roads and bring them into town because the BIA's all about urbanization of the smaller settlements, so we don't get any new concrete. They send day labor out on trucks to pull up shit out of the highway, that's what all the rubble is about."

"Yeah, I remember it being paved really nice before," Mom said.

"That was up before the last big crash," Gramma answered. "They renamed the bridge, too. Used to be the Ichiqi, but now it's Hughes. Vote came up last month and they ain't changed the signs yet, but that Garfish bitch came up with all her little Palmetto Roach girls and they did this big long speech about the future or somesuch."

"Garfish?" Pop asked.

"Marcy Garfish, she's in the Alligators' pocket right now, they worked together to get this asshole from Rutger into county, and now I swear they're tipping votes using the Andersonville laws as cover for all their little gerrymandering shit."

They crossed the bridge and rolled by an abandoned four story building that Gramma pointed at.

"That's going to be the new channel six building, it used to be Sunshine Palms hotel, back when it was owned by Marcia and Rob, but it's been empty since before you were last living down here."

"That reminds me. You never told me what happened to the house," Mom said.

"You remember seventeen years ago when you were pregnant with Eddie, after you moved off to the city and had your own business with Dan? I sold it and dumped all that startup in your shop."

"Is that where that came from? Why didn't you tell us when

we had a good profit? We'd have paid you back."

"No, ain't your place to pay back your elders for what they done, other than to take what they give you and run as fast as you can with it."

Ikasa narrowed her eyes and fingered the corn bag in her pocket. The car pulled into a gravel parking lot and stopped. Gramma loped out and stretched. She waved her hand up along the southwest.

"That's the fourteen, it's the highway you came in on, you coulda come in on the northwest, but I had you go around south because it's another road they're pulling up chunks out of, so it's all dirt if you get too far. Hear the state's going to come around and lay down new pavement eventually," she said, crunching her way up to the front gate.

The north mound was visible over the fence, rising up over the trees, covered in grass, with a big rectangular building on top, an old grass-woven longhouse with newer brick chimney and entrances into the pyramidal mound down below. When they passed by the outer fence and trees, there was a clear sand lot between two step pyramids that swarmed with alligator and bird imagery. The great mound had a spider and a hornhead surrounded by spirals on a big stone slab at the base. Ikasa could see that the complex wasn't straight north and south due to the shadows on the ground, but rather angled northeast. She looked at Gramma.

"Hey," she asked. "This is a heaven's pyramid. Is there another one of these directly east for Water, and one southwest for Fire?"

"Where the two rivers meet there's a Fire mound, and over in Leeseenoo just on the other side of the headsprings, there's a Water mound. There's another mound over by the Shimookooah airport."

"And one at the Chukto village?"

"So things actually happen in that shithole you call a head," Gramma said. "Think the shrine in Leeseenoo's maintained, but I don't remember. Don't matter anyway. This mound's dedicated to Losceohnah, a Wokadonah king, who helped ally with the Mokwepet during the Kaweekyooh war."

The family washed their hands at the front gate, where a girl with a horseshoe crab patch on her shoulder tended a small spring with natural rocks stacked around the banks. They entered the main yard between two stepped pyramids, a wide expanse made of packed clay and mixed gravel kept clear of grass in every direction. Multiple tall statues with the town's calendars sat at the northeast pyramid's base steps, and they were all well-kept, with clay, gold, and sacred blankets draped over their shoulders. Ikasa watched her parents head up to the primary house between the pyramid and the mound, and she jogged over to read the calendar.

The primary statue was tall and clearly representative of the current king of the United Tribal Confederacy, though he had with him a small statue that she assumed with the leader of the Wakwahnoo or the Ootsooduh, but couldn't figure out who the current council member of either of them was. She noted that his name was Thunder, though, and grabbed the travel flashlight out of her child's dress. As each statue moved down the line and around the pyramid, they would measure older rulers or heroes, which meant the oldest hero depicted here would most likely have the information pertaining to the cave under the towns, if at all.

Ikasa leaned back to look at the caretaker's house. Her folks had gone out of sight. She crawled a little bit up the oldest and rightmost statue to get a look at the town's origin. The statue looked wrong, squat and with very broad shoulders, not like the same culture as the others. She read the plate as "Nakoodah," taking the time to spell each letter out. Suddenly excited, she checked inside the statue's eyes, shining her flashlight across distorted lettering that she couldn't understand. She thought perhaps she would come back later with a notepad.

"I'd say it was blasphemy to climb up those things, but it's just a Spider," a voice called out.

Ikasa shuddered as the mana passed through her, and she whipped around like a bolt and stood up straight. Pacing around the edge of the dance field was the Alligator girl, wearing her turquoise headband and with a tall jade headpiece weighing down her hair. She had on a jacket with a spider pattern and wore the arm bands that indicated she was playing a part, rather than claiming to be a Spider family member. Ikasa squinted and huffed.

"You better take that off, I'm here now," Ikasa answered back.

Alligator girl drifted to the edge of the clay field and stopped short of the trampled yard.

"Holly Alligator," she said.

"Ikasa Spider," Ikasa answered.

The girl laughed, a deep, rumbling laugh, and pulled a tall pot around off her back; it was old, red clay with flaking paint and gashes, and one particularly deep crack sealed up with hardware glue on one side. Holly fumbled with it so she could hold the pot in one hand and put her palm on the lid.

"That's a bit presumptuous of your parents, isn't it?" Holly said. "Name your daughter after a planet. A name with mana like that shouldn't be owned by such a scrawny kid."

She screwed off the lid just a tiny bit, and Ikasa felt waves of heat pouring out from the lip.

"Or, no, I guess that's right. Ikasa was supposed to be skinny, and have hair like snow, and smell like guano," Holly said. "So I guess the name's perfectly okay."

Alligator ripped off the lid and cackled in a way Ikasa thought that only a Spider could, and the world devolved into fire; the heat was dry and made Ikasa's skin crackle and scream. The air caught fire, turning the world into bright yellow and red veins. She didn't recall falling, but she knew that she had somehow gotten down on all fours. The roar echoed all around her, and it took her a moment to realize that the fire wasn't lashing directly at her. She rolled and crawled around behind the closest statue.

"Just so you know!" Ikasa yelled. "My pop said giving me this name is a mistake!"

"Just like a spider, you get a candle too close and they run off."

The sound of another burst of flame echoed through the air.

"This jar is very old," Alligator said. "Our family got it from an crotchety man who traded it for one night's stay in our home. One night! For this jar. We had it independently verified by a Kuhdjoojoo Bird. Very expensive. Priceless, even."

She emerged from around the statue.

"Can you imagine the frame of mind someone would need to trade his family's greatest treasure for one night of food?" Holly said, popping the lid open again, releasing the fire at Ikasa.

Ikasa rolled away from the statues and started scrambling up the pyramid steps between two hissing alligator sculptures, using the outstretched arms of ancient magicians to grip on to. The stairs were always so steep that she had to crawl up them on her hands and knees, but the reliefs would make for good places to hide. More heat crested off her back, and she scrabbled up across stonework.

"Not even using the stairs? More blasphemy? You just keep digging yourself a deeper hole."

"Why are you doing this to me?" Ikasa wailed.

"I was told you'd come to take the jar and my place at the autumn dances," Alligator said. "I was told if I could scare you away from this shrine, you'd never come back. And Alligators are peaceful, shy, but very, very territorial."

"You used too many verys!" Ikasa shouted.

Another plume of fire lanced over her head. She tried not to show that she was sweating and swung herself up over the sacrificial block and hunkered down. She was certain Holly was coming up the steps now. Ikasa rubbed her temples and grumbled. The blood catch dug into her back and she moved to get out of its way, looking at the black stain in the bottom of the bowl. She briefly wondered if people still died on the rocks out here, and thought about blood being poured into the bowl. She quickly patted down her pockets and grinned, pulling out the corn bag. She put a few kernels in her hand and stood up.

Fire roared over her head again.

"Well, bug bitch, you scared yet?" Holly asked, laughing from halfway up the stairs, holding the cap on the jar.

"Yes!" Ikasa shouted back, cocking her arm and making one hard throw, letting the corn fly.

The kernels sprinkled around the Alligator's feet, and a few down into the folds of her dress. One caught in her hair. She frowned and looked up at Spider.

"Throwing corn is not," Holly said. "That was supposed to do what exactly?"

"Wait for it," Ikasa said.

"Wait for what?" Alligator asked.

Alligator's dress tore in several places as full-grown corn stalks erupted from each kernel. One rose up through her hair, knocking off the jade headpiece, and the rest burst out at odd angles from the stairs, and she yelped and rolled down the stairs all the way to the ground in a heap. She dropped the pot, and Ikasa jumped down the steps in just a few bounds to scoop it up and pick an ear off one of the stalks.

"Wait for that," Ikasa said. "You want to take some home for bread? It's my gift to you. I'll trade you an evening's meal back for this."

"That is your right," Alligator said, her voice muffled by clothing and dirt, still lying face-down at the base of the pyramid.

Ikasa rolled the jar around before finding there was a strap attached to it. She hadn't looked too keenly at it before, and now realized that it was rather slipshod for a pot, and was probably far past its use for anything other than the fire inside it. She slid it over her shoulder before remembering that Alligator was probably still on the ground. She turned to help Holly up.

"We're not finished," Holly said, once she stood and brushed herself off. "Next time we meet, I'll hurt you."

"It's our job to not be finished," Ikasa replied.

Holly Alligator smiled a genuine smile, teeth showing and her shoulders up. She slapped Ikasa on the left arm and grunted. Holly painted four white horizontal stripes on her own forehead with a compact from her pocket and pulled out an obsidian hooked knife.

"Roll up your sleeve," Alligator said.

Ikasa did so, and the girl cut her on the left shoulder, a coiled mark with triangles above, and two wavy cuts below, and rubbed dirt into the cuts.

"Ikasa!" called out Pop's voice.

Her parents came around the corner from the north as Ikasa was rolling down her sleeve. She looked at Alligator as her parents nodded and smiled.

"There you are, you didn't hear us calling?" her mother said. "Ah, good afternoon, Lady."

Momma Spider bowed and kept her eyes on the sky.

"It's okay, ma'am," Holly answered. "I was just giving 'Kasa some gifts for being new in town. Like this Spider jacket and that old pot."

She threw the jacket over Ikasa's head.

"And she was giving me some ears of corn she conjured up. It was very nice and proper of her," Alligator said.

"That's the first time she's ever been proper without being prompted," Poppa Spider said. "I'm almost disappointed."

"Daniel!" her mom said.

Holly waved as Ikasa's parents led her away. Ikasa watched until the Alligator was nearly out of sight. The Alligator smiled a toothless smile again. Narrowing her lips, Ikasa let her folks push her into the caretaker's house.

Chapter 10

A Creation Myth

On the western coast close to the beaches that give way to Death's Country they say there is a particular kind of spider that infests the caves all up in those areas. The Athamalco once lived there, and they explain that these spiders are created from the dark thoughts of the mother spider. One particular story talks about the warrior Kosalstakt, who lived in a city under the auspices of King Tsotsek Third-Cutter. According to the story, a floating skull entered the city and the king dispatched warriors to follow it, and subsequently found a strange palace in the forest.

Upon entering, they met a giant spider who spun webs over skulls and pits of corpse-fire. The men attacked it, but Kosalstakt challenged the spider, who laughed at him, saying, "you cannot slay me until a body in whose death I had no hand is brought before me!" The spider easily defeated the men, and the warrior ran out into the rain.

He went out to the nearby villages until he found a recent death that had not yet been burned. Making away with it into the night, he took it back to the palace and threw it before the spider, which was then quickly defeated and thrown into the pits, along with the girl's body. Kosalstakt returned home to his king and reported the death of the monster, and the queen there rewarded him with the chance to join their family, being introduced to their cousin, who had no husband.

Kosalstakt recognized the face of the girl.

Ikasa sidled into the kitchen rubbing her eyes. Gramma was standing like a skeleton in the open door of the icebox while Pop was pounding something thin and watery out a bottle that was clearly not labeled for water. Ikasa sat down at the table and shoved bones, feathers, twine, and wooden rings out of the way and hauled up a box of tumbled quartz. Gramma turned back around and dropped some beer bottles on the table.

"The trick is to loosen yourself up a little bit with something hard, four or five shots, then switch to a lighter alcohol," she said, then nodded at Ikasa. "Good morning, shithead. The little fucker is in the study room and the big one's trying to get laid."

Ikasa dug through the box of stones and grabbed some of the cracked ones.

"Can I have these?" she asked, waiting for Pop's nod. "Where's Mom and Kapu?"

"She and him took off to go get groceries. Stick around if you want to help haul them in," Pop said.

She stuffed the rocks in her pocket and got up. She dusted off her hands and started her way out the side door. Eddie was in the front yard leaning into some girl's car. She was fairly certain it wasn't a convertible, but it was missing the top all the same. She could see sawed-off metal with tape and spray paint to soften the edges. Eddie slid over to the passenger seat.

"Hey, bean-pole!" he shouted. "Tell Mom where I'm at!"

"I don't know where you're going!" Ikasa shouted back.

"Up to Barpost to swim!" he said, waving and beating on the side of the door.

"Don't get amoebas in your brain!" Ikasa yelled as the car pulled away to dust.

Gramma came out of the house, wielding a bottle and a scowl.

"Hey, come here," she said to Ikasa. "I know you meant to get out of here today, but your pop's going to work, my man's already gone with your mom up to town, and I ain't watching your little brother by myself."

"What? No!" Ikasa whined. "Why me?"

"Ain't nobody else."

Gramma's mana bunched itself into a tight little scarecrow frame and Pop came walking out of the house in a light daze. He hugged Ikasa once and gave a little smirk.

"What's going on?" Ikasa asked, as a truck pulled up into the yard.

The sad chunk of metal had no doors, and the flatbed was mostly just wood and metal welded poorly onto the frame. The bed was piled with men and women in canvas, and all of them had the look of great effort piled into their faces. The truck's mana was somber, and age in its tires spilled out over the road in thick waves. Ikasa felt the pale white of death slipping like fog between the eyes of the riders.

"I'm going out to pull concrete from the freeway," Pop said. "A couple more trucks are going to meet us on the way and they need breakers and lifters."

He climbed up into the back of the truck.

"I'll be back in two days!" he said, as that truck, too, pulled away into dust.

"Old freeway from before the crash, talked about it the other day," Gramma said. "Ain't nobody uses it anymore, going west anyway. Folks go out to break it up with hammers and picks, then load up the stones and bring them into town to patch up potholes or use in foundations."

She took down another sip of her beer.

"The irony is that by removing the freeway to help us make our town more civilized, the less connected to civilization we get. Gets harder for the government to drive supplies out here without using the train lines," she said. "Roads are like rivers for people. Is it any wonder they dam them up?"

"What?" Ikasa asked.

"Nothing. Get your little brother and meet me out back. I'm going to teach you a spell or something."

"Or something?"

"Just go get the littler shit."

Ikasa scuttled back into the house. While she was excited about the prospect of learning a spell, she wasn't very excited about having to drag Butch around while that went on. She found him tying knots in the back room, some place that clearly was meant to be a storage shed before it had been grafted onto the trailer. The sunken room smelled of cigar tobacco and mold. He had a small pile of masa cakes and stopped his work to make a dent in one. Butch wiped his hands off and dragged more string out of the sewing kit, going right back to doing overhands and figure-eights.

"Gramma says we have to go outside," Ikasa said. "Said she

wants to teach us a spell."

He got up and brought his plate with him. Gramma was setting up outside, knocking over buckets and grunting.

"Fucking Kapu, you stupid shit, I love you, but he's never lived in Ootsooduh before, keeps leaving all the bins lying out. Doesn't know shit about mosquitoes," she said.

The yard was a mess of grass and tarp, with bucketed highlights. Coils of rope so old the had become one mass artifact sat under construction spools and cinder block. Bundles of sticks and uncut limestone sat with breadboard, wiring, and piles of mussel shells and animal corpses in various stages of dryness. Feathers, useless and matted, sat on everything. Gramma picked up a basin full of rocks and fossils and dumped it out.

"The whole Ootsooduh used to be under water," the old woman said. "You two sit down over there and start going through them rocks and pick out some good ones."

"How do we know which ones are the good ones?" Butch asked.

"You'll know," Gramma croaked, filling a basin with water from the hose. "You all know what mana means, right?"

"Of course I do," Ikasa said. "I caught a lightning bolt!"

Gramma looked at her straight on and snorted.

"You know how to use it, but do you know what it means?" Gramma asked again.

Ikasa wasn't sure at that point. She just frowned and shook her head.

"It means prestige, honor, authority, and the potential of any one action or thing to have repercussions. Your little mana bag doesn't so much hold mana as it is a part of what you mean as a person," Gramma said. "Mana is the potential for intent. You have mana, an action has mana, a place has mana. Your room has the mana of safety, security, and personal space. Mana is the air of power. Sometimes, you can give something a pretense, and its nature will begin to resemble that pretense. Your mother knows this already and if she's any kind of woman she's at least taught you how to accept and understand the mana the world has over you. The fire-pot, that has powerful Spider mana behind it, in it, on it. It's possessed by the thing, but also by the idea of the thing. You're scared of getting hit by a car, yes?"

Ikasa nodded. Butch shook his head, but started nodding after a moment.

"It's because getting hit by a car has mana. It has a cultural and a personal meaning. Now, if you'd actually been hit by a car, it'd do a lot more than just scare you. That's the sort of mana it has. Cars especially, because they once made our civilization possible."

She put the bin of water down.

"Not so much anymore, I suppose. The more used to something people get, the less mana it has, but the more people talk about it, the more mana it has. You done figured out which rocks I'm looking for yet?" She asked.

Ikasa felt the thrum beneath her hands and wiggled her fingers through the stack, tapping a few when they sounded like the rolling sea or a strange prickling heat. She directed Butch at a few of them, but she picked some out that seemed especially wet.

"These," she said, handing them off to Gramma.

Gramma picked them up, sifted through a couple, and dumped them into the water basin.

"Why'd you pick these?"

"I don't know, they seemed the most watery?" Ikasa asked.

"Right. Mana gets built up as something interacts with its environment and the world. Most rocks have lives too big and too long for humans to really understand them. Animals are fairly easy for humans to understand, no matter their age. Your mom is good at talking to the earth, a trait it's likely you've picked up yourself, both of you. Not like your older brother at all," she said.

She stirred the water. Ikasa could smell salt and raw fish.

"The thing is, when you understand the meaning, when you get the mana, you can be affected by it long after, even if it's only to watch it."

The basin was deep; Ikasa could see a stretch of sand under the water, and watched fish swimming in lurid tinfoil schools. Some kind of ray or skate drifted among the little grasses along the sea floor. She was able to pick out a trio of puffers dogging after shrimp and angled herself to see if there was anything in either direction.

"This isn't what really happened, mind you. That rock mix covers a couple million years. Could be a shark tooth three million years old or a stingray barb only a couple thousand years old in there, but you'd get something similar. It ain't the distance of time what gives it a voice, it's the distance from idea to idea. Fish to fish is easier than fish to tree, even if they lived at the same time."

Butch shot his hand into the water and the image scattered; the smell disappeared, and it was just rocks in the bottom of a basin.

"And when you add people to things, it gets even worse," Gramma said. "So, you kids want to know how to do this? Make a window to someplace that isn't real?"

They both nodded.

"Good, back inside, we'll go learn what I mean by idea to idea distances, which is the spell you'll actually be learning."

Gramma dumped out the water and left the rocks where they were. She brought them back inside and brought up some magazines from the flower festival room, and dumped some scissors on the table. Sitting down, she knocked away a few wood chunks and tossed them in the corner of the kitchen.

"Pick out some pictures of things you like and cut them out," she said. "For this exercise you can use images of people."

"Isn't wonder-working harder to do on people?" Ikasa asked.

"Just about as hard as it is to work on any other animal," Gramma said. "Most plants are a little easier, and remains are even easier still. For this thing we're going to be working with the images, nothing else."

She cleared off the table and started setting out little pieces of quartz on her side while Butch and Ikasa chopped up images of city women and furniture and trees. Gramma surveyed the new wreckage on the table and nodded. She put her palms down.

"This is a game. Up here on my end is the sky," she said before pointing at the two of them. "Over there at you's end is down. I'll make the sky, Butch, you cut up things your sister looks for. Ikasa, you pick one of them people over there and put them under the sky."

Ikasa looked among the images and found a woman in a wool cap with a couple of feathers in it and an otherwise lineage-neutral jacket and dress, looking like she was going to work. Ikasa put her on the table, head towards Gramma.

"Now, Ikasa, what I want you to do is feel my mana as I'm asserting it on my end, and do what I'm doing. Butch, you too. Pay attention. Your penis is not an exemption from Spider business."

For a moment it seemed like Gramma had way more arms; she was weaving string on her side of the table and started moving her hands in a languid blur. The quartz dots closer to her didn't so much light up as the table darkened to a deep blue-violet, disappearing into a cloak of night. Ikasa felt fingers of cold sleep moving up into her arms as the table was pulled away to reveal the sky. She squinted and pushed back, aa Butch next to her did the same, a little stronger, but with less detail. There was strength to his push, but it seemed undirected. That was good, she'd always been better at detail; she took hold of it and made of herself a solid wall to put back the night.

"Ikasa is the fourth world from the sun," Gramma said. "Saykay-ah is your sister. Be the fourth world."

"I know," Ikasa answered, thinking of dwelling under the sky.

The woman in the cutout grabbed her hat as she started sliding across the table, falling in the image they were creating. Ikasa darted a finger out and pinned the woman's jacket, and she stopped falling.

"Butch, find me some ground," Ikasa said. She felt his push go away.

He put some actual rocks on the table, as well as getting out a pencil and drawing a horizon line, and scattered some stone cutouts he found in the magazines to the landscape. Ikasa put the woman down, and she brushed herself off, looking in either direction. Ikasa kept flooding the table with mana, gripping the sides and losing sight of the kitchen. The woman looked straight out and shrugged.

"She's not got any actual thought processes," Gramma said. "She's just an image that's acting how you'd expect it to act. Agayateni is the original name. Philosophers go bug fuck over this trick, call it the 'p-zombie trick.' We called it 'story table' back in the day. You picked up the idea really fast. Your mom says your good with specifics but that you're not good with strength. So, here's what you're going to do. Butch. Go get one of them pulp magazines from Eddie's room. Find me a big, mean, scary monster."

Her voice seemed effortless, smooth, without the croak she associated with the old woman. Ikasa was momentarily jealous as she felt heat and frost under her fingers.

"Ikasa, she's on your back, remember that. What's Ikasa like? Tell me about Sun and Spider's fourth child, but don't talk to me. If she stops moving before Butch gets back, you lose."

Without Butch's push, she felt like she hearing everything

through aspic. Her eyes were burning, her ears flooded with wax, and her arms were stuffed with cotton. She felt weight pressed down on her chest, and her toes went cold in her shoes. She wanted to squirm and fidget, to grab her hair and dig under a blanket and never emerge.

The woman on the table climbed up a rock and looked around before hopping back down into the dust and throwing up a cloud of little paper shreds and pencil marks. She started walking, and the scene followed her, rocks passing by like a scrolling wall, and she eventually picked a small one up to carry. After a while, she looked at the sky and pointed at a few stars with her forefinger and pinkie, making a little scooping motion before walking again.

Butch returned with a magazine and picked up the scissors; Ikasa was only vaguely aware of what he was doing. Gramma was saying something to him but Ikasa's ears had nearly gone out. Mostly she could just hear a rocky silence of the sort that came with still and thin air. Ikasa's arms turned to cold lead, prickling up to her shoulders and down into her palms. Her back groaned as if under a weight, and the woman stopped to check the sand and pebbles under her feet.

A great crash echoed across the wasteland, and something with too many teeth and thick albino hair pounded across the dust. All four of its arms were used in its motion, with tiny hind legs serving only to brace it. She'd never seen anything like it before, and what colors it possessed, other than thick black lines, were scattered like pointillist dots. The ground shook, and it was Ikasa's fault. The appearance of the thing threw her off. She took in a sharp breath. Some of the rocks rolled. The woman gave out a wordless scream.

Ikasa ground her teeth and took the weight completely on her shoulders. Somehow the woman had just taken to standing still, and she felt Butch's meaning pressing on her face, weighing her down like a muffled blanket. The beast pounded closer, and Ikasa wondered why the woman was just standing there, not doing a thing, sitting and staring as her doom barreled down. Ikasa pulled herself up out of the ground and urged the woman onward, and she suddenly jerked and shook herself like she was throwing away dirt, and she dove for cover behind a rock.

The monster tore away the rock and the woman was left bare; there was a moment where she held up her arms, and the whole image on the table froze. Ikasa fell back into her chair, sweating. Butch was panting and looking her way, and Gramma was just sitting there, grinning.

"Well, what'd you think?" the old woman asked.

"That was amazing," Ikasa said.

"Gramma, my arms hurt," Butch said.

"Yup," Gramma answered, standing up and wandering over to the ice box.

Ikasa worked her hands and knuckles.

"You were controlling the woman, weren't you?" Ikasa asked. "That's why she stopped. You let go. I had to take control of her actions while Butch was the monster, but I screwed it up."

"Yup," Gramma said. Butch is stronger, you have more finesse. Next time you play, we'll see what really happens to that woman."

"What do you mean?" Ikasa asked.

"Ha, that lady's not licked yet, you think? I bet if we give you some more time the next time around, you'll know what she should do."

Ikasa leaned on the table to prop herself up on her elbows and put her chin in her hands. The paper dolls were frozen in their last positions. The woman sat crouched with her arms up over her face, the white hairy thing had a fist in the air, and rocks were scattered around the landscape. She picked up the cutout of the woman and grumbled a bit, thinking that it wasn't fair to start up a game like this without telling her the rules. She tossed the cutout back down and pushed herself away from the table. Moving was like forcing a concrete block into place; she half-wondered if it hadn't been Gramma's plan to get her tired so there would be peace in the house.

She fell on her bed and listened to the chirping hopper chick in the shoebox next to her. She rolled over so she could look in; it was turning its head back and forth to check her out, and hopped up to sniff around in her hands and try to claw its way up to her neck, flapping little jerky arms while it stumbled around. The box, and, by extension, the hatchling, stank. She grabbed them both up and went downstairs to find that hose Gramma was using earlier.

Chapter 11

In the Rain

This is truly an old story of an old time. Once a young woman was whirled up by the roaring wind; she was taken up by a thunder-storm, and set down again in the village of Thunders. In after-times she described them as very like human beings, but all dressed in white with white hair and white clothes. They also wear wings made of lightning, which can be put aside. It is death for them to be caught in the crotch of a tree.

The great chief of the Thunders, hearing of the young woman's arrival, sent for her, and received her kindly, and told her that she should become one of them. To which the woman was willing, the chief called all his people together to see the ceremony where she would become one of them.

They bade her to go into a square thing, and while in it she lost all her senses and became a Thunder, and put on her back a pair of wings. She flew about like all Thunders, and followed their ways as directed. She flew with her new brothers and sisters, and wherever they went, there was a great roar and crash when they flapped their wings. They played with a great ball in the sky for their amusement, and often they would go and try to fight a great stork, which lived in the south, and made great trouble for them, but they could never slay it.

Eventually, however, the young woman wished to see her family again, only for a little while, and she told her new chief this, and he told all the villagers that their sister from the other world was very lonesome, and they should carry her back to the earth.

So she closed her eyes, and her brothers and sisters set her back down on the ground again.

Her family saw a great thunderstorm coming, and saw lightning flashing back and forth for over an hour, and when the storms passed and they ran up to the spot, they found the woman there, their long-lost sister who had been gone for seven years. She told them all how she had been to the world of the Thunders and how she had played ball with the Thunders and had even become one herself. They saw on her shoulder the mark of Thunder, and she showed them how to find the gifts the Thunders would leave, the thunder-bullets in the crotch of a tree or in the depths of the sand where lightning struck. Her chief on the land recognized her as the first of a new family, and her children bear the mark still, always walking back and forth across the land, carrying thunder-bullets in their pockets.

Ikasa was used to rain. Cahokia had a good amount of its own storms, especially downwind of the main city. Shimookooah took the city's stories of rain and laughed at them. Ikasa crunched herself into a corner reading what she could out of her comics, whichever ones hadn't been cut up by Butch or that her pop hadn't taken to claim for the whole family. She set up the hopper chick on her stomach and sat against her door, wrapped up in a feather blanket and needing a flashlight due to the darkness of the clouds outside. She was about halfway through her eighth alien invasion when there was pounding on her door.

"Open up, you little shit!" came Gramma's voice, and the door was shoved.

"Hold on!" Ikasa yelled.

She got up and put the hopper back in its box before getting fully out of the way. Her mom busted in through the frame and grabbed her by the shoulders. Gramma was scowling.

"What's wrong?" Ikasa asked.

"You told me you caught a lightning bolt the day you got here, didn't you?" Mom said.

"Yeah, I still got it!" she said.

"Get your ass outside now," Mom said.

"What?"

"March!" she said, pointing down the hall.

Ikasa stretched and started walking down the hall to the stairs. She was still trying to sort out what this was all about.

"Why's she got a hopper in there?" Mom asked.

"She got it from that Blue Crab boy, I told her she could have it," Gramma replied.

"You should have asked us," Mom said.

"She's fourteen, it's plenty old enough to have a pet, I was out fucking at that age," Gramma answered.

"Mom!" Ikasa's mom shouted.

"So were you, kiddo. Eddie's only, what, two years older than her? Look at what he's doing."

"Eddie's a slut," Ikasa said.

Both women cleared the ten foot distance instantly and slapped her in the back of the head. They didn't follow up with anything, but Ikasa tried not to roll her eyes and stopped at the back door of the trailer.

"Outside?" she asked.

"Yes," Gramma said, and her mom opened the door. The both of them had umbrellas.

"You're going to learn what it means to have lightning mana," mom said.

"Don't I get one?" Ikasa asked, pointing at the umbrellas.

"No."

She went outside and into the rain. At least it wasn't too cold, with big warm midsummer drops and a light breeze. There were questioning rumbles, but not nearly as many flashes as there ought to be. She squinted and looked back at her mom, astonished and no longer really annoyed.

"I have to help, that's what you mean, don't you? I have to make some of the lightning because I took that one bolt when we first moved in."

Mom nodded and pointed out into the yard.

"You get yourself a clear space and pay attention to them rumbles and try to figure out your part," she said.

Ikasa stepped into the yard proper among the tangled grasses and dripping bushes, in her shorts and undershirt, squinting in the falling water. Some droplets curled around her face and she felt the roots of her hair starting to get wet. There was a rumble directly over her head, and she looked back at the trailer-house. Gramma and Mom were still standing there, and she half-nodded at them before turning back to the woods and facing the wind.

A few more rumbles called over the rain. She brought her hands up and felt the tingle of cold heat prickle along the palms of her hands. More rumbles called through the clouds, and she felt water draining into her eyes. She pushed up, watching for flashes, trying to line them up with the noises rolling out over the forest.

She breathed, and water went into her nose. Her chest seized up, crawling with ants. She buckled over to cough and spit, and sparks rained across the earth. When she dropped onto her knees, everything erupted into a familiar pain; she tried to catch air but her chest refused to work. The world was a shade of red, washed in broad shadows. She crunched down into the mud, feeling nails and shards of glass in the ground or under her skin. She felt hands on her arm, and heard a grinding like rusty sheet metal scraping across the earth before she realized it was her own voice.

The ceiling over the couch sagged with a sort of amateurish depression when she was next aware of her surroundings. Mr. Armadillo was smoking and sitting in a chair, leaning over her body, singing as he placed coins on her forehead and cheeks. He caught her eyes and stopped singing.

"There we go. Told you," he said.

Her mom leaned into view and petted her on the forehead. Ikasa tried to speak but coughed instead. Mom sat down on the couch and took in a breath.

"I didn't doubt you," Mom said. "Just worried about the speed. You okay, sweetie?"

Ikasa coughed a few more times and sat up. Eddie was right there with water. She took it and drank until she felt like she could say something.

"I'm sorry, I think I fucked up," Ikasa said. "I tried to time it, but I snorked some water."

"Failure happens," was all Mom said before leaving the room.

Eddie rubbed her hair and laughed.

"Yahola says you're gonna be fine, shithead," he said, before heading for the stairs.

"You should be lucky your Gramma let me even touch you," Armadillo said. "At first she was yelling about all of us Ootsooduh motherfuckers at war with you. Convinced you'd pull yourself out of it. Anyway. Get some rest, kiddo."

He patted her on the shoulder.

"My earrings hurt," Ikasa said.

"You got struck by lightning that you produced,. You're lucky your teeth didn't explode," Mr. Armadillo said.

He brushed himself off and walked to where Gramma and Kapu were standing by the door. They talked about something before wandering off into the kitchen. She was alone in the living room, listening to rain outside, hearing rumbles but seeing no flashes. She could hear her dad's voice. Quietly, wrapping herself in the sheet, she slid off the couch and crawled under the table just outside the entry to the dining room and pressed her lips together.

"You should have fucking known," Gramma said.

"Known what?" her dad said.

"That it was a stupid fucking idea to give her that name," Gramma said. "You tentatived the name, saw the astrological and deep read reports, but you still kept that fucking name."

"It's been fifteen years, there could have been divergences," Dad said.

"Please, tell me how the fuck there's a divergence right now," Gramma said. "You tell me she hasn't seen that White Bird tooling around in the fucking neighborhood. You tell me she hasn't caught lightning in her hands. Go on and fucking tell me she doesn't have a fire-jar. You tell me-"

"Enough," Dad said. "It was your idea to make her wear the Ikasa regalia when we went down to the mound. Yours."

Dad got up and walked past where Ikasa was huddled under the end table, stomping up the stairs. She crawled away behind the couched and found her own way up on all fours. She knocked on Eddie's door until he answered.

"What do you want?" he asked.

"I want to lay down in here," she said.

He looked into his room and back at Ikasa.

"Okay, go get a sheet or some shit, you can sleep in here," he said.

She nodded and crossed the hall into her room, picking up her hopper out of the shoe box and grabbing a sheet and two pillows. There was a knock on her door. She could see Gramma's silhouette there in the frame.

"I know you heard what went on down there," she said.

Of course the old woman knew.

"You're going to grind into your future the same way a train slams into some boy walking home late and not listening to the tracks," Gramma said. "I know you seen the things underground.

The hollow place up in the ruins. This is yours."

She held an arm out to Ikasa.

"Well, it ain't so much yours as it is ours," she said.

Ikasa did not know what to say, especially since what she had been handed was a mummified star-plated box turtle, closed up and drawn all over with little symbols older than anything she knew. It radiated Spider mana so strong that it felt like a brick of solid ice.

"This is our shame. Spider's shame," Gramma said. She walked away.

Ikasa shook the mummified turtle. Whatever shame it contained was heavy and rattled. She stuck it in her shirt and dragged her stuff into Eddie's room. She curled up in one corner and wrapped herself up. Harsh light landed on her from Eddie's bed. He had a flashlight, the same one he had been using to read earlier.

"What is that?" he asked, waving the light at her hands. "I can feel the mana really heavy."

"You're a boy, I think this is," Ikasa looked down and frowned. "You know what. Okay. Gramma says it's Spider's shame. Whatever it is, it's inside the turtle."

Eddie got up and stuffed a sheet partially under the door before turning on his light.

"Let me see it," he said.

She showed him, and he took it over to his desk and pushed some movie monsters out of the way. He switched on the light so he could get a better look at the seams. He flicked his nail across the surface and Ikasa leaned in to look at what he was doing.

"There's something inside, do you know what it is?" he asked.

"Shame?" she said.

He picked up his carving knife and showed it to her.

"What do you think?" he said. "Should I?"

"Don't hurt the turtle," she said.

"Wasn't planning on it. These are land turtles, when they close up, they seal up completely, so they make rattles out of these sometimes," he said, scraping at the seams of the front end. "The hinges on the shell close it up completely. We should be able to remove just this one piece."

He worked at them for a good half an hour; Ikasa spent the whole time standing on an orange crate and leaning on the desk, watching as the dust came out bit by bit, and when one corner was opened to the dark room, she felt the air shift. The mana spilled out like thick fog in her nose, and she felt the weight of ages upon it. Eddie let out a whoop and held it at arm's length.

"My hands've gone numb, can you hold it?" he asked. Ikasa nodded dumbly.

She wrapped both hands around the turtle, facing it at him, and he switched to guide the knife with both hands, continuing to scrape and blow out the dust until the little angled front plate fell off. Ikasa quickly turned it upside down and shook out the contents. Tobacco dust and a tiny cylinder fell into her hand. It was light, but the mana made it heavy.

"What is it?" Eddie asked.

"I don't know," Ikasa said, rolling it around in her hands. "It looks like a battery."

It was a small cylinder, with just a slight band along the side to prevent it from rolling, and about half as long as her pinkie finger.

"Tiny battery," Eddie said.

"Yeah," Ikasa said.

She stared at the little white thing for a while, taking note of the little silvered end and pressed herself into it like the stones at the ruins.

"I don't understand, it doesn't feel like shame. It feels like pride on the inside," she said. She heard whispers from underground again.

"Objects don't feel like emotions," Eddie said.

"What do you know?" she whined, putting the cylinder back in the turtle and scraping up as much tobacco dust as she could. "Glue this up, please."

She watched as Eddie put everything back into place.

"What are you going to do?" he asked.

"I don't know. I have to hold onto it, but it. I don't know what to do about it," she said. "I'll ask somebody."

"Like Gramma?"

"No, she gave it to me, it's my job now," Ikasa said.

She curled up in the corner and wrapped herself in the blanket, listening to the rain pounding on the window. There was no flash from outside.

"Hey, man," Eddie said, turning off his desk light.

"What?"

"I know we don't get along as swell as we should, and I kick your ass a lot," he said. "But you know that if anybody fucks with you, all you have to do is tell me, right?"

"Yeah," she nodded.

"Alright," he said.

She kept her eyes shut for a little while, leaning on the wall. Staying that way until she could hear Eddie's regular breathing, she went back to her room and put the turtle down. The hopper chirped and tried to climb out of its box. Throwing a blanket over the box, she took her headdress out of the hat box and put it on. Taking a few steady breaths, she crept back downstairs and opened up the back door.

The wind howled an unearthly scream, and she saw something like slavering teeth in the clouds, billowing feathers, and streaming men made of thunder. She raised her arms into the rain and worked her feet into the mud.

"Let's you and me try this bullshit again," she said, calling lightning into her hands and watching it dance around the yard like a worm covered in ants.

Chapter 12
The Woods in Daytime

There are a big variety of fierce critters all over the countryside. The Puwomis believed in such strange things as the hun-gimmity, which was a little bit like a brushrunner but it had legs all over its backside so it could never be tripped. Travelers from the east often met with such odd peculiarities as the uplands trout, which made its nests in the hollows of trees, the rotagijjin, which had little paddle-like feet that it used to mimic the sound of a chopping axe, and the snoligoster, which was like an alligator, but had a big propeller for a tail that it would use to buzz along through the marshes.

The Kaweekyooh used to talk about things in their woods like the squonk, which was generally agreed-upon to be the most pathetic creature ever to exist. It was made of snot, they said, and constantly cried and bellowed about how poor and painful its life was. Like a little shieldface, they'd say, but with no big shield and not of very great size at all. The Hallawak to their north would say back that the Kaweekyooh have too many things to drink and too tall of any kind of hunting stories.

On the other hand, the Kaweekyooh say there's no point in telling a story if you're not going to add three feet, length, height, or otherwise.

The four of them were walking along the railroad tracks passing a joint around when they saw the tweakers for the first

117

time. Limpkin pulled everyone back a little bit and then hunkered down behind a great big oak. Ikasa was glad to not have to squint as Mary pointed out the five adults hunched over a bright red bucket under the bridge where a tiny creek running beneath and the shade from the big rocks cast over them. Limpkin rolled his rifle around and pulled out the ammo before dropping into the dust and looking through the sight.

"What's going on?" Ikasa whispered.

"Tweakers," Ehano said.

"Mary said her pop makes white junk for them. What is that, exactly?" she asked.

Ehano motioned for Spider to take his place, and she crawled up and took the rifle to look through the scope. The woman in the group picked a small piece of quartz, shining white like a lightbulb, up out of the bucket, and held it, staring into the center, until the bright glow flashed like glitter and disappeared. The stone turned to dust and crumbled. Ikasa looked back at Mary and frowned.

"Your pop infused the quartz with a momentary impression of euphoria, didn't he?" Ikasa asked.

"White junk," Mary shrugged.

Ikasa looked back through the sight. They looked a little wrung out, like they'd been twisted and squeezed one too many times, and once they'd emptied the bucket, they spent their time drawing on the concrete until they started roaming outward.

"What's going on?" Ikasa asked, watching them spiral out.

"We have to go," Limpkin said.

"Tweakers get bored easy," Mary said. "The white junk makes it so they can't really get interested in anything else, but they keep trying to find something to focus their brains. That's what daddy says anyway. That's why they start acting like that."

Ikasa looked back over her shoulder as the four of them were clearing out. One of the men was lashing at his own arm with a nettle plant, and one of the women was screaming wordlessly and running her hands over the black granite at the base of the railroad tracks. Ikasa wrinkled her nose at the smell of rotten meat, and quickly followed her friends.

"Your pop makes that stuff?" she asked.

"Yup," Mary said.

Ikasa said nothing after that, but just walked along through the scrub until they got to another creek. She picked up some broken shells from the midden along the closest loop and kicked around the dirt.

"So, what are we doing here?" she asked.

"When I was in the cyclops' office, I saw that she had a picture of them stalking a squonk out here, and she said they never actually could catch it," Limpkin said.

"A real squonk?" Ikasa grinned. "And who's the cyclops?"

Mary patted her right eye.

"She's the principal. She used to be an adventurer! She lost her eye when she took a .38 special to the face!"

"Nuh-uh," Ehano said, unrolling a burlap sack. "She put it out for magical powers."

"She wanted to scare a kid," Blue Crab said.

"Everybody has a story!" Mary said, laughing.

"You guys know that all of those could be the same thing, right?" Ikasa said.

Everyone looked at her with wide eyes and slack lips. Ehano swallowed and opened one end of the sack. He dropped it into the dirt and started covering it with leaves while Mary went to grab some vines. Blue Crab climbed up a nearby tree.

"Let me guess," Ikasa said. "You guys come out here and hunt brushrunners all the time."

"We got a system," Ehano said.

"Well, it's not going to work for a squonk."

"Why not?" Mary asked.

"Because a squonk is a scaredy-bird and super pathetic."

"Brushrunners are scaredy-birds," Ehano said.

"Brushrunners are also really alert, but squonks are supposed to be crying all the time," Ikasa said. "You should go listening for it crying, right? They're supposed to turn into snot when they get scared, so maybe you need to find it first, then hit it with a stick and knock it out before it knows what's what?"

Ehano looked down at his bag before sweeping the leaves back off it.

"She's kind of right," he said. "If it's out cold it can't turn into snot and ooze away."

"Yeah," Mary said. "Ronnie, go get a big stick, okay? Try to get a big oak branch, not a saw palmetto thing, that's gonna break."

He nodded and pushed off into the ferns. Ikasa looked at Mary.

"You and Ehano find us some metal or something so we can hold the bag open," Mary said. "I'll go watch Ronnie, is that cool?"

Ehano gave a two-finger salute and Mary wandered off into the brush.

"There's an old jungle camp up the stream a little bit, let's look there," he said.

They went up the river a little, watching fat boomerang-heads swimming around in the water and birds flit by in the trees. Ikasa hopped down and poked at some big three-toed footprints at the bank and trailed her eyes up the clay and limestone walls that framed each side. The water seemed so impossibly blue for a moment, and she looked back up the ridge at Ehano.

"Hey, what's this big but can crawl up and down the clay without leaving a scratch?" she asked.

He leaned over the side to look, but just screwed up his face and shook his head.

"Not hoppers," he said.

"And not a big meat-eater, either," she said.

"Yeah, it looks like it might be fat," he nodded.

She started climbing back up with an arm-wide root or vine, brown in color. The dirt there was loose and dry and under an old oak, the exposed roots striking down like an angry carrot. Soil fell in small clouds that stung her eyes, and she stopped climbing. Grains still fell, hissing softly as they hit the water.

"What's wrong?" Ehano asked. "You need help? You can climb those fucking power poles but you can't go up a river bank?"

He dropped onto his stomach and reached down a hand.

"No," Ikasa said, watching the dirt. "You see that?"

He pulled his hand back so he could drag himself out further. The thick drone was a pervasive, alien hum that echoed through the branches overhead and stirred the wind into a frenzy. Ikasa looked for it in the weather, but couldn't find it there. Some of the upper tree limbs cracked.

"It's the sound that's doing it. What's that noise?" Ikasa said.

There was a tearing like thunder, and Ehano looked back before flipping off the ledge into the water. Ikasa watched him as he rose. His body lashed through the air with purpose before he grabbed her by the shirt.

"Get down!" he yelled, and the bank exploded.

The soil and roots burst upward into a whirlwind and the

river followed, a churning mass that slowed before spilling every direction. Something heavy and definitely not wind landed in the creek. A long neck with a little stubby head attached to a fat and feathery body rose up out of the cloud of debris. Gangly arms tipped with three curved talons reached out impossible distances from rounded shoulders, and with an awkward gait, short little three-toed bird legs carried the fat beast up out of the water. A tiny little tail lashed out behind it, and the puny, beady eyes on the wedge-shaped head sought out the two of them before it held both arms out and started pacing ever faster in a circle.

"The water slowed it down," Ehano shouted. "What is it?"

"It's a whirling whimpus," Ikasa said. "It's going to turn invisible again!"

It went out of sight once it picked up enough speed, tearing up dirt and water, which went spraying in every direction before that weighty hum drowned out all other sounds. There was a ripple in the space between tree and earth where it moved with some terrifying speed. The pair scattered to each side of the creek and Ikasa shrieked when a good-sized log sailed over her head.

"What do we do about it?" Ehano screamed over the wind.

Ikasa flinched at the words, thinking that Ehano might know better than her. She'd only heard about it in stories, and most stories were remarkably short on how to survive an encounter with a whimpus; mostly they involved loggers and hunters just disappearing in the woods. It was pretty big, though, and having trouble actually striking them in the little ravine. There was too much clay to climb back up with any great speed. There were, however, a lot of little branching creeks not much wider than a car seat.

"Down one of these!" Ikasa said, dropping down to crawl through the mud.

She could hear Ehano following her, and the leaves and branches swallowed them up. Ikasa felt spiders crawling on her face, and she smiled quietly. Shoving herself deeper into the tangle, feeling water soak into her shirt and pants, she grabbed Ehano from where he was struggling and dragged him closer.

"Little sisters!" she cried out. "Help us! Wrap the sky in your webs and block out the light, hide us in the darkness and help us escape!"

She pressed her hands against the webs that were still intact, and Ehano grabbed her wrist and shoulder. His grip went warm, and it felt like her skin was being hurtled through the open air, enclosed safely in a tent of feathers.

"Together," he said. "A Spider asks her little sisters and a Limpkin asks his cousins."

If there had been any doubt among the orchard and banana spiders that the pair of them had the proper mana for making demands, adding that little wading bird tore it away. They worked like trapeze artists, throwing together a thick webbing that obscured the dim and scattered light from the forest floor. Ikasa and Ehano drew even further back into the little side creek. They tumbled back into a narrow hole covered in black trap door spiders, and Ikasa crawled down into the tunnel.

"Come on!" she said. "I bet it comes up a few feet down!"

She was right, of course; the tunnel popped up in the level ground and was scarcely bigger than either of them. Spiders scattered into the hammock every which way when they pulled themselves up, and she helped Ehano out of the hole.

"You are a fuckoff crazy magician," Ehano said in a low tone as they started to make a break for it, watching with wonder as the hole closed itself up.

"You should see my pop," she said, letting out a hard breath.

The river bank behind them exploded into a shower of dirt and leaves.

"Oh, man, it's still on us!" Ehano said.

Ikasa recognized the clearing where they'd sent Mary and Ronnie into the distance, and ran right for where she thought they might be. Hearing Ehano behind her shouting just made her pound her feet harder. She slammed down on her heels completely unlike she'd been taught until she saw the both of them, playing with a pair of sticks like axes.

"We gotta run," Ikasa shouted.

The tops of the trees flew off and sailed fifty feet over their heads. Ronnie covered his neck and turned away, running directly under the whirlwind.

"Where's he going?" Ikasa screamed.

"To the clearing by the bridge! If we cross the town line it can't follow us!" Mary said, following him.

"Oh, so he's doing the smart thing," Ikasa said, ducking her head as she ran.

Ehano waited until everyone had passed by before running again. They ran across the open ground with Mary and Ronnie ahead, breaking the tree line out into a grassy clearing with a tiny stone bridge. Ikasa saw Sadie Kaw crossing the path with four little corn sacks in her hands. She pounded up to the woman and grabbed her jacket, pointing into the forest.

"It's in there!" she shouted.

"What's in there?" Sadie Kaw asked.

"Whirling whimpus!"

"Oh, really?" the woman said, tossing the empty bags onto the ground.

Sadie Kaw cracked her knuckles and approached the tree line, standing and watching the leaves, head tilted as though she were listening to a distant sound. The ferns burst outward and tree limbs scattered like ash and coals from a tipped fire. Sadie Kaw stood unmoved by the whirlwind, at least until her body shattered into dry leaves, and the whimpus stopped spinning, loping into the debris and digging through with its massive talons. It speared something, a wet and bloody liver, amid the leaves.

"Oh, shit, man. That is serious shit!" Ehano said, his voice cracking.

"Did it kill her?" Ikasa asked, eyes wide.

"No, wait," Mary said.

Sadie Kaw strode up out of the forest from behind the whimpus, tapping it with two fingers on one flank and making a mocking cry. It whipped its body around so fast that its arms went invisible, tearing up the ground where she'd been standing. She was on its left flank now, and then tapped it with two fingers again.

"Skah-kraw!" she shouted.

It rolled hard to its left, clearly trying to flatten her with a mountain of flesh and muscle. She popped up at its tail, and grabbed it with a hand.

"Skah-kraw!" she shouted again.

The whimpus made such a loud fuss while turning to snap at her with a clawed arm that it tripped itself. She slapped it lightly on the head.

"Skah-kraw!" she laughed.

The children watched the spectacle, Ikasa feeling incredulous at Sadie Kaw's mana and audacity, forgetting how close they'd all come to death. Ehano laughed a little bit, and Ronnie had a huge smile on his face. Sadie Kaw gave the kids a nod and faced them, doing a little child's salute, thumb on her temple and waving with just her fingers while stepping left and right to avoid the creature's strikes. She reached up and tapped it on the wrist with each blinding attack.

"Skah-kraw!" she shouted each time.

Each time, it seemed a little more harmless, just a little smaller, and just a little more frustrated. Eventually it seemed small enough that she grabbed it by the head and pulled it over to the bridge.

"Now!" she said to the children. "What's so scary about this silly big thing that you had to run away?"

"Not a whole lot!" Mary said.

Ikasa lit up; she knew what the woman was doing, and laughed at the whimpus.

"Whimpus! More like a big wimp!" she said. "We came looking for a squonk and we found something even more pathetic!"

"Bravery is part of the wind, and is an even bigger part of winning, you know. A man in white paint is scary as a ghost, until he gets cut, so a whimpus is big and scary until you see it's just a little dope in the woods," Sadie Kaw said.

The whimpus had stopped putting up any kind of fight at all, and Sadie Kaw let it go. The four of them shouted, laughed, and threw rocks at the poor thing until it loped off into the woods, wailing and gibbering as it did. Ikasa watched it go before she'd realized that Sadie Kaw had disappeared as well.

"You guys saw the lady who was here, right?" she asked.

"Yeah," Ehano said. "The White Crow lady. She's been hanging around."

"The what?" Ikasa asked.

"White Crow," Ehano said.

Ikasa frowned at that.

"Listen, hey," he said. "Let's go get my bag, right?"

"Yeah," Mary said, and the three jogged off into the forest.

Ikasa knelt down and looked at the bags Sadie Kaw had dropped. A wading bird, a crab in blue thread, a crawfish, and a big yellow garden spider patch covered each one in turn. She shivered and the bridge suddenly seemed a thousand miles across. She hopped up.

"Wait! Wait for me, guys!" she shouted.

Chapter 13

The Woods at Night

Lots of little angry people live in the forests, and they range in size from no bigger than your thumb to as big as the tallest skyscrapers in the city. Many are good, many are evil, and many are no less or greater than ourselves. One time, there was a magician named Eeyehoh, and she lived mostly alone, at the edge of her village among the Amareekahs, and she would go out and walk along the river to collect berries and mussels to cook her meager meals and stones to make charms.

One day she was walking along and the sun had gone down, and she came across an injured man with many burns. Immediately she went to tend to him, and he reacted with great fear.

"You are a human!" he shouted. "Go away and do not eat my flesh!"

"You are a fairy," she said in response. "You should know that we only eat the meat of animals."

She tended to his wounds, and when he was able to move again, he smiled at her.

"This is such a great kindness, flesh-eater!" he said. "What shall I do for you?"

She looked at him, seeing he was beautiful, and nodded.

"How about if you become my husband?" she said.

He clapped his hands and laughed.

"That sounds like a fun thing! But, I have requests!" he said. "First, you must not let the rays of sun touch my body. Second, you *must not allow your friends and neighbors to set their eyes upon me. If they ask 'where is your man?' you must say 'he is out hunting today.'"*

"Will you catch animals and hunt tubers for me?" she asked.

"Of course!" was the answer.

So she nodded that this was acceptable, and they had a little marriage out in the forests at night. She made her house a little bigger and shored up the ceiling so the light wouldn't come inside during the day, and she changed the way she slept so that most of the day she was in bed with her husband. Every night, her husband would go out and hunt and come back with all manner of great game and berries, and they ate well and happy.

This gave her time to have children and to work wonders for the village while most of them slept, as well as repair the boats and make even greater charms. The other women would ask where this husband of hers was at, and she would tell them that he was out hunting. Of course she always had a big game carcass to show them, or her husband's arrows and tools, but whenever they asked to see him, she would say he was asleep, or out hunting. Even when the chief and her father came to ask if her husband would like to come to the sing, she would say that he was too busy.

Eventually, her neighbors got to gossiping enough that they would listen for the voice of anyone talking inside Eeyehoh's house. One day, her sister snuck around the back of the tent and listened for the voice of a man, and when she heard the lovers speaking over dinner, she burst through the back of the tent.

"Hey-yah!" she shouted, and all she saw inside was Eeyehoh's angry face and a man's clothing lying on the ground.

"You have made me break my wedding vows!" Eeyehoh shouted, and called up a wind that blew until all the game left the tribe's land, and Eeyehoh herself wandered back out into the wilds to find her fairy husband.

Ikasa was up against the back wall of the blue section of the trailer with Eddie's hand clamped firmly on her forehead. He pressed her into the plywood wall with one hand, causing dull pain across the back of her skull. He was strong enough and pressed heavy enough up against her body that she could do little else but kick and scream, and she knew she was getting in some good shots at his legs. He kept firing off a stupid grin and put the chocolate bar up to his face, taking the biggest bite he could muster, which was pretty much the whole thing.

"Mm," he said. "Tastes like. Success."

Ikasa wailed.

"That shit was mine, you said it was mine, you fucking shit," Ikasa said. She caught him in the knee good enough that she could wrap her leg around and start squeezing to pull herself out of his grip.

"Ow!" he said. "Don't you know, what I do and what I say are allowed to be different? That's because I'm older than you!"

"Wisdom," Gramma said as she walked by and opened the fridge.

Eddie took a step back, and Ikasa hit the ground. She whined a little and sat up, a tangle of brown limbs. Gramma slammed the door of the fridge and started guzzling down the orange juice.

"Hey," she said. "Go change the laundry and hang up the wet shit so it's out overnight and I can take it down tomorrow."

"What if it rains?" Ikasa asked.

"You'd better hope it doesn't," Gramma said.

She grumbled a little and stepped out into the carport over to the washing machine on the left; it was a big, avocado green deal with rust on the corners plugged into a socket made of more duct tape than metal and rubber. The clothes smelled lightly of mildew, and she was pretty sure Gramma had left them out all day and that it was the last night before they'd have to be washed again. She pulled out the clothes until they filled the wicker laundry basket so high she couldn't pick it up, and then dragged them over to the side yard to hang up.

Ikasa got about halfway through the whites before she heard something big moving in the forest. She pressed down the urge to be afraid of the whimpus again and crawled over behind some tires closer to the chicken coop. After a moment or two of not hearing anything else, she returned to the laundry, setting up the lines so they'd be facing the morning sun. Taking the basket back into the carport, she spotted Pop's flashlight up on the first shelf by the door. She thought about the whimpus, and the bags out by the bridge near the creek.

Looking into the house window, she couldn't see anyone in the kitchen. She brought her hands together and let the electricity dance between them. She grabbed the flashlight and shuffled into the dark. The railroad bridge was west across the creeks that fed into the Calabokee, and Ikasa recalled with certainty that the bridge where they'd encountered Sadie Kaw was a little stone ruin, rather than a modern path.

She checked the woods just outside Gramma's place first, digging around in the oak and pine leaves and the criss-crossed wild grape and air potatoes for sign of anything bigger than a brushrunner or a raccoon. A couple snapped tree branches made her slash the light around before the mosquitoes explained the need for her to get back out into the open yard. She turned off the flashlight and jogged out onto the road, using the soft blue light of the stars and moon to get across the street and wake up Mr. Armadillo's hoppers.

Grabbing the bigger one by the snout, she turned so that if it tried to back away from her, it'd at least get out into the middle of the road before she let go. They both chirped and checked her hands and pockets for anything edible before snuffling around and following her west down the road. She got to where she thought the trail might be and pushed into the nettles and sticker-vines and worse into the open forest. The hoppers took a little urging to follow, but she managed to coax them in after physically dragging the smaller one over the growth line.

She turned the flashlight back on and played the light around on the branches. She watched something slither away out of view. Her shoulders turned cold and her back stiffened up, and she resolved to get to the bridge quicker. She hugged close to the trees and tagged each one, making sure to mark which side she was facing when she moved to another one. After moving for what seemed like hours, she came across a small stone set in the base of a tree that pulsed warm when she touched it. The hoppers went ballistic, squealing and hooting and chirping, jumping up and down, and running in circles around the edge of the clearing.

A thing that was not like a tree at all walked on toothpick-skinny legs through the vines. Up the perfectly still, long body there were clusters of eyes, and the legs and thin tendril-arms wiggled in every direction until it came to rest, utterly still, in the darkness. Ikasa ran the flashlight over it, and all she could see in the light was a thin man in a brown herringbone suit, smiling without showing his teeth. She left the clearing as fast as she could, and paused only for a moment when she could hear nothing crashing through the forest after her.

She rolled down a bank, watching little two-legged things like skinny people run by, scarcely higher than her knees, fluttering in the night like fish beneath the surface of the water. When she rose to her feet, she found herself nearly knocked over by something trailing long sheet-like fins and gulping down little bursts of light that vaguely resolved into little mouths full of teeth before they were eaten whole. The flashlight revealed other aspects of such things - big stomping feet on the gulping fish-thing and lack of facial features on the tiny people, things that turned invisible in the dark.

There were few noises she could make other than a panicked shout each time she moved about and nearly blundered into a new terror, and all she could think was that she should have prepared herself to run into so many faeries. No one would dare think there would be this many in the city, and she realized that such a thing was likely because she had very little light. Stumbling amid another series of bushes and scattering a cluster of little eyeballs running around on three legs, she unscrewed the cap of the flashlight until it was at its widest, exposing the bulb and holding the cap down.

Suddenly she was alone. No hoppers, no faeries, nothing but trees and shadows playing across them. Screwing the cap back on, she turned it off once again after checking her path. She came out of the forest next to the bridge she recognized from earlier in the day, and saw bags under the moonlight still piled forgetfully at the western end of the bridge.

A cluster of four people were poring over the bags. Ikasa took note of their dark forms and then dropped to the ground, rolling up against the side of the bridge, feeling what used to be glyphs or reliefs of some kind grinding against her back. She stretched one long arm out along the stone to find a loose grip and tightened her fingers against it. Gramma would say that nobody could ever stop a Spider from climbing something she wanted to climb. Ikasa put her feet up and braced on the stone while slowly worming her way closer to the figures at the bags.

They were speaking, she was sure of that. What they were saying seemed almost intelligible, Izabellan, or maybe a little bit of Xiuteotl. There was something else that sounded familiar in there, as well, but the more she listened, the more it sounded like they weren't so much saying things as making sounds that recalled those things, rather than anything real. She crawled down under the bridge, hanging on the underside by chills and willpower alone, making her way slowly to the other side and taking a seated position just opposite where they were clustered.

Their whispers were louder, but still indecipherable. Each of them had a brown and dirtied set of clothes covering their entire body. They wore goggles and flight helmets of differing design, and carried guns that were not so much weapons as lumps of metal that looked like guns. Each of them had a long, corrugated tube through which it breathed in slow, ragged gasps, which seemed not to interrupt their speech in any way. They had a smell like wet attic rooms.

Ikasa realized they were likely faeries, and fumbled with her light quickly before turning it on and rolling it out away from her hiding place so that the broad beam spun around and struck the three of them. They vanished almost immediately, and only a few goggles and helmets clattered to the ground, which disappeared as the light struck them, as well. She picked up her light and walked out to the path, making sure to shine the light over all the forest and dim shadows before approaching the bags.

Almost at once she was surrounded by crows, which pecked and clawed at her arms and cheeks, and she wailed, waving her arms to defend herself. The swarm blotted out her vision and stunk like stagnant water. Dirty feathers washed over her body, trailing with them a raw and gritty sensation that climbed up over her arms. When she could open her eyes again, the bags were gone. Ikasa kicked the side of the bridge.

"Oh, come on!" she shouted.

She sat down on the bridge and fell back to look up at the stars, so much more complete than they were in the city.

"Whatever," she said.

Searching the sky for signs of Spider, she squinted to try and see the thick web she had been told waited behind everything, and then trailed her eyes off to find the open hand. She found the thumb star, but could never really see the rest of them. Constellations never really looked anything like their namesakes, anyway.

"Ikasa's the planet name in Nuwep," she said. "S'kea in Kaweekyooh. Eekshash in north Amareekah. Xiksosa in Mellegeny."

She pulled up her feet and stamped on the stone bridge.

"This is so stupid!" she said.

"What's so stupid?" someone said, voice hard and loud.

She jumped up and spun around, seeing the Alligators and the Saw Palmettos from the store at one end of the bridge. They had a little cage with some kind of dead hopper in it and a few cases of beer, most of which looked empty. There was a stink about them like a fertility ritual and she could feel the blood mana in the air.

"Nothing," she said, turning to walk away.

"No!" the Alligator-girl shouted, and Ikasa felt the wind rushing to close the distance between then, and the girl had her hands in Ikasa's hair-beads, wrenching and yanking.

Ikasa screamed.

"What the fuck did I tell you about the next time we met, huh, you little shit?" Alligator said, and bounced Ikasa's head against the stone bridge. "We ain't finished with our little bleeding. Hey, this is a river. Don't the motherhood god for the Xiuteotl say something about kids with white hair? They're fucking witches and they need to be drowned?"

She yanked Ikasa by the jacket.

"Well, you little fucker?" Alligator said, as she pushed Ikasa into the Saw Palmetto. "Hold this little shitskin for a second, bring her down here."

There were too many. She thought about shooting someone with lightning, but didn't think anybody would survive the experience, and that would put her in too much shit. She struggled a little until the Alligator brother slammed her into the mud next to the riverbank.

"This is going to be fucking great," Holly laughed.

The older boy put his knee on Ikasa's chest, and she coughed. Ikasa couldn't come up with any kind of mental directive, her mind jumping confusedly from one point to the next. She knew perfectly well what was happening, but couldn't find a way to take back control.

"Yeah, fuck you, you stupid little cunt," Holly said. "Punch her in the head!"

Saw Palmetto obliged, and struck Ikasa across the temple. She felt someone else grab one of her arms and press down into the mud. Saw Palmetto punched her again.

"Keep your head fucking down," he said.

"Got it," Alligator said, and waved the corn bag she'd taken from Ikasa's belt. "This is the shit I was talking about."

She tossed it to her brother. He dug into the pouch and

pulled one out.

"Let's stuff one up her nose," he said.

There was laughter all around. She could feel a shoe on her wrist, and grinding wet sand swallowing up her fingers. She coughed and spat when river water drizzled backwards down into her nose.

"Don't you fucking spit at me!" Saw Palmetto screamed, jabbing his elbow into her throat.

She tried to say she was drowning as her chest went raw, but couldn't choke out a word. Instead, she closed her eyes and dragged her hand under the mud before letting the lightning out. There was no throttle. Every time she'd let it go, it always came out the same, a searing polychaete of white light whose direction was that of an uncontrolled torrent of water. She screamed as always, voice going dead in the air.

Pushing up, she pulled herself from the muck and broke the quickly-cooling fulgurite in her hand over Saw Palmetto's cheek. They'd all been scattered like tinder, picking themselves out of the riverbank like groggy lungfish. Ikasa howled, barreled into Holly, and grabbed her corn bag back as Holly snapped down on Ikasa's shirt.

"Got you, you little cunt!" she said.

Ikasa replied by testing her fingers again, letting light spark over them. Holly let go with a pained scowl and hiss. Ikasa scrambled up over the bank, feeling a few paws on her leg, but she forged ahead, losing herself in the forest and running past the slippery shadows of the faeries. She took the long way around the western forest, following the path until she saw the Oehtkohtokuhn merge with the Calabokee, and ran all the way up the road until she saw the lights of her house.

The Alligators were at her door. They were talking to Pop. She ran to him, face hot and tears coming down her face, choking as she did. A few of them had burns and were smiling as she ran up. Pop grabbed her quick and socked her in the jaw.

"Get the fuck inside, you little shit!" he said. "Not only do you run the fuck off but you're stealing from the fucking nice folks? What's this bag, now?"

"It's a little corn bag, I got it from my gramma," Holly said, pleading strongly. Her eyes welled up with tears. "It's real important."

"Do you have her gramma's bag?" Dad said.

Ikasa opened her mouth to say something, but just tightened her nose and pointed her lips at Holly.

"I threw it away in the woods, into the river," Ikasa said. "It's probably halfway to the sea by now."

Her dad punched her again.

"See? She fucking attacked us, shot us with lightning!" Saw Palmetto said.

"Don't worry, I'll deal with it," pop said. "You fucking go into the fucking backyard where all that junk's at and you pick out something for me to beat you with, five whacks. If I don't like it, it goes to ten. If you whine, it goes to twenty."

He stopped her.

"One more thing. Apologize to these people," he said.

"Okay," Ikasa said. "I'm sorry they're all lying cunts."

Pop slammed her up against the trailer wall. The Palmettos giggled.

"Ten! I'm sorry, folks," Pop said. "You go on home."

"Sure thing, Mister Spider!" Holly chirped, and they walked away, pumping the air and pointing back at Ikasa from behind her father's back.

"March!" Pop yelled.

Ikasa wandered into the backyard scrap head to find something that at least wouldn't give her tetanus.

Chapter 14

Witness

A turtle was the first creature appointed by the other things to watch over the world. The hope was that turtle would be able to see everything everywhere, and report back to the court what he could find. Unfortunately, his legs were too stubby, so he came back to the court and apologized.

"My neck is long, and my intent is true, but my legs are too stubby to make a good census," he said. "You should let someone who can fly try it."

The court agreed with this, and made turtle the master of doorways and keys instead. They appointed a raven to watch everything and report back what he'd learned. He did his job well, but he had a tendency to give orders, and talk about everything to everyone, even to people who didn't want or need to hear about what he'd seen.

"Then give my job to rootscraper!" raven said when they told him he was no longer the watcher. "She has a big long neck, and is undefeated in battle! She is also very quiet and is very careful about everything."

So it went, but Rootscraper was too quiet and too careful about everything. She also had a terrible temper, and while it took a long time to make her angry, once she was angry, she never rested for a moment, and was very scary to everyone. When the court called her back, she agreed with their decision.

"But wait," she said. "I think you should make Spider do this."

"But Spider does too much already!" the other animals cried.

"Hear me out!" shouted Rootscraper. "She is small, has a tiny voice, eight eyes, can climb nearly anything, and has no real passion for violence. She is perfect for being a watcher. She already sits in her web all day to do all her things. If you're afraid of Yellow Spider, then make Brown Hairy Spider do it. He's not actually doing anything at all."

The court agreed with this, and they haven't had any problems with Spiders being watchers since. Of course, Spiders being Spiders, sometimes they set traps, and of course, they always help each other - it's not just Brown Hairy Spider that does the watching.

Ikasa fiddled with the fashion magazine cut-out of the woman she'd sent to another planet, drawing on it with a black marker that was nearly dry of ink. She added armor, a family name, and a few tools on the woman's belt. The woman's name was Hornhead, and she now carried a knife and rifle, a flashlight, a wrench, two screwdrivers, wire cutters, and a bit of padding for her chest and head. Eventually satisfied, Ikasa picked the Hornhead woman up and took her over to where her folks were watching television.

"Hey, mom, check it out!" she said, and handed her the cut-out.

"Oh, you're playing story-table. I used to do that," Mom said.

"My Hornhead is so cool! Next time Butch and me play, I'm going to win!" she said.

"You can't win agayateni, that's not how it works," Mom said.

"They're kids, they'll figure it out somehow," Gramma said. She took the cutout from Mom.

"You know what you need to do?" Mom said.

"What's that?" Ikasa asked.

"Giving her some more stuff is good," Mom said. "But you know just like if you spend all the time painting toy soldiers or little models like your big brother, you get better at models. You can play story-table by yourself on your wall."

"Yeah," Gramma said. She coughed while taking a drink. "Your mom had her whole room done up as a little obstacle course and neighborhood for all her agayateni stuff. Like how rich kids have fucking dolls. You get good enough and you can add things in real time."

"Sometimes people get so good they do it with movies they're watching. Have conversations back," Kapu said. "Introspection and all that."

"And the mana it brings!" Gramma said, and raised her beer to Ikasa.

Ikasa nodded and held out her hand. Once she got the Hornhead back, she jogged up to her room and pinned her up on the wall, taking a moment to draw a little open box underneath her. She planted her palms on each side and pressed into the wall. She let the cold prickles work out from her fingers and then washed the wall in herself. The woman dangled from the pin and looked up, yanking at her work jacket. She looked down, took the knife from her belt, and cut herself down.

Hornhead dropped into the box and looked around as Ikasa looked down at the pencil on the ground. Her focus suddenly gone, she watched the Hornhead flutter to the ground a moment later, and picked up both of them. She put the woman up on her nightstand and took the hopper out of its box. It was losing down and starting to grow long shafts on the arms and back, turning into a prickly little ball with sharp claws. It ran around and chirped plenty well on its own, though, and refused to sit right in her lap.

Ikasa dug around her comics before deciding she didn't want to cut any up. She picked up the hopper - big enough now that she could barely use one hand - and wandered back downstairs, into the backyard. She put it down, and it followed her like a chick after its mother while she gathered up some of the rocks in Gramma's piles, whatever she could spot as trilobites or shark teeth.

"Mom, Dad, I'm going to the trading post!" she shouted when she came back through the sun room.

She showed the rocks to Gramma.

"Is it okay if I take these?" she asked.

Gramma looked them over and took one of the trilobites off the stack.

"All of them but this one. Hurry up," she said.

Ikasa nodded, happy to have some trades, and stuffed them in her pockets. She picked up her hopper again and looked around the front yard real quick before grabbing a sash off the hat rack just inside the trailer to make a little sling. It nestled down into the sling and wiggled its butt before tucking a long neck into the folds of fat and down behind its shoulders so it could still look out.

She went across the street to Armadillo's trailer, and he was passed out among a pile of cans. She picked up a good long palmetto branch and tapped him with it.

"Hey, Mister Armadillo!" she said.

He did nothing. She opted not to whack him, but to try a few more times before he grumbled, rolled over, and buried himself a little deeper in the cans and magazines in his car. A wave of some horrible stink washed over her face, and she opted to just walk.

The road up to the Nokaha was a white dirt worm surrounded by slash pines, with scrub oak and saw palmetto fighting one another before thicker trees swallowed up the open areas to offer shade far away from the road. There were brown and green grasses that rose chest-high growing everywhere. Exotic peppers and tall, skinny trees with angry leaves were scattered amid the mix, and Ikasa always spotted a few stones clearly taken from the large ruins nearby embedded in the road. She liked stepping on them, feeling their mana echo up through each footstep like a deep drum or like plunging her leg into a fire.

When she'd been down this way in the car, she had spent more of her time reading a comic or messing with her brothers to really take a good look at it. When she was riding with Mister Armadillo, he was telling a story, or else she was always walking the other direction, back toward the river. She stopped and dug through some of the clutter along the roadside a bit, picking up a hubcap and wondering if she could make a hat out of it with some twine or something.

Then she found some poop. She'd seen remains from smaller animals and knew that's what she was looking at, but this was as long as her arm and as thick around; she felt a momentary tingle of fear roll through her shoulders and she used that palmetto sword-branch to peel it up a little. It was a deep reddish-brown, and with a bit of exploring, she saw the remains of pine needles and berries buried within. She looked up around the sandhill and didn't see anything bigger than the plants, but she did see a lot of flattened and broken trees far under the pines.

She followed the path of destruction as it wound around trees, finding big footprints with a large central toe and a smaller one on each side, round and filled with ants still running about looking for the culprit. Craning her head, she listened for cracks and snaps over the cicadas, and checked the direction. She decided the tracks went north, and went from tree to tree, noticing that there were several paths going around the trunks of the slash pines.

Entering under the cover of the trees, she noticed the missing bark on the old oaks some seven feet in the air, though they'd obviously been through the scratching process several times, with healing marks all over them. There she found branches stripped of foliage and hanging bare in the wind, and began to hear low-tone hoots and the grinding, heavy drumbeats of gigantic padded feet.

There were about six of hornheads out there, each of them her mother's height at the shoulder, with their heads twice that height, browsing on the oaks and the slash pines. They pranced about on four legs or two, all covered with shaggy, wispy feathers, half a dull reddish-brown with a black stripe running the length of the flank. The other half of the herd was lighter-bodied and had brilliant rust colored feathers with red and black bands across the back, and their magnificent, branching crests stretched with skin were marked by bright eye-spots and stripes. The outer edges of the small herd were tended by some small two-legged cutters - predators with whipping tails and broad jaws, which caught small animals the herd was kicking up. They shouted warnings to the bull hornheads when Ikasa came out of the trees.

The cutters nipped and chased the young hornheads into the center of the herd and hid with them, while the bulls made coughing, hooting booms, getting up on two legs to threaten Ikasa. She clenched her teeth and backed up, wanting no part in being crushed by the animals. She climbed up a nearby tree to get out of the way, and the bulls honked and bellowed until the herd moved on. She watched them go with a stupid smile, skin shivering and eyes aching like they might roll out of her head any moment. She had to tell Mary.

Forgetting all about the store, she dropped back down out of the tree and rushed back to the road, flicking a tick off her shirt as she went. She jogged down the other direction, making the turn down the white shell road that went right up to Mary's airstream. She heard yelling as she approached, mostly from Mary's pop. Mary was lying on the ground, crying and trying to crawl away from her pop, who stomped with a purpose up to where Mary was blubbering. He grabbed her roughly by the arm.

"Do you realize how dangerous this fucking shit it?" he yelled, shoving his fist into her face. "Just a fucking rock to your little shit brain!"

He opened his hand, tossing a piece of quartz into the air; he grabbed it with his thumb and forefinger when it came back down. There was a soft glow to the shard.

"Or are you fucking doing this shit? You better not be fucking doing this shit!" he roared, and kicked her so that she rolled. "These little pieces, all these little pieces are just the potential for fucking you up!"

He threw it with an underarm swing, following up with a backhanded sweep of his arm, and the quartz detonated with a monstrous howl. Ge squinted in the white light and slowly falling glowing motes it left behind.

"See that shit?" he said, and smacked her in the face. "You see that shit? That shit could be you!"

He dumped Mary on the earth and kicked some dirt around.

"Fuck this shit," he said. "I do all this shit so that you can be better than this and what do you fucking do? You fuck it up! Your little shitskin friend is here. Go see her."

He disappeared inside. The smell of rotten meat followed him. Ikasa helped Mary up.

"That was scary," Ikasa said. "Are you doing the white junk?"

"No," Mary said, and wiped some blood from her nose. "I just wanted some broken rocks."

"I believe you," Ikasa said. "You don't smell."

Mr. Crawfish came back out and handed Mary a five dollar bill.

"Take this, get your asses over to the store or something," he said. "Just don't be here."

Mary took it with a yank and stomped away.

"Come on, 'Kasa," she said.

They headed back down the trail toward the store. Mary didn't look like she was sad or upset, and instead looked more like she was annoyed or angry. Ikasa was pretty sure people were supposed to feel sad when their parents punished them.

"Are you okay?" Ikasa said.

"Yeah," Mary said. "Pop sometimes blows up. Just like the rocks. That's why I said it didn't do no good to mind him, he ain't minding himself. He pulls all his happiness away from himself into the rocks, so what's left for him?"

They showed up at Wilmer's with a somewhat legitimate five

bucks, which meant they felt and acted rich, ordering the most expensive chocolate stuff off the dessert menu, using the jukebox, and flipping through magazines with full color photos.

"I meant to ask you if we could go back to the Wohona cave," Mary said. "The one with the room and the cot? Or at least near there. There's a cave called Young-People-Meeting cave a bit of the ways down the river. There's another pad there that looks like the one you opened, and I think it's a sort of back entrance into that room."

Ikasa shivered, but managed to keep the magazine held tightly.

"Sure," she said. "I need to go back there to look around, but I don't want to do it by myself. Will Ehano be there?"

"We can get him. Wouldn't think it was right since he got cut out last time."

"Cool," Ikasa said. "Hey, what do you think about this?"

She showed Mary some pictures of a house and a few green trees, clearly from up north.

"About what?" Mary asked.

"Oh, I have a cutout I use for aga. Aya. Something. Story-table."

"Agayateni!" Mary said. "You're such a dork. That's a game for nerds."

"Magician nerds," Ikasa said. "Anyway, do you think my cutout would like it?"

"I don't know, it's your cutout. Those trees look cool," Mary said. "But it's agayateni, you're not worried about how expensive or cool it is, I say you go for broke."

She flipped through another magazine on the table and showed Ikasa a comic with a huge splash page covered in tubes, pipes, wires, giant electrical arcs, five airplanes, and a shelf with a rocket belt. There were ray guns hanging on the wall, and a collection of capes hanging over the back of a chair. Ikasa grinned from ear to ear.

"Go for fucking broke," Mary said.

"Yeah!" Ikasa nodded.

"I mean, really, isn't the only rule that you can't bring anything you personally drew from scratch?" Mary asked.

"I don't know," Ikasa said.

Mary dug around on the table and picked up a magazine that looked like it was nothing but empty stock images and text articles titled *Exploring Tables*, and flipped through.

"Here, like this. 'It is considered bad form to bring one's own artistic ability to the table, since anyone with a decent grasp of artistry could have very well brought their own convictions in regards to their pieces that muddy the waters of implicit group activity,'" Mary read. "What's 'implicit?'"

"It means, like, nobody actually said it, but they all agree on it anyway. Is it okay to draw on stuff you already have?" Ikasa asked.

"Uhm. 'Adding detail to one's prepared cutouts allows for some degree of stacking the deck in a woman's own favor, but such a person is not to be ostracized, for she has taken some degree of fate into her own hands - it is a borderline issue, and one that should be discussed at length with her group.'"

Ikasa leaned over the table and reached for the magazine.

"May I see it, please, readmaster?" she asked.

"Oh, yeah, sure," Mary said, passing her the magazine.

"Can we get this?" Ikasa asked, paging through stock photos and articles about centering and how to avoid applying awahakah connections into scenes, and an interview from some magician who wrote a book about how to make paper servants that could leave the table entirely.

"It's like a quarter," Mary said.

"And that means?"

"We can so get it," Mary said.

"Avos!" Ikasa said.

"You sound like you're from the big city again," Mary nodded.

"With avos? What about copacetic?"

Mary giggled.

"Oh, don't listen to that gum-flapping dewdropper's applesauce, he's just feeding you a line hoping to score a little ambo for an eye opener, but he flushed all his iron mans at the meet last night!" Ikasa said. "Now, this here funny paper's only two bits, but it's got a real howler in it!"

Mary broke out into laughter. Ikasa smiled, wondering if it was forced, but let herself laugh along with a genuine burst of mana. She felt the awahakah tighten, and briefly wondered if she should tell somebody about Mr. Crawfish. She waved that thought away before burying herself in more comics.

Chapter 15
Back in the Hole

The Spider and the Burrowing-Rotting-Caterpillar are famous for having arguments. A lot of their debates over how things should have gone. As an example, after Frog had gone off and ruined immortality for human beings, Caterpillar and Spider tried to figure out what should be done with human souls and bodies.

"I think they ought to be buried in the ground and rot, so everybody gets the parts to eat." said Caterpillar.

"Well, they didn't get immortality," Spider said. "But! I think you should burrow a hole with a flap door on top. When they die, they get buried, and it makes the body heal and change into a whole other body, then the soul gets put back inside and they crawl out somebody new as a young child, but all still remembering everything right."

"That sounds like too much work. What if they just remembered one thing?" Caterpillar said.

"Well, I think it would be a very nice world if everyone could always be learning new things and such. I agree with Shield-Bone-Headed-Thing," said the Spider.

"Everyone already agreed with Frog that humans don't get to be like that!" Caterpillar said.

Spider sighed and agreed, and crawled up into her bush and spun her webs. Burrowing-Rotting-Caterpillar crawled around on the ground until he realized all his dead brothers and sisters weren't coming over to visit any more. He realized why this was, and just crawled down into the meat under a rotten log and stayed

there, alone and surrounded by darkness.
Spider spins trap doors, still.

Ehano handed Ikasa a flashlight.

"Heard last time you guys went down a cave, you didn't have this," he said.

"Yeah, I had to use some limestone," Ikasa said, taking the light and pointing the beam down into the crevasse.

She cast the light over pale eggshell-yellow outcroppings and lowered herself down across the broad surface of something that looked like a melted wedding cake. She grabbed stalactites and skittered over a pit, then wiggled her way down a column until her feet touched a bottom lined with beer bottles, magazines, and a musty stink.

"Holy shit," she heard Mary say.

"See, you say that because you don't remember she has a spider tattoo," Ehano said. "Hey, 'Kasa! We're going to throw a rope to you, because we can't crawl across that shit upside down."

Ikasa was confused for a moment, but when she looked back up, she saw the terrible angle of the stalactites, and how they were covered with water and blue-green streaks. She found few sharp edges; clearly there had been structures along the path at one point, though they had been swallowed by growing rock. A thick vine fell down next to her, and Mary was the first to appear. She immediately went over to a small pool of water underneath a massive series of graffiti and adulthood seals in spray paint. She stuck her hands in the terraced pools and fiddled with something. Ikasa brought the light.

"It's five-three-eleven-seven, right?" Mary asked.

"Yeah," Ikasa said, pointing the light into the pool.

About elbow-deep, there was another flat panel, like the cover of a sarcophagus with seals and numbers, covered with limestone. Mary finished tapping out the sequence and the sarcophagus shuddered, the limestone cracked, and a portion of the nearby wall fell away. The chamber there was filled with stale air, and the caves kicked up with a strong, momentary wind as the room beyond them breathed for the first time in aeons.

Lights came on, smooth as the walls and arched, vaulted ceiling, illuminating the cavern beyond with a soft glow. What wasn't under an inch of water and carpeted with deposits was still seamless and clean. No graffiti decorated the pale walls and no damage seemed to linger.

"It looks like it was just poured into shape and left there," Ehano said.

"And it's white. Like dead people," Mary said.

"How old is it?" Ikasa said.

"Doesn't look that old," Mary said. "It would be deeper if it was old, right?"

"It could be from a way older world, but we had to use Xiuteotl numbers to get inside," Ehano said.

"So it's from just the last world," Ikasa said. "The Hundred Cuts World."

"What's that?" Mary asked.

"Story goes?" Ehano said, shining his flashlight at Ikasa.

She nodded.

"Story goes," she said. "There were four worlds, four countries, before this one. Their great cities were ground down into mountains, river stones, and dirt paths. In the fourth age, the world was fertile again, having been left over from a time when humans never touched the ground, and the waste of the previous world made for strong compost. Even as they learned to coax corn out of the ground, the humans in that country also learned to make totally new materials from the thin air. Despite this, it was said that their power was in the sea, and they had tiny devices that you could fill with seawater and fuel any number of strange wonders."

Ikasa looked around behind the massive stele in the center of the room. Her flashlight shone across a strange relief that depicted a white-haired witch casting a wonder that made the sky boil. She shivered.

"They sent ships out to sail among the stars, and find other worlds not just across time, but across the great ether, as well," Ikasa said. "The legends say they could make the sky crossing any time they wished. But they slowly killed the world with all their magic. They cut the world a hundred times, and it slowly bled until the world turned again, and the fourth country ended."

Ehano backed away from a flickering light hanging in the air.

"What is this, an art gallery?" he asked.

"No, this is the entrance to a magician's lodge," Ikasa said.

"Your lodge," Mary said, pointing at the relief with her lips.

"Yeah, it's scary," Ikasa said.

The image of the magician was certainly older, with much longer hair, but she had the red beads in her hair, and her dress was black and gold with little streaks and spots made of white. Her skin was dark red-brown, like rust or clay, from her arms issued fire and wind, and she chased boats across the sky. Her wings were made of silk and spider legs, and in one image, she rose above teeming throngs of people, sheltering them from sickness and plague. Water dripped from the ceiling.

"Maybe it's depicting her because the magician who worked here liked spiders?" Ehano offered.

"No, she worked here," Ikasa said. "I worked here."

To emphasize her point, she reached out and waved away some of the hovering ghost lights.

"The lodge paqui knows me," she said. "Is this what you thought would be here, Mary?"

Mary shook her head.

"I was thinking, maybe. A little kiosk. Or a dead end," she said. "Hey, here's ritual space."

Mary pointed at a little rotating dais surrounded by dust, dirt, and several jars, some clay, some metal, others of some unearthly make. There were little rivulets in it the shape of an orb web where sand or blood could easily be poured. Above it, the ceiling was done up in a copy of a night sky.

"I know the thumb of the hand, that constellation there," Mary said. "Why's it so low to the horizon?"

"Because it's from another world," Ikasa said. "According to Gramma, anything that isn't now, anything that's the past and the future, that's another world. You are not who you were or will be, there is only the you that you are now."

She stepped out in front of the spinning table and stuck up her arms.

"What should I do?" Ikasa said.

"Do the dance of putting the stars right," Mary said.

"Okay," Ikasa said.

She clenched her fists and held out her left arm, opening the palm to the sky. She drew her right hand to her chest. Ikasa reached up to mimic plucking a light gently with her thumb and forefinger, and she pulled back with a tiny star. She looked up, seeing it gone from the ceiling, and gazed around the room at her friends.

"Hey, uh. I don't know where they go," Ikasa said.

"Dumb Spider doesn't know where the stars are?" Mary said, and laughed.

Ronnie stepped up to the dais, tapped Ikasa's arm, and pointed to a space slightly higher.

"Thumb star," he said.

"Oh, shush," she said. "Everybody knows where that is."

Ikasa put it back in the right place. A few of the other stars started drifting into more familiar spaces, and they watched as the entire setup shifted.

"It's like an orrery," Ehano said. "It's calculating where the stars are based on what she changed."

"That's cool!" Ikasa said.

"What else can you do?" Mary asked.

Ikasa put her arms out to the side, stretched out her fingers, and lifted up her arms. She moved herself until she could see a star between each finger on her hands. Taking in a breath, she pushed out into herself and felt a heavy thud run through the bones in her arms. The world creaked and groaned like a great beast rising from the sea, and she heard a slow heartbeat.

"There is a vein of the world's blood, teotl, underneath us," she said. "I can feel the edges of the lodge. It's not very big, much smaller than it once was. It's mine, but it's not mine."

"What's that mean?" Mary asked.

"I think I can turn on the lights," Ikasa said, and the room warmed with brilliant golden illumination, both in symbol and glow.

The walls came to life, with old scenes playing out like slow dances. Ikasa put up the stars in some, and in others she roared across the heavens in magical conveyance. Ikasa traveled to other worlds. Ikasa demanded the mountains part for her palms. Ikasa touched the great machines in the center of the world and tore apart gears to grant herself supernatural power, and Spider watched all of it, her eyes stony and old enough they had no reflection.

"Did Ikasa build this?" Ehano asked. "The historical Ikasa, maybe?"

"If she did, she was mighty up herself," Mary said.

"Seems like that's all I can do," Ikasa said. "Just make the pictures move."

"Let me try," Mary said, and Ikasa nodded and stepped off the ritual circle.

Mary stepped up and held her arms out to her sides before making clipper-shapes with her fingers. The images on the walls lit up again. Crawfish deeds scrawled over the walls, but they were different Crawfish. Jimmy Crawfish fought the living dead. Megan Crawfish chopped down a whole forest of man-eating trees. Guapo the Mud-Lobster cast spells to destroy evil. Spider watched all of it, her eyes stony and old enough they had no reflection.

The pictures changed and moved, always on the different tasks and stories of the Crawfish family, skittering through the mud and working magic hidden from prying eyes. Ehano touched a wall.

"One of you's got problems," he said.

The pictures went out and Mary stepped back up to the group.

"It's cool," she said. "But I think 'Kasa's right. We can't do anything except make pictures. Maybe if we went back to the room with the cot?"

Ikasa shivered, wondering why Crawfish got so many varied images from different heroes. Spider had different heroes. More than just her namesake. She let the thought wallow in the shallow river of her mind until it was well and covered and then she punched a wall. Everyone else jumped.

"I'm Ikasa," she said.

"What?"

"Gramma says. When people die, their souls get picked up, and their memories get taken away from them," Ikasa said.

"Yeah, this is basic shrine stuff," Ehano said. "Supposedly, Death comes and takes the soul and the memories inside you, and takes them to the White City on the shore of a huge sea, called 'Matla.' There are a lot of dead people there, and in a lot of the southern tribes, the memories get put in Xigoltocl, the Vault of Whispers. But before that, you see lots of judges, and the judges can be bribed with your mana and things your relatives bury with you. People have lots of judges to see, so they go and build cities and towns out there in that country, and what you burn with people is carried with them out into the places there."

"That's why the Xiucuscu built such huge tombs like the catacombs and junk, instead of just mounds, huh?" Mary asked. "That's why crawfish build chimneys in the swamp. For the dead who didn't get a tomb."

"My gramma tells these stories, too. And the judges say what your soul gets used for next. And you get to keep one memory," Ikasa said.

"Five-three-eleven-seven," Mary said, nodding.

"Yeah. Which. I can't help but think this is some part of this Ikasa's plan," Ikasa said.

"You mean like from the last age? Before the nehaghee, or even before the last turning of the cycle?" Mary asked.

"Yeah," Ikasa said. "This Ikasa, who became the mythical Ikasa, she was real, she lived here, on this land. And she kept sending a message to each of her incarnations, 'five-three-eleven-seven,' and so here I am. Holding her name, her mana, her message. It's a little creepy, but I think I'm using her soul."

"That's a pretty mighty claim," Ehano said. "Is there a way to test it?"

"Other than the four-number code, no," Ikasa said.

"No! There is!" Mary said. "My dad has a translation reader at home, we could go into the cot room or find something that used to be hers, or something, then do a read on both of them. Did your parents have an astro done? We could totally use those numbers to calibrate the reader!"

Ikasa struggled for a moment, not sure if she should be excited or angry. Her shoulders burned red hot, but washed over with the ice cold of dread and fear.

"Yeah, they were talking about it last night," she said. "I also think I know a thing that used to be hers. Should I go get them?"

"Saturday, Spider-girl," Mary said. "We'll do it Saturday at the mound."

They filed back out to the main chamber, and the doors closed behind them. Ikasa was the last one up, and she used the rope. The green world above was a far cry from the drab, gray emptiness of the world underground. She listened to the sound of distant thunder and heard questing voices in it. Thunder heroes, likely, or sky-people. She looked off at the horizon with a tight jaw. Mary tapped her on the shoulder.

"What's wrong?" she asked.

"I'm scared," Ikasa said.

"If it's true, then the you from the past is trying to send you a message. She must have a good reason," Mary said. "And it makes sense for us to try to find that reason, right?"

"I guess so," Ikasa said.

She looked at the storm line coming in.

"Hey, a long time ago, people used to hold counsel with sky people and Thunder and all them," Ikasa said. "Magicians did, anyway. Do you think if I made an offering and shouted really loud, I could get one to come down here and talk to me?"

"Maybe," Mary said.

"You've got to be feeling extra magical if you think you can call down a thunder-woman," Ehano said.

Ikasa laughed and faced the clouds. Half the sky was brilliant blue, and the other half was blue-black, studded with constant flashes in the dark. The trees whipped themselves into a frenzy while an alien scream resonated across the slash pines. She held out her arms and brought her hands together as if she were gripping a tall pole, and the lightning struck up from the ground, through her hands, and into the clouds.

The force of the emergence nearly struck her off her feet, and she dug her heels into the ground. Vaguely aware of her own screams, she squinted in the brightness and averted her gaze from the dirt that was slowly turning wet and red under her. The other three shielded their eyes and stepped away, and Ikasa grabbed enough awareness to silence herself for a moment.

"Thunder-women! Sky-people! Brothers and sisters made of air and fire with no smoke!" she shouted. "I'm your sister! What proof do I need to present other than this bolt of lightning? Will you make me form thunder-wings, too? Please, come and speak with me! I must ask a question about the country that came before this one, the country where humans flew through you in great numbers in the belly of metal eagles!"

She held the lightning further, until her chest went numb and her feet felt hot through the rubber soles.

"Please! Come before me!" she screamed.

A few echoing rumbles in the clouds issued forth, but no one came down.

"I implore!" she began, before she let out a pained breath and threw herself down. The lightning escaped into the ground.

She remained there, on all fours, coughing and wretching while her body felt as though it might turn to stone and fall apart at any moment. Slowly, she stood, and the other three gave her sympathetic grimaces. She shrugged.

"Sometimes the magic works, sometimes it doesn't."

Chapter 16
At a Mound Festival

People used to not know anything from anything, you know. We ate our meat raw and terrorized everyone. This tribe would attack everyone and smash everything. At the same time, when it rained, our children would get sick, and when we drank water from the river, some of us would slowly die. We would say that was fine, because Spider's third daughter is mean to everyone, and that is acceptable, the harsh world teaches us all to be strong. Eventually, though, one girl got fed up with all this and left behind her family. She would have told them she had enough, but no one could speak back then, either.

So this girl goes up to start wandering the songlines back and forth, and nobody knew what those were, either. And she makes noises on the road, like "choo-whoop! Choo-hah! Choo-ki-yi-yi-ya!" since nothing like that existed.

Then, suddenly, in front of her appeared a big tapering trunk, like a tree trunk, and it had crackling legs and long hands, and it screamed out loud, like "gyaaa-kya-KYA!" and it knocked her over.

"It's so good to stretch!" the big glowing pillar says, in a voice like rocks grating over each other.

"Who are you?" the girl says, suddenly able to throw what she was thinking into the world.

"I'm Shee-joo-tay, the spoken word!" says the glowing thing. "I went to sleep for a long time, but somebody got the 'idea' to say something so I got back up!"

"Did I make you?" she asks.

"Yes and no! It calls back. You made up the spoken word, but you're not the first one to do so. Either way, I went to sleep before, but you made me up, so I woke up, and here I am!

"So my noises can make things like a spoken word?" she says.

"Your noises were sings," says the Spoken Word.

To emphasize its point, it starts singing and dancing.

"What's that you are doing there?" Raw-Meat-Girl goes, and copies it.

"Something you are much better at," says Spoken Word.

"I can tell," Raw-Meat-Girl answers.

So they go about, singing and dancing, off down the songline looking for more ideas.

Ikasa didn't know half the people that turned out, but that didn't really matter. She slammed her foot down and swept her arms in tune to the drums, staying in her space in line with the other clans. Toad, Wind, Hornhead, Cutter, Kuhdjoojoo Stork, Long-Necked-Swimming-Snake-Bird, and Yam were all in her line. She couldn't make out the signs on the other dancers across the yard, but she could feel Alligator and Thunder's presence over there. All rich kids, mostly.

The drums broke, and there was silence. Mr. Armadillo started saying something into a microphone to the crowds in the bleachers and on the blankets, but she couldn't hear the words he spat, at least until he began singing. Hornhead came out from her line and wandered aimlessly around the yard, bobbing his head and tapping the ground with his fingers until he knelt down on the ground and closed his eyes.

The mountain clan boys and girls came up and clustered around him. Ikasa stepped up and reached into her pocket for the little quartz marbles and threw them up into the air, clenching her teeth and keeping her arms outstretched until they slowed in their arcs and hung still, catching sunlight and shimmering. The crowd clapped and cheered, and the drums started up again, low and hushed. The mountain kids bustled about, singing to themselves.

"Hah! Shih. Shih. Ha! Ha! Shh. Ssssst," they said, making sounds like a prelude to an earthquake as two of them began groaning with deep throat voices.

Mr. Armadillo kept singing and took the microphone right up to Hornhead boy, passing it down to him.

"Oh! I have slept so long I slept backwards!" he shouted. "Look still! The mountains are having a congress about where they ought to go!"

"Mountains are indecisive," Mr. Armadillo said. "But so lazy! Look over here, Spider grandmother has put up the stars, at least. And the rivers are starting to flow. But where is your Mother?"

"That's right, the first time I had this dream, our Mother was here," Hornhead said. "Let me sing, and maybe I'll make her appear again."

Mr. Armadillo nodded and stepped away, and the Hornhead boy started to sing. Spider heard nothing but a mélange of voice and drum. She held her eyes on the marble stones she put up in the air, thinking that their layout was wrong, but not doing anything about it because that might disrupt the sing. She waited until the drumming stopped and the stories ended before letting the marbles drop from her hands into the dirt.

Other kids scrambled off after them, and she wandered back to the payphones on the north side of the western pyramid. She settled down into the dirt and tried to catch her breath. Ronnie came by, his hair enormous. He was wearing a blue, white, and brown jacket adorned with crab shells.

"Hey, man," she said as he sat down against the wall.

He handed her a couple of marbles.

"Did you grab these when I dropped, or did you sock somebody?" she asked.

He smacked his fist and just grinned.

"Tools people use in the sings end up with a lot of power. Pop wanted me to make a star-catcher thing, but I didn't want to just hand spider magic to some other kid. I get enough trouble from them Alligators," Ikasa said.

She put them in her pocket.

"Summer's almost over," she said. "I hope this thing doesn't follow me into the school year, but I don't want to finish my trial before school is over. It'd be hard to be an adult and still be going to school, wouldn't it? I'd have to get a job or something."

Ronnie nodded. He counted the change in his pocket before he got up and wandered off to the youth building. Ikasa thought about following him, but he was probably just going to win at pinball and buy a soda. She went around the back of the pyramid and sought out her folks. Eddie was banging out a cadence on a truck hood for some older girls while Butch was danced with them.

"What's up, fuckhead?" Eddie shouted. "Get over there and shake your feets!"

She smiled and whooped before jogging up and joining in.

"Got no problems in my eyes," Eddie sang. "Got no problems in my ears!"

"Got no problems in my throat, or nothing about my years!" Ikasa sang back.

"Nothing about my momma, no nothing about my poppa!"

"Plenty on my knuckles, though! We all got no problems, because we kicked some ass!"

"Hey-yey, kicked some ass!"

"You got a problem with me, brother-man?" one of the girls sang.

"I got no problem with you! You got a problem with me?" Eddie sang back.

"Got one problem here!" a girl yelled.

"Then step on up and take a free shot, sister, then we'll all have kicked an ass!" Eddie said.

Ikasa clapped and laughed, until she saw her parents up over on the north end of the field, waving her down. She broke from the free dance and clapped her way over to her mom and pop. They were with the mound keeper, some old lady from a wind clan Ikasa couldn't recognize, and whose name she forgot. Her mom waved.

"You remember Laura," she said. "From three weeks ago."

"Yeah," Ikasa said. "Hello, ma'am."

Laura nodded back at Ikasa.

"She's so good," Laura said. "Our local Spiders other than the Gramma don't remember any of the dances or have practically any of the mana they gave up during the unification."

"Oh, I know," Ikasa's mom said. "Cheryl around here's my cousin, and they made out with more money, but most of us in the northwest kept the family's mana locked up. Honestly, the old Spider dances are the only ones Ikasa and Butch know."

"There are man dances for Spider?" Laura asked. "See, I didn't even know that."

"Yes, I have a second cousin up near Pohroy in Ortelia who does a lot of the Spider man stories," Ikasa's mom said. "He's one of the best storytellers in the area, and a good magician to boot."

"I hear your Ikasa is becoming a magician, too."

"My mom's teaching her, and she's doing some tutoring with our neighbor, he's in Armadillo clan. Plus, she's been doing a lot of learning on her own, I think."

"She needs to keep her ass out of fights, she keeps antagonizing those Alligators, I keep having to kick her ass," Pop said.

"I do not! They jumped me!" Ikasa said.

"You expect us to believe that, even with the amount of respect that girl's been giving you?" pop said.

"Whatever," Ikasa said

Pop slapped her on the back of the head. Ikasa pressed her lips together and readjusted her squirrel-bird headdress.

"So stupid," she mumbled, walking off.

"She's still a kid, I'm so sorry," Ikasa heard her mom say.

"I love how you integrated the Spider regalia with the Xiuteotl historical regalia," Laura said.

Ikasa went back to the statues of kings at the eastern pyramid and kicked a serpent head stone lightly. She found Sadie Kaw smoking and leaning against the back of the first king, holding a conference with blackbirds and fried potato cakes. Ikasa frowned.

"I don't think you should be leaning against that," Ikasa said.

"Says who?" Sadie Kaw said, lighting another cigarette with the one she'd almost finished.

"Says anybody."

"You're the one who was crawling up on this one a while ago," Sadie Kaw said. "That's even worse. Sticking your hands down in his mouth and pawing with your feet all over him."

"How did you know that?"

"First, never be surprised by anything a corvid does," Sadie Kaw said. "Second, you're carrying a fucking corn bag I gave you. And I. Am a powerful magician. Anyway, what's in this king's eye?"

"Who? Nakoodah? I didn't get time to see last time," Ikasa said.

"You got time now," Sadie Kaw said.

"Yeah, but the festival," Ikasa started.

"Festival nothing. Climb up the ancient king Nakoodah and look into his eyes, and tell me what he sees."

Ikasa shook her head and looked around. She couldn't see

anyone watching at the moment, so she swung herself up onto the king's shoulder. The statue didn't so much have arms, as it was a pillar carved into a man. He held a bowl in his hands, up to his chest, and fresh blood had been painted on his chin and poured into the bowl for the festival. Ikasa stuck her feet on his belt so she could lean off the side and turn herself to where he was looking. Seeing nothing special in that direction, she pulled out her flashlight and went looking into his eyes for the carvings she'd seen earlier. It looked something like names, but she didn't recognize anything else.

"I don't think I speak this language," Ikasa said. "It doesn't look like Ootsooduh or anything, but it's not pictures like they put on codexes or anything."

"Well, I didn't think about that," Sadie Kaw said. "Is there anything you do understand written in there?"

Ikasa pulled herself up closer and looked in the other eye. She saw something in Xiuteotl scrawled over the letters.

"Yes," Ikasa said.

"What's it say?" Sadie Kaw asked.

"Hold on, it's hard to read and it's really old. Uhm. It says. 'This one has,'" Ikasa started. "Hold on. It says something like 'I farted on the bowl when I sacrificed the king's daughter.'"

Sadie Kaw laughed.

"Okay, that's funny, but it's not what you're looking for, is it?"

"No," Ikasa said. "Why would someone-"

"Write that down? It's naughty. People like breaking rules and then hiding the secret somewhere. I know an axe-smith who writes dirty poems inside axe heads before he puts the handles in. Everybody whispers naughty secrets to their own personal hole under a tree."

"Really?"

"Oh, yeah. Nearly everyone does something dirty. The super nice old guy on the bus? He might have eaten his own shit off his woman's nipples by her request. Every nice old lady choked on a dick once. A magician might pee behind the spirit houses. I like drawing scars on myself of things I didn't do. Everyone you see has a dingy secret, and you'd be surprised how many of them have those secrets in common," Sadie Kaw said.

She laughed to herself, manically, almost with a sort of deviant glee.

"This sacrifice leader? I bet she didn't make a habit of farting in the blood of her offerings, she just wanted to do it once. If I told you the things chefs do, you'd never want to eat in a restaurant again," Sadie Kaw said. "Keep that in mind."

"Why?"

"You're a Spider, why am I telling you that you need to think about what sorts of naughty things people do when they're all alone? Isn't that half of Spider's deal? Spider stole the food out of an offering plate for an old stone and got run over. Spider stole fire from the Sun and got married to him. Spider stole a hundred ducks from a whole tribe. She and Hopper are like trickster sisters who aren't even supposed to be clowns. That's not even getting started with all the dick and pussy jokes both of them get up to."

Ikasa hopped down and put away her flashlight.

"I forgot about clowns. We don't really see many contrary clowns in the city," Ikasa said.

"That's the problem," Sadie Kaw said with a firm nod. "You don't know what it's like for clowns to have to keep topping the secret misdeeds everyone gets up to. You have to make someone laugh who's probably already done terrible things secretly, but you can't be so contrary you make someone angry. It's like trying to smile but all your teeth have fallen out."

"You're not a clown, how do you know this?"

"I am a powerful magician!" Sadie Kaw said. "So powerful I need no house or blood other than my own! I will never marry, nor visit the Lodge of Lost Faces!"

She raised her hands into the air.

"Let me show you a powerful trick!" she said. "You got your pot of fire with you?"

"How do you know?"

"Spies!" Sadie Kaw shouted, jumping right into Spider's face. "Now, go fetch it!"

Ikasa grumbled a bit, but went back to the car to get the old cracked pot out of the trunk. It was heavy with clay and mana, and she had a little trouble hauling it back out to the far side of the pyramid. Sadie Kaw had gotten a stick and was busy setting up a circle in the dirt, with stones tossed around. She directed Ikasa to put the pot in the off-center, and put Ikasa up in the middle.

"Now, your Alligator friend," Sadie Kaw said.

"She's not my friend," Ikasa said.

"I know. But your Alligator enemy was able to pull off the lid and shoot the fire every which way, and that's all. You, though, you're a Spider. Not just any Spider, neither, you're a mother's daughter, too, and you have a really powerful name your folks gave you. It might not have been theirs to give, but that's how it goes. So! I have taken the liberty of making up a sign that they use in power plants nowadays to drag off extra energy and throw it off into the ether. If we're lucky, when you pop that cap, combined with the fact that you're, well, who you are, it ought to not just explode."

She pointed.

"So go on, pop open the lid."

Ikasa thought maybe she was being taken for a ride, but then looked around at her feet where she was standing and, while it was enormous, it was certainly a match for the stuff she'd seen etched into the back of the battery pack of her brother's radio. She stuck her hands around the edges of the keyed lid and lifted straight up. There was a moment of flashing, snapping red fire, and it arced beautifully into the ridges and stones of the circle.

"The stones can take a lot of heat, but they'll melt before too long, kiddo. Listen up! Take control of it just like you took the lightning bolt!" Sadie Kaw said.

"Okay," Ikasa said, taking in a dry breath.

She coughed in the soot and heat and squinted. She didn't feel particularly confident about not burning her fingers off, but she saw a little bright yellow clump of something in the center of the pot. It had to be the fuel or something important to the fire. Clenching her teeth and pulling back her elbows, she jammed her hands into the clay pot. When she felt her skin prickling likes pins and needles rather than pain, she relaxed just long enough to hear and smell her hands being consumed by fire.

"Don't you dare scream!" Sadie Kaw said.

Ikasa bit her lip and wrapped her hands around the source. It squished in her hands, like clay, and when she pulled a thumb-sized portion away, she couldn't see a reduction in that bright orange-yellow lump. The heat was dying down into a warm and numbing sensation in her palms, but so hot on her face that sweat was turning straight to steam. She took out the little bit she'd pulled off, and it burned in her hands like a crackling camp fire. What fire remained in the pot no longer leaped and screeched, but instead billowed softly up through. Sadie Kaw dragged her foot across a few parts of the circles.

"Looks like you got it. Neat trick," Sadie Kaw said. "There are a few thoughts on family treasures. Some people say they ought to belong to the families who inherited them, and that they ought to be locked up in little rooms and covered in cinnamon bark and dried squash and have spirits evoked only in their names. Some people believe they ought to be out and used, because that's where they're happiest. Other people say they ought to belong in museums."

She stepped up to Spider and looked into the jar, taking care not to get too close.

"What's this sun-jar think about any of that?" she asked, and the fire flared. "Oh, no, I'm with you, but I want the Spider to tell me."

Ikasa squeezed the white-yellow gunk in her hands. She thought about smearing some on her face like makeup. The mana was strong enough that even with the heat gone, she still felt her wrists grow distant and her heart speed up.

"I think," she said. "I think it's happy it gets to come out every once in a while."

"Well, then," Saide Kaw said, putting the lid back down on the jar. "Let's go on over to the leather trash and see if we can't make a strap for you. It's got these little handles on it so Spider could carry it around on her back."

Ikasa giggled and nodded.

"Okay, cool."

Chapter 17
Slash Pine Day

There was once a village that lived way up in the mountains, and up in there was a stream that, although small, was a very important thing for the village. It was so clear and delicious they would talk about it to any stray traveler they would see. Eventually, though, came the day that it started to slow down and get thin, and one day it became as dry as a pile of ashes. Now the people were wondering what had happened to their pretty stream, so they sent a man up to go to the village above them in the mountains to see what had gone wrong, and he found a great big dam, and sitting on top of it was a big fat bloated thing with stick arms and big bowlegs.

"Hey, thing up there!" he shouted. "My people suffer without water, you and your village have too much!"

Seeming to be amused by this, the big bloated thing poked a hole in the dam with an arrow and laughed.

"There is your water!" it said, and the man went back into his village.

After a few days, this tiny trickle again disappeared, and they wondered what they should do. The people do not start anything, and only finish what has begun, and no one had shot an arrow or thrown a stone. Eventually, though, Waksenakee came down into town, and he was ten feet tall and his hair was made of fire, with a thousand feathers in it, and so much clay there was a little village of tiny brothers inside, and there was a big stork sitting on his back with its long beak and furry body hiding his things.

"What problem do you have here?" he said, and the villagers pointed him up into the mountains, where he went, and saw the village with the dam and all the people in it.

He sat down on a log out on the edge of town and began to smoke, until people took notice of his countenance and approached, asking him what he wanted.

"Just a small drink," he said.

"Oh, no one gets a drink here unless the chief says so," a woman told him.

"Then go to him, and tell him I want a small drink, so I'll know why he is such an ass."

The woman nodded, and came back with a tiny half-filled bowl of dirty water that smelled like piss. Waksenakee poured it on the ground and stood up, walking up to the dam, and shouted up at the thing there.

"You, bullfrog, I know who it is!" he shouted, and when the big fat thing appeared he struck it with his spear, and clean water poured out every down the mountains.

Waksenakee grabbed the bullfrog with his hands and squeezed it until it was a tiny wrinkled thing.

"Now, all of you! What will you do with the water?"

"I'll live in the mud where it's always wet and safe and comfortable!" a woman said, and Waksenakee turned her into the leech.

"I'll drink all the water forever while I swim!" a man said, and Waksenakee turned him into the fish.

"I'll skitter around on top of it!" a woman shouted, and Waksenakee turned her into the water-spider.

"And I'll stay here on the dam and keep pinching it so it stays clear!" the last man said, and Waksenakee turned him into the blue crab.

"Now!" he said to the bullfrog. "Get out of here!"

Bullfrog hopped away into the water and hid in the mud.

Ikasa had taken to carrying the fire-jar around wherever she went. She took the straps Sadie Kaw had made and tied them to part of a backpack so she could stow snacks and changes of clothes in case anybody decided to go swimming, too. She'd also begun collecting about near everything that was loose and looked cool, and for everything else she had a pocketknife. Ikasa wanted to cut her hair so that she'd look a little less manly, but her mom had vetoed that idea with a line of knuckles and a chest-splitting scream so loud that Mr. Armadillo came running over to make sure there wasn't a possum being gutted in their back yard. She decided to bind her hair up in red beads instead.

She sat in front of the Wilmer's eating bean soup out of a paper cup, at least until she ran out. Then she just sat in the heat and rubbed sweat and oil off her forehead. She saw a few people she recognized going in and out, but otherwise she didn't bother to pay attention until Ehano walked up. She waved at him and he sat down next to her.

"What's up?" he asked.

"Nothing, Pop is still out with the breakup labor, so only my mom and gramma are at home," she said. "And my mom's being really strict lately. I thought I might play some pinball but they had bean soup, so I bought that instead."

"Shit, they made bean soup today?" Ehano stood up. "Hold on, I'll be right back. Oh, Mary and her pa've gone into town for the next couple days, he's making a big sale down at the airdock. You want to go down to Ronnie's, get him, and go up to the ruins or go fishing?"

"Sure," Ikasa said, and Ehano disappeared inside.

He came back out with another two cups of soup and some sodas, tossed one to Ikasa, and she picked up her bag.

"It's a Nuwep type soup," Ehano said. "They don't make it out here very much. There's that Nazro guy who works here, and he brings these freaky giant spores to put in the soup."

"Is that why it's a little less spicy than usual?"

"Yeah, they give it this weird light sour taste, like limes, that's hard to get around here unless you order Nazro food specifically. It's so good."

"I guzzled it down," Ikasa said, popping the cap off her soda and smelling sweet mango.

"That's such a stereotypical Spider thing. Beans, huh? Did you burn off all your hair trying to get some baked beans out of a crock your gramma was cooking?"

"You're a shit," Spider shook her head. "And my mom won't let me cut my hair."

"That's too bad, it's so long you look like a boy," Ehano said.

"And your crew-cut girly hair makes you look like a princess!" Spider shouted.

Ehano laughed.

"Oh, man, Mary doesn't joke like you do," he said. "She keeps trying to be responsible. But I guess. I don't know. I've heard a lot of man-stories about Spider, but not a whole lot about the actual family. What's your clan orahjoo?"

Ikasa took a drink and a breath. She let it out and burped.

"Spider is the patron of technology, magicians, the stars, and trickery. She's like a clown, but she doesn't act contrary to teach anybody anything. She does it because she has her own agenda. Loyalty is the most important virtue a Spider has. Our family is all strong magicians. Back in Cahokia, we used to fix broken washers and computators and junk, and summon spirits and have wonder-working services. We might start doing the same thing out here, once we get enough mana to the locals," Ikasa said.

"Okay, that makes sense. Is Spider etheric or fiery?"

"Etheric, but with a strong connection to fires," Ikasa said. "She put up the stars, but there's a story that one day Spider will wrap the world in a wide web made of invisible wires. It's a very fire-heavy story."

"Sounds it," Ehano said.

The air shimmered over the concrete and birds refused to call, sitting tired in the tree branches with their mouths open. A few brushrunners in the nearby bushes didn't even run when the pair walked by them. They were just lying in the shade with their heads on the ground, breathing heavily and wondering at them. Ikasa thought about going back to the store and getting some water for them, but it seemed a million miles back the other direction. Her own hopper refused to walk itself, having instead crawled into her backpack and gone to sleep.

"Are feral hoppers a problem around here?" she asked.

"Not really, I carry an air horn just in case, but there's maize-cutters around here," Ehano said. "And since they hunt the same thing, they usually kill off the wild hoppers."

She had forgotten about that. She stuck her hand in her pocket and felt the broken knife. Shivering, she watched the tree line.

"Do you know where they are?"

"Nobody does," Ehano said. "Law says we can't cause cultural contamination, or something. But I know where they camp sometimes. You want to go there?"

"Yeah," Ikasa said.

"Then it's a plan," he said.

They crossed down into the sandhill and ducked their way through blaring cicada orchestras and down through the saw palmettos where the Blue Crab house sat. Ronnie was out back by himself and in the process of shoveling dirt into a hole, surrounded by hoppers that swarmed on him like he was the pack leader.

"No!" shouted Andy Blue Crab's voice.

Ehano grabbed Ikasa and held her down under the palms.

"Nope," he whispered. "We got to wait this one out."

Mr. Blue Crab exploded out of his house and closed the distance to Ronnie in seconds. He back-handed Ronnie across the face and pushed him down into the sand under the slash pines. He put both feet on either side of the boy and flipped him around so he could punch Ronnie in the nose. Hoppers screeched and ran for cover in the bushes, while others grouped up a few feet away and screeched.

"You listen to me! You don't ever hide my liquor!" Andy screamed.

He huffed and looked around, seeing the shovel and the hole.

"This? Is this where you been putting my shit?" Andy shouted, picking up the shovel.

Ronnie started to get up, but Andy slammed the shovel down into the dirt next to him, spade first. Ikasa flinched when it sounded like he'd cut something. Andy pulled the shovel back up and beat it on the tree. Ronnie covered his eyes.

"You fucking shit! You don't ever hide none of my shit! You understand me? You fucking understand! Don't you ever hide my fucking liquor!"

He threw the shovel at Ronnie.

"Dig it up, you shit!"

Ronnie stood up and Andy kicked him in the leg.

"Did I tell you to fucking stand up, you little cum-stain?" Andy said. "Crawl."

Ronnie was visibly crying, but he still hadn't shouted or screamed like Mary had.

"Is everyone like this?" Ikasa asked.

"My parents don't give me no mind period," Ehano said. "Andy's a drunk, he's been in jail a few times, his sister and his brother-in-law are in jail right now, so he takes care of Ronnie."

"Don't you ever talk?" Andy roared, as he kicked Ronnie in

the stomach. "You ever fucking talk? You stupid shit, there is something the fuck wrong with your brain. I should have never fucking agreed to take you. Should have left you in the jungle like an old lady. Hurry up, dig that shit out, the sooner you get me a bottle the sooner I stop kicking your ass."

To emphasize the point, he kicked Ronnie in the ass. Ronnie clawed with hands and shovel to dig up a couple of bottles, most of them broken.

"You busted that shit on a tree trunk, didn't you?" Andy said. He picked up one of the intact bottles, tore off the cap, and took a swig. "Mother fucker, you lost me eight dollars of liquor, get the fuck inside. I don't want nothing but the house to see how bad you're going to catch it."

He squinted and staggered a bit before walking back into the house. Ikasa stood up and waved over at Ronnie, who ran up into the palmettos and sat down. One of the crab claw bead strings he wore in his hair was broke. He was covered in dirt and snot from the fight.

"Let's get out of here," Ehano said, still crouching below the palmetto fronds.

"Yeah," Ikasa nodded.

They crawled, at least until they were under oak cover, and then ran most of the way into the woods to where Ehano said the maize-cutters met. Ronnie sat down next to the little pile of charcoal in the clearing and finished crying while Ikasa gave him a towel and a shirt.

"There's a spring right over here," Ehano said. "We can go swimming."

"That sounds cool," Ikasa said. "The water's clear?"

"Best-kept secret of the area. If they're not phosphorous mines, they're clean, clear water," Ehano said. "Come on, Ronnie, let's go for a dip, get you cleaned up."

Ronnie stood up and brushed himself off.

"Thanks," he said, as they went over to the edge of the spring.

Ehano had said the water was clear, and it was true. There was a huge hole under the water in the center, a big limestone boil littered with bones of enormous animals down in the bottom, and a shallow little lake with one big river flowing down and away to the Calabokee. Bluegill and boomerang heads swam or walked along the bottom, and Ikasa was sure she could see turtles down in the depths. The water was cold, too, fresh out of the aquifer and swirling like a lazy snake.

Ikasa could see the two-toed footprints all along the mud of the northwestern shore, and when she slipped into the water, she swam over to look. The remains of rope-making, a crude needle and some sharpened quahog fossils, sat along the bank, and she reached out a hand to touch them. They throbbed with waste mana, and she felt her mouth holding a needle, weaving in and through and around a central thread, wrapping tight and thick into coils that were spun into other coils. She took her hand back, hissing and giggling.

"What is it?" Ehano asked.

"They were here!" Ikasa shouted back.

"I told you!" Ehano said. "They come here to make knives and rope."

He swam around over the boil.

"They come and get the bones out of here and sharpen them, too," he said.

"They can swim?"

"Of course they can swim, they have to, right? They haul bones out of here."

"Weird," Ikasa said.

She looked around over the water and saw fleeting images of what she thought was a turtle, but which moved oddly, only flicking two of its flippers. She smiled at the crab.

"Ehano! Catch that blue crab going that way!" Ikasa shouted and pointed.

"Oh, shit!" Ehano said, and dove.

Ronnie grabbed a stick from the bank and circled around to send it back their way.

"Don't let it get into the river!" Ehano said, trying to purchase his feet on the limestone bottom. "It gets into the river we'll lose it!"

Ikasa looked up to where the clear water turned swiftly into dark tea from the cypress and oak trees before she remembered the bucket of water in her backyard and the fossils and stones in the bottom. She thought about trying something, but remembered the enormous bones in the boil. She shook her head to clear out frightening thoughts of ancient monsters rising up from the water. Diving under, she opened her eyes to the sting of minerals in the water and swam forward, keeping herself focused on the blurry movement of the crab. Ehano lanced down, putting his hands on top of the shell, and Ikasa surged forward, grabbing it by the back legs. She came up.

"I got it!" she shouted.

Ronnie threw up his fists for victory, and he started making his way to shore.

"Wood!" he chanted. "Wood! Yes, wood!"

"We'll make a fire and bake the thing," Ehano said.

"New claws for Ronnie's hair," Ikasa cheered.

Ronnie stopped and looked back at Ikasa for a moment. He looked confused before he smiled and shouted.

"Wa-kyah!" he said. "Let me count some on it first!"

"No problem!" Ikasa said, emerging from the water.

She dangled the crab over the sand on the shore and let Ronnie hit it with a stick and shout a few times before Ehano broke off the claws.

"What kind of spices can we use on it?" Ikasa asked. "We don't have anything."

"Sure we do," Ehano said. "You're learning to be a magician. Which plants around here do you rub in your eyes to make wonders?"

Ikasa thought about the comment before smiling and dance-picking peppers from the edge of the clearing. It was the best crab she'd had in a while.

Chapter 18

A Dime

Brushrunner is a little bird with no wings and a striped tail. He likes to snack on just about everything, and one night, he was out looking for something to eat. He spied a crawfish out crawling along the shore and got a plan to catch it in his mind. So he snuck up to the bank and dropped over and took a deep breath so he looked bloated and dead.

"Oh, look here!" the crawfish said when it found him. "Such a great thing to eat, a dead creature like this!"

Crawfish went over to check with his claws and see if the brushrunner was really dead. He pinched the brushrunner on the nose, and the rubs, and the soft feet, and the brushrunner nearly cackled out and giggled, but managed to stay perfectly quiet.

"He is surely dead!" the crawfish shouted with joy, and skittered back to his village to tell his chief.

All the villagers cheered and were called down to the feast. The chief called up the warriors and told the young men to dress in their finest clothes and paint, and the men marched right up to that brushrunner and started to form a great big circle around him.

"A great feast we'll have on this feathery beast!"

"He is dead, and we will dance to our hunger running away!"

"A good time! A feast of flesh!"

And as they danced, the brushrunner suddenly shot out his neck and picked up the chief before gulping him down with a crack and shake of his head.

"Who did you say you were going to eat? The soft-feathered

dead beast? I'll break your ugly backs and crunch your pincers!"

The brushrunner ran among the crawfish, killing and eating them by the scores, and at the end of the night, as the sun was coming up, the brushrunner walked back into the forest, tail swishing and belly full, and left behind a river bank full of the broken.

Ikasa sat under the trees with her hopper reading funny books. A few blue-black storks were sharing the shade of the great cypress with her, mostly puttering around on all four legs and prodding bushes with their beaks or sitting around with their mouths open. The hopper lounged completely on its side. It had lost most of its down and in the process of turning into a prickly ball of growing feathers.

She had already run out of water and left her backpack a good ten feet away. After enough sweat had dropped from her face to loosen the staples on the pulp she was reading, she gave up and fell back against the tree with her arms out to the side. She rubbed a layer of oil off her face and took a moment to look over at the nearby river, seriously contemplating refilling her bottles. She remembered something Gramma told her about brain-eating amoebas and she figured better.

Collecting her bottles, she stood up and groaned. She looked back down at the issue of *Thrilling Air Stories* and let out a small whimper, but just left it there. The storks didn't bother to fly away, instead satisfying themselves with the loud croaks and clacks of their beaks. Her hopper got up and followed, loping and pointing its open mouth at the ground. Ikasa felt like she was carrying a hundred pounds of soaked cotton on her shoulders.

She trudged up along the creek until she found the Calabokee and followed that north, lamenting how fresh and cool the water looked, all blue and green and catching the sunlight like hobby glitter. Animals all along the other bank lounged in the water or drank deeply, and even the turtles didn't climb all the way out of the water to sun themselves. Eventually, the forest line on the other side of the river ended, a large fence complex pushing the Stetson forest to the south, and the open pine scrub and sandhill to the northeast took over. She recognized one pine in particular as being near Mary's house, and looked for a place to cross the Calabokee.

She waded across a somewhat shallower curve and swam

when she got to the big furrow cut in the limestone to artificially deepen the river. She crossed up over the other side, feeling more thirsty than when she got in. Pressing through palmetto fronds, she saw her hopper coming up behind, holding its little wings on the surface of the water as its hind legs went ballistic to try pushing it through the water, cheeping constantly at her. He made it to the other side and shook himself off before dropping at her feet like a tossed rag. He was getting a little too big to actually carry properly, and the feathers coming in clearly marked him as male. She was starting to think of a name, but couldn't figure one out. She wanted it to be something awesome.

Ikasa scratched him on the head and ran her fingers through his pinions to get more water off them. He tried to gnaw on her sleeve.

"Papatlaca means 'to shiver,'" she said. "Maybe I should call you that."

She stood up and looked for the path around behind Mary's neighborhood.

"Tzahualli is a spider's web, Gramma says that's what we used to call magician powers in the Xiuteotl, before Izzabellation," she said.

She looked back down at him.

"All you hear is 'blah blah blah food blah.'"

He chirped and looked up at her before ruffling his wings and wobbling his body back and forth, his fishing-pole tail bobbing up and down.

"Yeah, see."

She shoved her way through a particularly tight set of saw palmettos and out onto the trail, following it up the way to the remains of the paved road. Hearing shouting up ahead, she figured the neighbors were yelling at an animal or something, but it had quieted down before she arrived at Mary's.

Mary, as usual, sat outside in the yard, pulling nails out of broken boards and tossing them in a pile to her left. She waved through some tears as Ikasa walked up. She had a black eye.

"What's up, Spider?" she said.

"It's too hot for anything." Ikasa sat down and grabbed a spare hammer. "Are you okay?"

"Yeah, Pop just got stiffed for a couple thousand dollars and he needed to talk to me about something. It got a little out of hand, but it's okay now."

Ikasa thought about how often she came over, and about how often Mary's pop got a little out of hand. She turned her attention to the hammer and grabbed a piece of broken board.

"Seems like that happens a whole lot," she said.

"Don't your folks smack you?" Mary asked.

"Yeah, but. My pop doesn't go that far."

"How far would he go?" Mary asked.

Ikasa let out a breath and tried to imagine her pop punching her in the eye. It seemed impossible, like the universe might stop spinning for a moment if he did it, even Gramma didn't seem the type, and she felt her guts squirm in place.

"Never a black eye," she said, standing up.

"Wait," Mary said.

"Mister Crawfish!" Ikasa shouted, stomping at the house.

He appeared in the doorway of his trailer, in penny loafers, slacks, and his under shirt. He was busy adjusting his suit jacket. Ikasa started walking faster.

"Yeah, what's up, shitskin?" he said.

Ikasa stopped walking.

"You're. You're an asshole, and I hope you get struck by lightning!" Ikasa said.

"Really." He put his jacket down and came out of the trailer. Mary rushed between them.

"Daddy! Daddy, don't!" Mary said.

"Fuck I will, I will not take shit from this little friend of yours anymore. She has been a little snail-foot cunt since the first day I saw her. You got a problem with the way I keep my kid safe?"

Ikasa closed her eyes and started breathing faster. Her body didn't want to move. His mana rolled over her like a stinking cloud of kitchen garbage, and she shivered. Lightning would be so easy, but she clenched her teeth and made herself bigger than lightning.

"You're a black magician!" she screamed, turning to run away. It was the worst insult she could remember.

She felt Mary grab her.

"Spider, wait!"

Mister Crawfish picked Mary off Ikasa and wrapped his arms around her.

"Oh, no, you're not going off after that shit, good fucking riddance."

"Daddy!" Mary said.

Ikasa caught him throwing Mary against the trailer and bringing his fist down on top of her head before the bushes swallowed them all. Ikasa ran straight east, despite the sticky miasma of the day.

"Shitskin, I'm gonna look for you next! Good thing about you is ain't nobody going to see your bruises when I'm done with you!" she heard Mister Crawfish shout.

That made her run even faster, and she felt her face burning with more than just the sun. She was slick with more than just sweat and could barely see the blurred world, instead feeling the familiar mana of Wilmer's on the north end of the Ichiqui bridge. She pushed herself inside and saw Andy Blue Crab just in the first aisle. He ignored her and went back to stocking shelves.

"Do you have a phone?" she asked.

Andy pointed down next to the pinball machine. It was relatively new - a big boxy black thing with a rotary dial and an "any number, 10c" label just underneath the Wodara logo on the top. She fished for a dime in her pockets, finding one that had been in there since school ended. It was the dime she'd been told to buy juice with at lunch instead of getting water. She looked in her pocket for other change, but couldn't find anything left of the five dollars she'd gotten from Gramma.

Ikasa looked down at the dime in her hands. For a moment, she briefly entertained just dumping it into the pinball machine and walking away, or just going home and crying in her closet. The sound of a bottle breaking jerked her back, and she saw Andy. He was scooping up the shards into a dustpan and picking dried peppers carefully up and onto the counter. The manager had given him nothing but a stern look and a question about whether or not he was okay. Andy apologized profusely, saying he'd take care of everything.

She scowled in disgust, figuring the only reason Andy was being nice was because there would be a consequence for it. People had to be polite if some bigger and badder fish was watching them. It was so stupid. The Alligators acted nice, but they were really just assholes, Andy and Mister Crawfish knew just what and how to say to anyone to get away with whatever they were doing. Ikasa wondered briefly if she could even do anything about it, and she pinched the dime in her hands, pressing her mana into it. People seemed so full of shit, deserving nothing but hardship and pain, just for that moment, and she caught herself before thinking of something terrible.

Suddenly, without bidding and warning, she realized the amount of power the dime actually had. It would not accept mana; it already had the mana to stop everything that was happening to Mary, to change her life so completely that it burned Ikasa's hand just to hold it. Mister Crawfish had the apparatus for white junk in his trailer. It didn't matter what he said about anything once anybody from the BIA or the police office got a look at that.

She walked up to the phone and looked at the number on the side. There was a phone book hanging on a busted cord underneath, most of the B-listings torn out. She idly fumbled the bulky tome around in her hands and felt dusty ink rubbing off on her hands. Finding the number for the Fort Hammock police, she narrowed her eyes and bit her lip. An icy pair of hands reached out from inside her shoulders, as if she were casting a wonder. She believed it to be fear, though she couldn't figure out what she was afraid of.

She picked up the handset and slammed the dime in the coin slot. Dialing the number, she tried to keep a hold on her breath as it quickened, starting to come fast as it did whenever Holly beat her up. Each ring seemed a thousand hours apart, and when a voice picked up on the other end, she winced and clenched her teeth.

"Hello?" came a woman's voice.

"Mister Crawdad makes white junk in his trailer, and he beat up his kid!" she screamed into the phone, and slammed the receiver back down, hearing her dime clink down into the machine.

Standing there, breathing heavily, she tried to make sense of the rolling, queasy rage stuck in her throat and caught herself on her knees. When the phone rang, she ran out of the store, slamming her feet down in all the wrong ways. She couldn't tell the difference between sweat and tears as she crossed into Stetson and all the way down the dirt road to Mary's house, so tired when she got there that she couldn't stop herself when she emerged from the brush almost directly into a boat-shaped black and white car, all fresh and clean, and where black and white men in black and white hats were pulling a pile of metal and glass out of the Crawdad airstream.

One of the men stopped her and patted her on the shoulder.

Ikasa could see Mary between two officers, both of her eyes black now and her arm bound in a pillowcase. She heard an ambulance coming up the way, and Mary's eyes flickered up to see her.

"You!" she screamed, and tried to get up.

One of the officers grabbed her by the good shoulder, light enough that she was able to tear free and make it across the yard before there was any real reaction from the cops. She punched Ikasa right in the nose, and Ikasa went down, hearing the crack more than feeling it.

"You fucking stupid shit, you called the cops, didn't you?" she said, kicking Ikasa in the ribs a few times before she was picked up. "Why? I told you not to! You stupid bitch, now I don't even have a dad! I don't even have a dad now!"

She howled indiscriminately when one of the officers grabbed her by the slung arm. They picked her up and put her in the back of the ambulance while another helped Ikasa stand.

"You okay?" he asked.

"No," Ikasa said.

"You and me? Not friends," Mary screamed. "Never! Never ever!"

She grabbed the pillow off the ambulance bed and shoved it into the driver's face.

"Leave me alone!" she said, and took off into the palmettos.

"Somebody stop her," one of the officers said with more exasperation than desperation.

Ikasa just sat down in the dirt and cried. She felt mana both leave and come to her through her mouth and eyes. Her hands turned numb; it was not a pleasant loss.

Chapter 19

Odd Jobs

One time Spider and Hopper were out looking for something to eat. They came across a big, round boulder that had a sacred rope tied around it and a bowl out in front that had some food inside. They knew it was forbidden to eat food left for the boulder, but they were very hungry.

"Hey, you!" Hopper called out to the boulder. "Hey, are you listening?"

The boulder did nothing, remaining silent.

"Old man! Say something if you are there!" she shouted again.

The boulder did nothing. Hopper ran back up to Spider and snickered at her.

"The old man isn't saying anything, should we take the food?" Hopper asked.

"What food?" Spider said, walking up with her head in the sky.

She kicked over the bowl and looked down, as if surprised.

"Oh! This food that is all over the ground!"

She and Hopper snickered at each other and stuffed themselves. Shortly they became aware of a great rumbling nearby, and slowly turned to the boulder. With a great crack and a woosh, it came free, and rolled off after them. They ran and ran as fast as they could, but eventually, the boulder overtook them and crushed them both flat as a pancake.

Ikasa grunted and leaned on the old icebox. She heard

tearing vines and roots ripping up from underground, and the weight shifted and ran away from her, falling over into a pile of leaves and sending chickens scattering in a panic. Stepping back, she looked at the uncovered square of dirt that was beneath the rickety old wood. She spotted a few worms, some roaches, a bunch of ants, some holes, and a fat red-and-brown snake.

"There's one!" she shouted.

Butch dropped down and tried to grab it by the midsection. Its flat head, buried in the dirt and grass, dove further down into the soil.

"It's trying to get away!" he said.

Tiny little back legs pumped furiously in the air as he picked up the wide body. Ikasa put her hands down in the cool dirt and felt around until she found the bulges at the back of the head and pinched.

"I got it, I got it," she said. "You want it?"

"Yes," Butch said, and he let go long enough to pick up a big jar with about three more snakes of various colors and shapes slithering around.

"This one's cool, it's got little back legs," Ikasa said, and coiled it into the jar.

"Maybe it's not a snake," Butch said.

"Kapu said sometimes snakes have little tiny back legs. It has long scales on the belly, right?"

Butch picked up the jar and looked.

"Yep," he said.

"Then it's a snake," Ikasa said, and crossed her arms.

"Okay, what kind?"

"Ask Kapu," Ikasa said.

They picked their way back across the yard to where Kapu was sitting outside cutting leather into fringe strips. Butch put the jar up on the picnic table.

"Hey, what kind of snake is this?" he asked.

"Which one?" Kapu asked, without looking up. "I see some rat snakes, a cricket snake, and a mole snake."

"So it's a mole snake?" Butch said.

"Yep, you're lucky, those aren't very common down here. The little mice they like to eat don't usually come this far south," Kapu said.

"Cool," Butch said.

"Let's find something other than a jar for them," Kapu said, leading Butch off to the side yard with all the water bins.

Ikasa watched them go, stretched her arms, and climbed up the pots against the back wall of the trailer into her room. She wondered what Eddie was doing, but it was probably building models or getting fucked, and she didn't want to walk in on either of those. Mom was likely still with Gramma up in Fort Hammock buying supplies, and that meant she had time to herself again. She stretched, picked up her hopper like he was a fat chicken, and went into the carport. Early morning chill clung to her skin, feeling like a layer of shortening ready to be cooked off by the day's heat.

The car pulled up into the driveway and Gramma and Mom got out. Gramma snatched a paper bag out of the back seat and went to the side door into the kitchen.

"Well, it's a male," Gramma said. "That hopper. He's going to have some nice patterns. Black and white, with some other bits of colors, due to his breed."

"What breed is he?" Ikasa asked.

"Useless," Gramma said.

"I still don't know what to name him."

"Ompohualli on chicome," Gramma said, opening a beer.

"What?" Ikasa asked, immediately thinking Gramma was talking about numbers.

"You heard me."

Ikasa stopped and looked down at her hand.

"Omome, omei, onnahui, ommacuilli," Ikasa counted. "Forty-seven?"

"When I was growing up, that's what we'd call mutts like that," Mom said, coming in through the door. "Forty-seven flavor sauce."

"Huh," Ikasa said. She put him down, looking in the icebox for some chicken to cut up.

She got a knife and sliced the chicken she found into strips while the hopper ran around by her feet.

"Chicomay the mutt!" she said, throwing him a piece. "Chicomay!"

"Go get the last bag of supplies," Mom said.

"Yes, miss," Ikasa said, and walked out the door. "Chicomay!"

She threw the rest of the chicken out into the yard and he ran off, sniffing it out of the grass and tearing it down before dropping down onto his flank and pushing himself along the dirt.

He jumped up and flapped his little wings to cover himself in grass and sand. Ikasa went around behind the car and looked in the bag. She saw mostly boring adult stuff, but there were some new boxes of string and beads. Ototsooduh was really hot, and she thought about making a shirt with beadwork on it instead of the jacket she liked to wear. She spotted a box of copper wire. She brought the bag inside and put it on the kitchen table before picking up the box.

"Hey, can I have this?" she asked.

"No, you can have a piece of it," Mom said, snatching the box out of her hands. "Kapu needs it to fix the washing machine. I'm sure he'll give you a bit when he's done. What do you need it for?"

"That backpack I made! I need to make more hooks on it for bottles and some cook pans."

"Cook pans?"

"Yeah! I'm going fishing with Ehano and Ronnie in a couple of days, and because we caught a blue crab the other day, I want to make sure I have a mess kit for it. And I want to fix the cage on part of my pack so it can carry my fire jar better."

"I still don't think you need to be walking around with that," Mom said.

"You don't get a say in it, it's my jar!" Ikasa said, and stomped off.

"We're heading back out for some groceries!" she heard her mom shout.

Ikasa stomped all the way up to her room and picked up her box of agayateni stuff. She saw the magazines she got the day she and Mary were hanging out at Wilmer's. She almost put the box right back down, but took in a strong breath and went back downstairs into the sun room. Chicomay stuck his long snout in the box. It was empty so he hopped up on the edge. The box fell over, and he crawled inside so he could scratch cardboard with his back feet before settling down and gnawing on his hands. Ikasa put out her magazines and scissors out on the coffee table and started about cutting up trees and facades, putting the Hornhead up on top.

She pressed both hands on the table and felt the weight and the cold, and the Hornhead animated, looking about confused again. Hornhead brushed herself off and turned left and right before walking along into some trees. She looked a little odd interacting with cut-out drawings and photographs, but she collected a lot of things, picked up an umbrella, put some books in her pack, deflated a few beach balls, and grabbed a few other bits before dumping them together. Ikasa wondered what made Hornhead do that, she was hoping the woman would interact with the background a little more.

The side door opened and Pop walked in, covered in dust and stinking like alcohol, piss, tar, and sweat. He shook off dirt, put his hat on the rack, and stomped into the sun room.

"Hey, Pop," Ikasa said.

"Hey, man," he said, falling onto the couch.

"Are you okay?" Ikasa said.

"No," he said. "Get your mother."

"They came by to drop some stuff off, but they left a couple minutes ago."

"Ah. Playing with your paper dolls thing?"

"Yes," Ikasa said.

"Go get me a beer," he said.

Ikasa got up, went out into the kitchen, and opened the icebox, seeing something like four brands. A bag with about ten thin joints sat atop one of the boxes. She grabbed one of those, too, heading back into the sun room and tossed the beer to her pop.

"You're not going to smoke that shit by yourself," Pop said. He sat up just a bit to get his lighter out of his pocket.

Ikasa shook her head and caught the lighter after he tossed it. Pop got up and came over to sit down next to her pile of magazines while she cut out a few of the houses. He dug through one while they passed the joint back and forth.

"Why are you back so early, anyway?" Ikasa said. "You said you'd be gone a couple days."

"There were some guys hogging the water rations and I sort of," he said. "I pissed in the bucket the other night and ruined the whole batch, so they had to come back early."

"Oh. So you're just home until they fill back up?"

"No, I got told there was no point in coming back if I was gonna act like that."

"So you got fired?"

"Something like that," he said. "Your mom says not to worry about it, but I don't know."

"You're like me," Ikasa said.

"What?"

"You just do stuff you think is going to fix things without actually fixing anything, and then it blows up. It's got to be a Spider thing," Ikasa said.

"It's your fault I had to do this shit in the first place. We had to hold on to the store until you were done with middle school and now we're so fucking buried in the red. I don't think we can dig out. We're living on favors and loans, you know? Fuck, if I just had a store."

"So get one," Ikasa said. She didn't like being blamed for things she didn't know about, but decided it was better than being hit.

"It's not that easy. You need space, inventory, licenses. Sure, I still have licenses for another five years, but I don't have the space or the inventory."

"You're kidding me, right, Pop? Have you looked in the backyard? All them fossils Gramma's got is just waiting to be used. Plus, there's a lot of abandoned stores on the other side of the bridge, right across from Wilmer's and shit, you said the Andersonville bill will let you just claim one. You can figure out inventory or something. If you need some help, Mr. Armadillo has a lot more wonder-working junk in his yard, too."

Pop looked at her and slugged down the rest of his beer.

"Why do you got to be so fucking smart?" he asked, taking a long drag off the joint.

He stood up and coughed, then staggered his way out the side door.

"Armadillo man!" he shouted. "Where are you at?"

Ikasa cut out a tree and put the Hornhead on the table. She animated Hornhead, and the cutout walked around a little and picked some acorns out of the tree before cooking a few in her kelly can. She used some of their shavings on some catfish and saved the rest. Chicomay jumped up on the table and tried to catch Hornhead with some jabs. She ducked and rolled out of the way. Ikasa let go, and the scene held still. She looked back up at Chicomay, grinned, and reanimated everything.

"That's great! Try to catch her again!" Ikasa said.

She laughed as Chicomay failed to precisely catch the little cutout lady, but with each peck, she got a bit more used to the attacks. Ikasa smiled as she thought about what to do in regards to Butch's four armed monster the next time they played. Chicomay managed to catch her, but couldn't get jaw purchase on the table, and just rubbed his snout around while Hornhead flailed across the table, Ikasa acting as the source of gravity. She cut the animation off when Hornhead looked like she was panicking, and started packing things up, leaving Chicomay with his head turning sideways in each direction, trying to figure out where the small animal had gone.

Ikasa slid the box under the table and dusted off her hands. She wanted to go check on Ronnie. Grabbing her backpack from her room, she locked up Chicomay in the bathroom and headed out the side door to find Kapu and Butch busy making a terrarium out of a ten-gallon glass box.

"Hey, I'm going out," she said.

"You going camping or something?" Kapu asked.

"No, just over to the Blue Crabs!" Ikasa said as Kapu waved.

She crossed the trees into the forest and followed the trail up to the creek where she first met Ehano and Mary and jumped down to walk along the clay and sand bank for a little bit, until she had to get her feet wet. She climbed back up into the woods and listened to pine needles and leaves crunch beneath her shoes, watching animals scatter as she walked.

Smiling, she picked up a stick and swung it around as if to block with while making clashing and buzzing sounds, pretending it was an axe and there were enemies all around. She jumped up with a spun and slammed the pine stick down onto the ground hard enough that it broke in half, and a bit of it whipped into the air. She thought that was cool, and started looking around for another stick to try that again. That's when she saw Holly and her friends.

Holly's brother snickered.

"Well," Holly said. "I have a feeling this time is going to work out a lot different."

"You are correct, ma'am!" Spider said with a salute, and she ran the other direction.

"Get her!" one of the boys shouted.

Ikasa looked up into the sky. Mid-afternoon, sun was slightly west, just enough to know where she was running. The pines and oaks whipped by as she crawled between a set of saw palmettos that seemed like they were trying to grab her and hold her up into the air.

"Where the fuck do you think you're going?" she heard Holly yell in the distance.

Ikasa was not thinking about going anywhere; she was looking for the trail of herbivorous destruction she'd seen the other week. She rolled down a limestone slide and popped up between some grass. Holly burst out from the palmettos like they we thrown open to her, and it took Ikasa a moment to realize that they probably had been. Ikasa flicked a tick off her arm and kept running. For the barest hint of a moment, she felt a hand on her backpack, but a quick jerk to the side and half-crawl up an oak tree put her out of reach.

She fell to the ground, smelling fresh sap and wood, running, and a quick glance behind told her that a Possum boy was gaining. She jumped a creek, rolled over the side of a moss-covered foundation block, and landed right in front of an enormous hornhead. She could see the cutters and the young behind it, and she ducked behind the block, crawling on all fours around to the other side.

Holly and her crew ran into the clearing and stopped. Ikasa pressed her back up against the shadow of the block. The bull hornhead bellowed so loud that it shook the dirt on the ground. It dropped to all fours and stomped off toward the other kids. Cutters flanked the bull to back it up, flashing sharp teeth. The kids screamed and took to trees or else they ran back out into the forest. The group was scattered. Ikasa waited until things quieted down before peeking out. She saw Holly in a nearby tree.

"Worked out a lot different than last time, innit?" Spider asked.

Alligator just scowled while the bull paced in circles below her.

Chapter 20
Wonder Workings $5

The family of Corn is a big and powerful one. Once, a long time ago, at the start of the age, several tribes once lived around the Wahkepoh, who were the first growers of corn. They used to sell it at very high prices to everyone around them, and they would carefully go about the other tribes and rip up every corn plant they found. One particular man, though, kept hiding his corn plant because he grew it in a pot and would only put it outside on days the Wahkepoh weren't walking around.

Eventually, it grew so big and tall that it produced ears. They were tiny and not very good, but he called all his friends from the other tribes over to see it and to join in feasting on a soup he made. When they finished the soup, a woman none of them knew arrived, but because she was wearing a white dress, they didn't ask her to leave, thinking she might be an evil witch.

At the end of the night, she thanked them for their soup, and told them about a secret song and dance. It was one where they would turn into blood and dirt at the end, and the man asked what that would even do, considering that if they turned into blood and dirt, they would surely die.

"Yes, you will, but you must do this dance or I will put a plague on all your tribes for defying the Wahkepoh," she told them. "Go now! Do it while your bellies are still full!"

And so, fearful, they did as asked, and as they did, they found themselves bursting up out of the ground and screaming, having grown out of the earth and falling to the ground out of corn-

husks. The woman smiled at them as they did.

"There, now you are made of blood and corn, and now the Wahkepoh cannot prevent you from growing the corn," she said. "Because what kind of terrible tribe does not let a thing's own clan keep that thing among them?"

She broke apart into a thousand white-colored ravens, and the Corn clan knew they had seen Death, who had given them the ability to live.

Ikasa kicked over a bent and rusted can.

"See, Pop?" she said. "Empty store. I saw it when we first moved in. I saw the store spirit, too."

"We got to see if anybody owns it up at city hall," Pop said. "I'll go check, you try cleaning some of the mess up anyway. It smells like piss in here."

"That's because people pee in here," Ikasa said. "It's right across from the Wilmer's, I bet people fuck in here."

"Ha!" Mr. Armadillo said.

She picked up a big piece of plywood and kicked it out the side door.

"This needs a new door," she said.

"Start a list," Pop said, getting in his car. "I'll be back in a couple hours!"

He drove off. Ikasa frowned.

"Hey, Mr. Armadillo, do you have any chalk?" she asked.

He tossed her a small pouch with a bead work armadillo on the side. Opening it, she found some chalk, wax, tobacco, and coffee beans. While he started moving glass bottles out into the alley, Ikasa drew some stick figures of people buying things at an old store, getting their hair cut in old barbershops, listening to music, and ordering food at old diners. She drew pictures of the sun, and a spider up in the stars, spinning little webs. She put her hands on the wall and burned the tobacco. She felt the eyes of the building bore holes in the back of her head.

She turned to see a burlap figure, scarcely human-shaped, with a big, bulbous head made of swirling, swarming screws and nails like a colony of ants. A pair of long, skinny legs like rusted pipes held it up, and it was covered in graffiti and stank of wet dirt. Her first impression was that it wept guano out of its head in pain.

"Are you owned?" Ikasa asked.

It gurgled and ground away, making sounds like two pieces of sand paper rubbed against wet meat.

"Are you owned!" Ikasa shouted, and it just got louder and rolled around on the ground, spraying foul-smelling liquid on her shoes. "Why are you not answering me?"

"It's a piece of technology what ain't doing its job," Armadillo said.

Ikasa got an idea, and slapped it on the shoulder, then stomped on the ground four times. The thing flickered like a television set and stood bolt upright.

"Are you owned?" she asked.

"No," it said.

"Okay! Then you're a Spider building now, okay? Spider and Armadillo."

"Why are you asking it? It doesn't understand that shit," Armadillo said. "You'll just confuse the thing."

Ikasa nodded firmly.

"Then you are a Spider and Armadillo building now. Go and tell city hall!" she shouted, pointing up the road.

The burlap phantom, covered in screws and nails, ran on its rust-pipe legs out the door and down the street. She watched it go and took note of a man in a suit watching as well. He moved up into the door frame, realized that was broken, and instead stepped in through the front window. Ikasa noticed it was a city suit, probably from a high-rise. There were no patterns on it except for the herringbone on the jacket and the triangles of a professional in their field on his cuffs. He had a bit of a smile on, but it was a toothless, lips-only smile of a government official.

"Ikasa Spider?" he asked. "Bradshaw Armadillo."

He nodded at Mr. Armadillo. Ikasa frowned. She nodded anyway.

"That's me," she said.

"Well, hello! My name's Mickey Kenson, I'm from the Bureau for Implementation of Andersonville," he said, picking his way over a coil of chicken wire. "I have a few questions to ask you about your friend Mary, if that's all right."

"Like what?" Ikasa said, suddenly suspicious.

"How long did she know her father was manufacturing CC-938?"

"What?"

Mr. Kenson looked confused for a moment, but shook his

head.

"White junk," he said.

"I don't know," Ikasa said.

"Do you know where she might be right now? Did she or her father have a safehouse of any kind that you know about?' Mr. Kenson asked.

"No, I don't think so."

"Then did any of your friends know anything about what was going on? Is there any reason we should know why you or your friends didn't report what you knew as soon as you were able? Can you tell me to whom he was selling?"

"How do you know I had friends? How do you know who the fuck they are?" Ikasa asked. "How would I know who he was selling to? Why do I care?"

She stepped up and shoved him.

"A stupid disbeliever walks up to me and starts asking stupid questions about fucking drugs, what the fuck?"

"Look, I'm just trying to help," he said.

"Fuck you! You're not trying to fucking help anyone! Trying to protect us from shit we already know about. Not trying to help us, just chopping us off like little globs of hanging fa on a big piece of meat. Fuck you, fuck the BIA, you don't want to help, you just want to chase us out here to flop around like dead fish, and when we stink, you come out and try to bury us!"

She shoved him again and ran out of the store.

"Spider, wait!" she heard him shout.

She ran across the street to the Wilmer's, going around back and punching the dumpster so hard she saw a flash of light before she screamed and dropped to the ground. Mr. Armadillo came around the side of the building, followed by Mr. Kenson. Mr. Armadillo crouched down, clearly at great difficulty, and took her hand, checking the knuckles.

"You're okay, you didn't break nothing," he said.

"Kid, you don't have to answer anything," Mr. Kenson said. "I really just want to know how deep the problem is."

"You don't care how deep it actually is, you just want to throw a blanket over it and tell people there's nothing to see here," she said.

"Is that you or your folks talking?" Mr. Kenson asked.

"Maybe a little bit of both," Ikasa said.

"They lost their home to Andersonville," Armadillo said.

"Look, if I knew the right spells and was magical enough, I'd wave my hand and send away the BIA. Snap my fingers and the Turmek never invaded! I'd caw up at the sky and the tribes are all in little pieces again, and shout at the mountains and everybody forgets the war and the Black Monday. The Nehahgee is gone away!"

He patted her on the shoulder.

"But that's not going to happen, and unless we all work together, even people like Mr. Kenson whose family doesn't believe in orahjoo, nothing's going to happen."

Mr. Kenson rolled up his right sleeve to expose a tattoo, a bluejay inside a clock, with square wings and an even squarer beak.

"But your name?" Ikasa said.

"I got it from my dad, he raised me pretty much by himself. He used to wander around out in the wilderness, and when I graduated college, I got this tattoo because I got a dream from the blue jay in it that I should put it on. Since then I've worked really close with all the Blue Jays trying to get food and supplies out to towns like this," he said. "And besides, you're all Spider's kids. I shouldn't have to tell you that because I have a Sun name instead of an orahjoo name, you're supposed to at least talk to me."

Ikasa laughed.

"It's true, I forgot," she said.

"But that's okay, I know the stories, I understand. Who names their kid Ikasa and doesn't expect trouble?" he said, smiling with his teeth out.

"Okay," Ikasa said. "Look, nobody else was making white junk that I know about. And nobody else really knew except for my friends. Nobody talks about that stuff around here, we all just know."

"Yeah, but I have to tell the office something. They're trying to protect you from sex, drugs, blood, and they don't know you live in it. Get that store cleaned up, next time I come up here I want to see a good strong magician business," he said, handing her a card. "If there's any trouble, you call me. I don't care who answers the office phone, you ask for me specifically and don't stop until you get me. I'll know who you are. The witch that almost put a hole in my face."

"What?"

He pointed at the dumpster before he put his hat back on.

"You just punched it, right? You put a hole in it and a burn on the backside. Looks like you moved it about a foot, too."

He nodded, scraped something off his shoe with a coat hanger, and walked back out to the street. Ikasa looked over at the dumpster while Armadillo wrapped her knuckles in a strip of cloth. There was a clear line that lacked garbage where the dumpster had sat before, and a burn hole right where she'd but her hand. There was also a spidery pattern of burns across the back inside wall. She laughed, then felt a sharp stab run down her arm. It hurt to laugh.

"I'm ready to go back in now," she said.

"Yup," Mr. Armadillo answered.

They walked back across the street and started picking up trash again. She started moving some of the bricks outside, stacking them and realizing there were a lot more than she thought - most of them still with cardboard wrappings over chunks.

"Hey, could we a make a smoker with these?" she asked.

Mr. Armadillo came over to look and nodded.

"Yeah, you bet," he said.

"Prebeest," she said. "Should I start digging?"

"Wait for your pop to be back with the papers," Mr. Armadillo said. "Come back inside, I want to show you something."

He drew a pair of circles on the ground and handed her the chalk.

"Do you know how to draw a reservoir diagram?" he asked.

"Yes."

"Do you know what chalk is made of? Calcium?"

"A little bit. Dad told me it's a metal, and it's what our bones are made of, and when we draw in chalk, we draw in the bones of plants that lived millions of years ago."

"It's an alkali earth metal. Not Earth, but. Well, it's complicated and periodicity is only a theory anyhow."

"Perio-what?" Ikasa asked, drawing little circles on each end and connecting them with long narrow mazes.

"Don't worry about it. Energy is the ability of something to do work, and mana is a property of the potential for work. Lots of people confuse mana with energy, but that's not really the case. Mana is more like the hand that slaps the water than the ripples created. Your spiritual body, lineage, friends, respect, and, in a black magician, fear and pain. A king's mana resides in his footprints, and could kill you. Paqui is what we call the energy produced. Paqui also means balance. So this ring of circles is for what?"

"It's a diagram for funneling paqui produced by mana from the actor in the center."

"You betcha," Mr. Armadillo said. "That looks good, now hand that back to me."

He pointed at the smaller circles.

"So what do those do?" he asked.

"Well, the little channels make the paqui ripple into them. I did it once with my fire jar, they suck up the extra energy, but they explode if you don't have something there to soak up the energy, the paqui."

"Well, it'd be out of balance if we didn't put anything there, if there's no medium, there's nowhere for the energy to go and something horrible will happen to you," he said. "What if we did this?"

He erased the sides of the smaller circles and drew in a little line just on the outside, coupled by a few dollop-looking shapes and some hopper-looking symbols. Ikasa tilted her head and tried to imagine ripples in the surface of water blocked by pieces of floating wood.

"The energy will just get out, but strong waves will be smaller when they come out the edges," she said. "But it'll just be going nowhere. You'll be able to collect a lot because you turned the building into the reservoir medium, though."

"And if you collect a lot of paqui, what happens?"

"Powerful spirits show up to eat it, but unless you do a calling dance, you don't know what will show up to eat it."

"Which is great if you just need something good done. Now, I know a dance that alerts the spirit of the end of things that you need her for something," Mr. Armadillo said. "Usually you only do this when something is over and everything needs to move forward."

"Death?"

"Yeah," Mr. Armadillo said.

He got a pepper out of his pocket.

"You want to rub this pepper in your eyes with me, dance the Death-calling song, and tell her that this building's days as a lonesome box are over? I'll spill my blood as an adult, and you sing as a child and dance like you was up at the mound, we'll put in all our mana and make so much paqui she could summon up a whole feast for herself."

"Okay," Ikasa nodded. "We should give her a lot of different kinds. If you're the kind of spirit everyone is calling for and only ever to get rid of things, then you think she needs a good snack and a nice break."

"Well, I think you're right. When people die, a form of their memories passes into her realm, and she picks them up and takes them to her country. So, imagine what it is like to shovel so many little tiny insect spirits into great big trucks and how much work that might be!"

Ikasa laughed.

"Okay! Come stand in the circle with me, and let's see if we look like fools when your pop comes back!"

Ikasa dusted off her hands and stepped over the circle line.

Chapter 21

Fishing

Once all the spirits did not know where the animals should be. It was right after the animals had got made that a particular being thought they would get fed up very quickly with all kinds of chaos, so they went to the first hunter, Utchusu, who was out looking for food to bring to his wife, for she could get very irate if she had nothing to cook.

They said, "listen, you will need to make us an axe shaft for every animal, and each one must be a different size" and Utchusu agreed, not wanting to offend these beings. They went to his wife Hetchea, and they said "listen, you will need to make us a axe head for every animal, and each one must be a different size." Thinking this might be hard to do without a forge, she agreed anyway, and when Utchusu returned home, they both talked about making the axes.

So they began, working for a thousand years to make them, and when at last they were done, the beings appeared before them again. "Now," they said, "you must take them to Pyahkoo mountain and present them to the animals. Give the biggest to the strongest animal, the next biggest to the next strongest animal, and so on until you have given the smallest one to the weakest animal.

Now, hopper had heard all of this from the window of the hut of Hetchea and Utchusu, and she ran off as quick as she could go to where all the animals were. When the spirits came and told the other animals, they all decided to try and get some sleep so they would be well-rested come the morning. Hopper wanted to be there first, so she thought she'd make it hard for the other animals to sleep.

She jumped all around, throwing rocks and banging sticks and howling and screeching, but the other animals just kept right on sleeping. When at last the morning came, hopper was so worn out she could hardly stand. She took a stick and put splinters in her eyes so that her eyes would stay open, but all that happened was that she fell asleep and the splinters pinned her eyelids together.

When the animals came to the mountain in the morning, the man and his wife handed out axes to all the animals so the beings could see who was the strongest. He gave the biggest one to the maize-foot (who had normal feet back then), and the next biggest to the rootscraper, the next to the deathwalker, and so on, all until only the smallest axe was left. They asked where the last animal was, and all the other animals woke up hopper and brought her before the man, who could not see because sticks were in her eyes.

They laughed, the man and woman and the animals, all at hopper's misfortune, but the being saw that although she had made a mistake, that hopper had at least tried to be cunning, so they gave her and her descendants some more, even at Utchusu gave him the last axe.

"Even though you were late and the weakest," Utchusu said. "You are a proud and hard worker, and a good and sneaky hunter. If you wish, you can come and live in my hut with me, but you must leave half your cunning outside."

Hopper, upon hearing this, immediately used her axe to cut herself in two, each with one half of her cunning, and while one bit of cunning ran off into the jungle, the other walked into the house of humans, and has been there ever since.

Ikasa drew chalk circles on the walls under the bridge where she'd seen the tweakers so many weeks ago. Chicomay hunted for things in the bushes and failed to catch them. Ikasa used Eddie's model glue to affix some railroad granite on the medium circles and double checked the vortex effect by sitting down at the ring around the kelly can where the tweakers were juicing up. She released small bursts of electricity, and watched the flash of light leap into the circle before disappearing altogether.

Ikasa laughed and clapped. She didn't figure the setup would prevent them from airing themselves out, but it would at least make them look for a new place to do it.

"Come on, Chicomay," she said, climbing back out.

She stretched and jogged down the rails, up over the palms and scrub to the Blue Crab house, where Andy was passed out on the porch and where Ronnie was eating out of a giant garbage bag of popcorn. He was surrounded by his hoppers, who kept stealing snacks out of his hands.

"Hey, big talking man," Ikasa said.

Ronnie waved back.

"Do you want to go out shooting with me? I promised we could a while back," she said.

He nodded, dumped out the rest of the bag, and dusted himself off. He gave a small grin and tapped the new crab claws dangling down in front of his ears.

"You're welcome, no problem. Come on," she said. "Let's go find some power poles."

They walked over to the railroad tracks and watched the poles for wires that got knocked down during storms and big vacuum lamps with swirling light inside.

"Oh, that's a nice one," Ikasa said, under a pole that had a large nest of them, some as small as a thumb, others as large as her arm. The shining bulbs grew like a cluster of barnacles, and the spirits inside ranged from formless globs to odd-looking salamander embryos. She shimmied up the pole and popped some off, then threw a bunch of them into her pack and slid back down.

"Some of these are really cool," she said.

"Are we going to shoot them?" Ronnie asked.

"Yeah, back when we lived in Cahokia, sometimes the darkest alleys would grow these things, as long as one fell from a high distance and didn't break. There are lots of little clusters that have ones you can just break off," Ikasa said. "When you pop the glass, the little spirits inside break out and fly around before disappearing, so it looks really cool!"

"So they don't die?"

"Nope! The bullets pass right through them like they're not even there."

Ronnie seemed satisfied. He smiled and fingered the pistol on his belt. They went out to one of the big fences and Ikasa tested the cabling until she found one as firm as an iron bar and started tying vacuum bulbs to the underside, dangling them at various lengths.

"This is what we used to do in the junkyard," she said. "There's no. Well, I guess half the town is an open junkyard, huh?"

She came running back and tapped Ronnie on the shoulder.

"Okay, it's not like watching a movie at all," Ikasa said. "Don't try to look cool, just try to pull the trigger smoothly."

Ronnie took the gun out of his belt.

"Check your cylinder by popping it out, then look down the barrel from the cylinder chamber to make sure it's clear and see if you need to load it," Ikasa said.

"It's not loaded," Ronnie said, and took some bullets out of his pocket.

"That's good, but never assume," Ikasa said. "Load it one by one, unless you wanna use my loader cylinder."

He filled each of the six slots of the cylinder, locked it back in, checked the spin, and pulled back the hammer.

"Keep it pointed down until you're ready to shoot," Ikasa said. "And remember, smooth pull."

Ronnie squinted and pressed his lips together.

"Stop," Ikasa said. "Put it down."

She stood up, walked over, and stuck her thumb between the hammer and the pan. She picked the pistol up and checked down the barrel.

"Don't squint. You can't look away when you do it, you'll miss," Ikasa said. "The point isn't usually to hit anything, it's just to make a loud noise. A cutter or a deathwalker isn't going to go down from this, but it might think you're too loud and annoying."

She removed her thumb and aimed at a big bulb. The glowing salamander inside swirled about and shed blue motes of light.

"Point at something you think you might hit, relax, breathe normally, and pull smoothly," she said, and popped a shot off.

She missed; the bulb wobbled and spun.

"Also, I am only a decent shot, I just passed my cert last year," she said, and tried another shot.

The bulb broke and the little salamander-thing wormed around in the air for a moment before disappearing in a glittering zephyr.

"Cool!" Ronnie said.

"That's why I picked those things," Ikasa said. "Focus on how cool the little critter will look rather than the loud noise or anything else. Really, we should have earmuffs, but you're not shooting close to your head."

She watched Ronnie pop off a few more shots before sitting down on a ruin block. Ehano emerged from the bushes with his rifle pointed at the ground and waved at Ikasa.

"What's up, I heard gunshots, and now I see Ronnie still can't hit anything," Ehano said.

"Oh cool, a rifle, can I shoot it?" Ikasa asked.

"Yeah, sure," Ehano said, putting it down on the block.

He stretched and looked around the clearing and over at the fence.

"Bamboo!" Ehano shouted. "Oh, man, let's go fishing! Ikasa, knife me!"

She pulled the knife from her pack and passed him the handle.

"With bamboo?"

"I always carry a roll of line, some sinkers, and hooks on me. It's fucking Ootsooduh."

"Nice," Ikasa nodded, and took a shot with the rifle; another bulb exploded.

"You get those from the power lines?" Ehano asked, rolling out some fishing line.

"Oh, yeah. Found one that was growing a huge batch of them like bananas."

He nodded and went back to cut down another piece of bamboo.

"Have you seen Mary?" Ikasa asked.

"Not since the radio said her pop was arrested," Ehano answered. "At least, that's what I think they said. Our radio's busted and the only Spider who used to be around to fix it charges either an arm and a leg or, no offense, your gramma."

"Nope," Ikasa. "Can't find offense unless I dig through the shit, and I refuse."

She missed again. Ehano stacked up three bamboo rods and threw them over his shoulder.

"Come on, let's go up to Fish-head hole," he said.

Ikasa slung the rifle, making sure it was barrel-up. Ronnie followed as Ikasa showed him how to put the safety back on. Fish-head hole was one short trail north, and it was big and round like most of the other lakes nearby. This one has a foggy haze to its depths, and tiny boils along portions of the shore.

Ikasa saw a few alligators wallowing in the far end. She shaded her eyes with a hand.

"It's all murky, see, so the catfish and junk can't see our hooks, but they can smell the bait," Ehano said.

"What bait?" Ikasa asked.

"Lizards," Ehano said. "Or whatever else we can find. Go turn over some rocks or something. I also got some sandwich, you can ball up the bread into little dough globs."

He tossed it out, and they sat and rolled the bread in their fingers until the little bits were gummy and stuck on hooks, and swung lines out into the water.

"Do you know where she is?" Ehano asked.

"Of course I do, she's in the hole. The first one we found," Ikasa said. "She knows it connects from the spring. East of here, that's it."

"And she's hiding there why?"

"The things all turned back on. There's some kind of cot or chair looks like it came out of a pulp book," Ikasa said. "There's a place to sleep in one of the corners, lights, all kinds of stuff. Either that or she's camping at the ruins."

"No, I meant why. Did you call the cops?" Ehano asked.

"I did. I didn't mean to make her mad. I just saw her dad beating on her and I couldn't take it anymore," Ikasa said.

"I understand. I ain't done it because I thought maybe," Ehano said. "I don't know, it just seemed normal to me."

"Does it still seem normal?"

"Yeah, it does," Ehano said. "But you make me think, Spider."

She said nothing and let out a breath. She wasn't sure what to think, and watched a boil for a few minutes. There were a few tugs on their lines. Ronnie busied himself with catching lizards and throwing them into one of Ikasa's jars. He'd come back to a pole every so often, pick it up, slowly press his lips together, then go get another lizard. Most of them were little green ones, but there were some with bright blue and orange heads. Ikasa wondered about what type of lizard they might be, and thought that if any survived the day, she'd take them to Kapu and find out.

"Got something!" Ehano said. He stood up, his pole turning as round as a bow being pulled. "It feels big!"

He stepped back up the bank and tilted the bamboo rod,

dragging the line in. Something black and with a big armored head broke the surface, and Ikasa saw whiskers before something bigger and darker appeared beneath the wriggling form.

"A catfish!" Ehano said.

"No, it's a snapping turtle!" Ikasa shouted.

"What?" Ehano said. An enormous mouth closed around the fish, hooked beak grinding down into flesh. "Whoa! I've never seen one before!"

The shell was enormous, as long as they were tall, and it took all three of them to haul the massive form up onto the lake shore. The instant the cleaver-jaws came out of the water, all four meaty, tree-bark legs went into overdrive, and the beast surged forward across the sand and limestone, hissing and gurgling, the hook still stuck firm in the lower jaw. Ehano screamed and backed away. Ikasa stood transfixed. Ronnie came running back from the woods with an enormous branch - too large for him to lift over his head - and gave the weapon to Ehano, who then let Ikasa take the pole.

"Smash it on the shell!" Ikasa shouted.

Ehano brought the branch down on the turtle's back. There was a terrifying crunch. The branch exploded into a thousand splinters. The turtle dropped like a puppet with torn strings. Everyone dropped to the ground and panted. Ikasa put the pole down and crawled over to poke the carcass. She figured that the whole thing had to be as long as Ronnie was tall, if not bigger. The shell seemed like she could hide in the empty space if the meat was torn away. Chicomay ran up, then ran away, chirping and gurgling. Ikasa worked the jaw open.

"Be careful!" Ehano said.

She slowly pulled the remains of the fish and the hook out. What seemed like long and painful minutes went by as she tried to work the hook out of thick brown gums. When at last her fingers cleared the jaw and the final bits of fish were nearly out, the jaw clamped shut. She screamed. Ehano screamed. The turtle hissed and rose up on all four legs, tail flopping about and mouth opening wider than anything Ikasa had ever seen. She lashed out with a foot or lightning, and the turtle scuttled at them, gurgling and spitting drool or water. They all made for the edge of the woods, and half climbed trees before the turtle huffed like an old man tired of games, waddled back into the water, and disappeared. The alligators approved.

Ikasa crawled back down from the trees and sat in the sand. One of the bamboo poles was broken. She cradled her cheeks in her hands and looked at the remains of the fish.

"You know, Gramma says you have to fight a dragon to become a true magician," she said.

"And take the forehead stone," Ehano said. "I heard that too."

"Listen, I want to try to get Mary to like me again," Ikasa said.

"She's mad?"

"Boy, is she ever. She's probably so mad at me we'll fight when we talk next. She said we'll never be friends again."

Ehano let a long, slow breath.

"Try taking her something she likes, maybe tell her a story?" he said. "She's a sucker for stories. Make one up if you have to."

Ikasa kicked around in the dirt and gave Ehano his rifle back. She was pretty sure she could come up with something where crawfish was a hero, or something about how sometimes people do stupid things because they think those things are right. She wasn't sure she believed that, but it was something to go on. She rubbed her face.

"Don't over-think it," Ehano said. "My mom, when she deigns to speak to me, tells me that nothing worth doing was worth getting it wrong for trying to do it too well."

Ikasa sat down and heard the turtle shell in her pocket rattle. She took it out and looked down at the old brown thing while running her fingers over the remains of old yellow star patterns. Whatever was inside was so obviously full of wisdom, perhaps it was enough to help her get back Mary.

"Is that the thing I keep hearing about?" Ehano asked.

"Yeah," she said.

"It's strong. We never did do the reader thing," he said.

"It's okay. I'll go talk to her," she said.

She wrapped the turtle box up in her hands. The innards felt alive, still moving and breathing. She felt like Ikasa could reach out across the ages and touch her, filling her with knowledge borne on the breath of a lifetime. Her fingers started to slide through the shell, and she fumbled to catch it before putting it back in her side pocket.

"I'm going right now," Ikasa said.

"Hey!" Ehano said, tossing her a sandwich.

"Thanks."

"You need any help, you come running to mine or Ronnie's place, okay?"

"I will, thanks," Ikasa said.

She walked into the jungle.

Mr. Armadillo (60+?)

Doesn't bother with his makeup anymore

Grows fat

lives in his car

← hood ornament!
Deathclaw footprint
Mufflerdeath (not shown)

Mr. Armadillo's 1933 Weevely Motors Thunderbeast (manifested)

Dirty mouth

KAPU (25)

← grannie's husband

No IDEA why they're married

Homeless!

→ Mystery!

Sadie Kaw (??)

Many beads

has old lady powers

NEVER swears

Ehono Limpkin (13)

Another gov't standard hairstyle!

When grown his nose shall have a MIGHTY Hook

Doesn't Talk Much Ronnie! (9?)

Clear sign of hanging with the wrong crowd

plays a mean pinball

Blue Crab!

"Javelin White-White-Green" (??)

← Sir not-Appearing in this book

Lost his knife in the woods

Chapter 22

Crawfish Heroes

Many years had passed since the hopper had given up half his cunning to be with human in their home, and he had prospered above all the other animals. Shieldface looked in on them often from where he was in the world, and wanted to prosper so well himself. He wandered off into the jungle, seeking out the other half of hopper's cunning, which was also a hopper, and found her chasing dragonflies by a waterfall.

"Hopper," he said, and she turned to see him.

"What do you want?" she asked, "to play fivestones? I will win."

"I want to live with human, too," Shieldface said. "I want to prosper like the other half of your cunning."

Hopper thought for a moment.

"I will help you," she said. "if you give me your horns and your size so I can make a frightening disguise. If you live with human, after all, you will not need them."

Shieldface so agreed and gave Hopper his three horns and his great size, and when it was done he was small and had only a beak to defend himself. He shivered at the thought of his new form, and looked sternly at Hopper.

"Now, Hopper, use your cunning!" he demanded.

"Very well," Hopper said. "Challenge the man Utchusu to an eating contest. Whoever wins shall be the other's servant."

"But I will win, I am the greatest eater in the jungle!" moaned Shieldface.

"You must trust me!" Hopper replied, and so the Shieldface, with no other option after giving up his most valuable defenses, relented and walked up to the hut where the first hunter and his wife were living with the other half of Hopper's cunning.

"Utchusu the hunter! Come out!" he cried.

Looking outside after the shouting, Utchusu saw a very small Shieldface, no bigger than his table, hollering and bellowing outside. He turned to his wife Hetchea and said "look there, it is dinner," and with that, he stepped outside.

"There you are," shield lizard said, "stay your spear. I challenge you to an eating contest, and whoever wins will become the other's servant for ever and ever."

Utchusu so agreed, for he could hunt any time, and a servant like Shieldface, with a good nose for tubers and truffles, would always be welcome. He called his wife out and the two prepared a sumptuous feast of all they could find in the jungle.

First came the fruits, and Shieldface easily ate twice as many as Utchusu. After that came the vegetables and roots, and once again, Shieldface ate twice as many. Shieldface began to get worried, for he so wanted to lose. That night, he sought out Hopper again.

"Give me back my size and horns, for I am winning!" he screamed.

"No, you have already lost," said Hopper. "Go back tomorrow and I swear to you that Utchsu will beat you five times over."

And so Shieldface went back, despondent. He climbed up to the table like the last two days, and on this day, the humans had prepared a feast of meat, cooked, boiled, broiled, fried, and even grilled and still hissing from the cooking fire. Utchusu ate his legendary fill, and Shieldface nearly gagged at the smell of it and could eat none.

It was true, for by the end of the day, no meat was left, and Utchusu had eaten it all. Shieldface accepted defeat, and followed the first hunter and his wife into their hut, where he prospers to this day.

Ikasa picked her way across the Shimookooah basin, crossing deep gouges in the limestone across fence beams and fallen tree branches. She clambered over soft moss and dropped down walls coated with vines when she found them. The familiar complex of the Oksachee spread out before her like a maze, and she found her way back to the main square with the fountain. The spider amulet was still in the pool and the gate into the cave was still closed. She followed a few ancient halls lacking any semblance of roof, and found the remains of one wrapped in green and with a small tent or overhanging blanket pitched over the side of what used to be the second floor.

"I know you're here," Ikasa said.

She threw a rock up into the mossy boughs.

"Go away!" Mary shouted.

"Aha, knew it!" Ikasa said.

"Didn't I fucking tell you? We're not friends. Go home, Spider, or I'll come out and you'll be sorry."

Ikasa backed off to the edge of the ruin and sat down.

"You don't sound like you're leaving," Mary said, emerging from behind a tarp, dirty and eating something she clearly took from behind a restaurant.

"I thought you'd be down in the hole," Ikasa said.

"It's evil and scary down there."

"Well, I heard, a long time ago, that there used to be evil everywhere. Black magicians given mana by deathwalkers hid in the jungle and stole blood and mana from hard workers and good people. They wove a big blanket over the woods, and nobody could actually see the evil taking place, because they were blinded by the blankets and the darkness. Then, up from the mud, comes all these little crawfish warriors, and they cut through the blankets and showed the people where the evil was living, and even though all the little crawfish warriors got crushed by the bigger, meaner things trying to fight evil, they knew that would happen, and kept cutting away the evil anyway."

She sniffed and wrapped her arms around her knees.

"Crawfish lessons tell us that sometimes we do things that we know are going to get us in trouble or do stupid things, because if there weren't stupid people in the world, there wouldn't be anything worth protecting or doing," Ikasa said. "So I did something stupid. I was just trying to help. But your pop was doing something stupid, too."

"And he was just trying to help," Mary said.

"Are you still angry with me?"

"I stopped being angry with you two days ago, you shit head," Mary said. "Mana and pride just dictated that be who I was."

"So, are we friends?"

"No. You have to earn that back. Step one is not telling anybody where I'm hiding."

"What's step two?"

"Get me five buds, a kelly can, another tarp, and something to read," Mary said.

"Not something to eat?" Ikasa asked, waving the sandwich Ehano gave her.

"That works, too," Mary said.

Ikasa threw the sandwich up. Mary kicked a rope ladder down, and Spider climbed up.

"Not like you couldn't just crawl up the wall," Mary said.

She had a little campfire setup out in front of the tent with a few tarps layered over the top, with some poles to keep up the whole little frame, and lots of little pillows and blankets like a nest stuffed in the back.

"Oh, this is pretty cool," Ikasa said.

"Yeah, I got a screen I can put down to keep out the bugs if the fire doesn't work,"

Ikasa opened up her pack and put out her kelly can, flashlight, a pack of buds, some rolling paper, a spare waterproof sheet, and some of her pulps.

"Step two," Ikasa said.

"Step three is giving me more time to think," Mary said.

Ikasa started to get up to climb back down.

"I didn't say you had to go, but you better," Mary said with a nod.

"Yeah," Ikasa said. "I'll come over tomorrow with some more stuff. And some real food. My mom makes awesome tamales."

Mary nodded, and Ikasa dropped back down. The jungle was always foreboding, but today the leaves seemed especially quiet. Ikasa thought maybe there was rain coming, or else she was lost inside her own head, trying to figure things out. Mr. Crawfish had been hitting Mary too much, and she knew Mary was still mad at her. She feared what calling the cops about Ronnie might do. The power of a dime still burned her hand when she thought about it.

She looked back up at Mary's makeshift house, and the mana thrummed in its folds, enough that Ikasa had to squint when she went looking. Ikasa shuffled on down through the ruins, up until she came to a place where the water flowed only an inch or two deep across ancient stones and welled up in little square pits where fragments had been torn up or broken down.

Ootsooduh was flat, and that still continued to strike her. When she was out in a scrub the horizon was a perfect line like a kid in art class that hadn't figure out how to draw mountains. All the ponds and pits were either dug by people, shallow, or else they looked like giant acid burns in the limestone that filled in with rain or water from below, and there were alligators in every single one of them.

Salamanders and frogs were everywhere, and fish seemed to be teem in the strangest places, from water stuck in the crooks of trees to buckets in Gramma's yard. There was rarely a moment in which she couldn't hear insects or birds. It was easy to believe that Cahokia's lights and gray streets were a dream, or that this was the dream, and the city was real, either one in totally different worlds from one another. She crouched and watched something crawling across a stone, headed by long antennae that seemed too enormous for its tiny body. Bright blue shone across the surface of the reflective carapace.

"The present is subjective," she said, repeating something Gramma said.

She put her hands in the water and pressed against the cold stone. She closed one eye and squinted until the world looked flat. The reflection in the pool was clean of moss and lichen. People shuffled about in opulent and complex clothing, full of long sashes marked with the images of station, wearing badges on both shoulders. She watched them go back and forth, doing nothing in particular, and she realized she couldn't see what they'd do because she had no expectations of what she could potentially see. She splashed the flow and it rippled away.

She stood up, reorienting herself to the world, and knocked her head at Chicomay. He dashed up and checked her hands. His feathers were coming in as patchwork and the colors looked like they might be brilliant. He splashed around in the water, washing himself and taking a drink every now and then. Ikasa wobbled a bit before climbing over another stone. She saw a trail of ants running along between some lichens and followed them back to their nest at the base of a tree and watched them for a moment.

Sitting down, she noticed that they weren't going to their own nest, and instead were raiding the nest of some much bigger ants that seemed to have trouble keeping up with the little swarms rolling all over them. She looked over a few, watching them tear each other apart. The big ants balled up the little ones into tiny clusters of limbs and crushed them, and the little ones swarmed over the big ones and tore off their antennae and legs. She watched for another few minutes, at least until the smaller ants started winning, before slamming her hands into the tree bark and scowling.

"Why?" she yelled.

Everything had to have fucking meaning. She kicked over some dirt. The turtle shell in her pocket throbbed. She looked back down the causeway and stomped all the way back to the fountain, fishing out the spider icon. The lines were thick and she felt them moving like slow rivers under her feet. She set the icon into the image of Xiucuscu and drew her face up into an angry pinch as the passage opened. She crawled down inside, flashlight in hand this time, and Chicomay sat up at the entrance, chirping in alarm.

The tunnel was as she left it, narrow and dripping with water. Clambering over little cake layers, she opened the door at the far end into the chamber with the cot. With the light she had now, the room looked much smaller, consisting of the tiny cot and the papers as before. She passed the light over the stack of books she knocked over when she came in the first time, dug a couple of codexes out, flipped through them, and noted that people must have been down here in the interim. She wondered what other kind of people would know the code, and looked at the handwriting in the margins of the books. A thought occurred to her, and she dug through the pile for a book with a red cover.

The interior was scribbled with a variety of notes on how to operate various apparatus in the room. Ikasa stood up and matched the first diagram with a nearby altar. She looked back down at the book, flipped the corners around, and screamed before pitching the book into the dark. She stomped on the floor, giving the cot a kick. The frame shook, and the book slid back. Out of the long swell of the cavern there emerged a figure on four legs, like a stork, wrinkled and with a toothy maw. Her general impression was that it was walking on long fingers with a web of skin stretched between its four limbs. The hind legs were tiny in comparison. The beak cracked open, and the whole thing rippled like the surface of a puddle.

"Ikasa," it said.

When the ripples gave way, she saw one of the men from the bridge. His breathing was loud through his mask, and each heave of the body inflated the little safety valves on the side. The jacket he wore seemed to be more buckles and clips than bare fabric, and the unit patches were garbled, nonsensical, but so near a meaning that they still radiated mana. He reached out a gloved hand and the cavern flickered, lighting up as if there were evening sky above. The horizon was flat and fraught throughout with little reflective patches of swamp.

"You've figured out what's in the rattle, haven't you?" he asked, his voice croaking like a thousand frogs.

She pulled the box turtle from her pocket.

"You're not a spirit, who are you? What are you?"

"I'll answer yours if you answer mine," he said.

"I think so," she said. "It's the old Ikasa's memories, isn't it? She recorded them somehow, kept them out of Death's hands."

"Not just memories, but all of her mana, her skill, her power," he said. "She flew to the stars, to the world of her namesake, she gave birth to spirits, changed the very fundamental nature of the world several times. As befitting one of Sun and Spider's daughters."

"Her namesake? She wasn't the planet?"

"You know as well as I do that a myth is a cultural truth, rather than a historical truth," he said.

"And who are you to know that?"

"That is an immaterial matter! I mean nothing. I'm devoid of metaphor, an outsider to your events," he said. "Go and check your lines of confluence if you wish. Should you find space for a role, I am yet one more senex in your life."

"Fine!" she said. "Tell me more, how do I get this power she left behind?"

"You already know," he said.

She turned back to the cot, sitting in the middle of the swamp.

"I do," she said. "I lie down in that, and I do something with the little battery, don't I?"

He stepped up beside her and nodded.

"So, Whispering Man, what do I do?" she asked.

He let out a horrific, unearthly scream as she named him. He dropped to the ground, twitching and gurgling. He clutched his chest and took in one long, slow, loud breath.

"So be it," he said. "You do what you feel you must."

She knew the turtle could fix everything, the little battery.

The mummy told her that, like a spiritual being descending on a rope at the end of a mystery dance to wave away the pain. She also knew that it might not be her decision, that perhaps Ikasa had made the decision long ago and carefully arranged what memories she might carry so as to force the hand. She looked back at the Whispering Man.

"So, if someone could get their incarnations in a line to remember specific parts of their life somehow, could Ikasa be manipulating threads? Could she have created stories to form a destiny? Is it possible I might have to lie down there?"

"The thing I'll tell you about destiny and astrology and all that other shit is that those things are nothing but an excuse not to act and remove blame from yourself for the bad things that happen, and to steal credit from heroes by saying it was inevitable. Not that the right birth at the right time could cause some of the similar effects of hard work. Just that if you start thinking it's your destiny to sit in that cot and gain all those powers and restore your life to what it once was, then it's definitely going to happen. I'm with your grandmother on this."

"Alright, I understand," she said.

She actually did. She put the turtle back in her pocket and smiled a big, toothy smile.

"Thanks a lot, that really helps," she said.

"Thank you for the name. I haven't actually had a proper one in a couple thousand years," he said, and reached out his hand.

She shook it.

"You're not so scary when you don't look like a stork from a pulp story. I'll make you laugh one day, too."

"I expect it."

She nodded firmly and bowed before heading back out into the hall. She contemplated the power in the turtle before trying to think on the potential of the rattle a little more. Gramma said it was Spider's greatest shame, and she wondered why that would be. A mystery for another day, she decided, and climbed back out into the world of the living.

Chapter 23

Crawfish Villains

Spider was crawling along at the edge of the swamp one day when she came across Alligator. The Alligator roared and stomped around, and surged up out of the water.

"I'm going to get you for what you did to me!" she screeched.

Spider nodded.

"That's fair, but, ah, I've just got done meeting with Makan-tahay the king of demons," Spider said. "Do you know what he said about you?"

"No, I have never even seen Makan-tahay," Alligator said.

"Well, he said you were afraid of him, that you'd never come up and see him in the face," Spider said. "That when he comes over tomorrow to say 'hallo hallo' to me and bring me cocoa cakes you wouldn't come to see."

"That is pointless rubbish, of course I will," said Alligator.

"Very well. Tomorrow I will go and see the king of demons. I must warn you of a few things. If you see a lot of black smoke, do not be afraid, that is just Makan-tahay walking along."

"I will not be afraid."

"Oh! And if you see a lot of birds circling around and little stripe-tail bush eaters running away, they are scared of the king of demons, so don't you run off!"

"I won't run off!"

"If you hear a fire crackling and some smoke very nearby you, that is just Makan-tahay coming very close by. That's when it's best to get a look at him! So be ready."

"I'll be ready," Alligator said finally.

Next day, Spider told Alligator that the king of demons was coming, and when Alligator was all good and hidden, she fished a bit of fire out of her fire-jar and set it among the bushes a distance away. The smoke very quickly rose into horrible black spirals over the scrub.

"Spider, where are you?"

"Don't be frightened, it's just the king of demons moving about!"

The fire roared across the field.

"What is that sound?" Alligator asked

"That's just him breathing hard!" Spider shouted.

Soon the grass around Alligator began to catch fire and burn beneath her. She twisted and roared and growled with the pain.

"He's so very close now! Just wait a few more moments and you'll get a good look at him!" Spider shouted.

Alligator could not stand the pain any more, and ran all the way back into the water and thrashed about to put out the fire.

"What's the matter, Alligator? I thought you weren't afraid. You're in such a hurry all the time."

Alligator sank into the waters and stewed in her hatred of Spider.

Ikasa was playing curse pretty hard-line with Mary in the old store when Pop came in and disrupted the whole thing with his stomping around, making the curse jumped right straight up into Ikasa and suffuse her whole being. She felt itchy as it crawled under her flesh and watched ants drip-dropping out of her fingers until they went away. Mary laughed while Ikasa ran around screeching and laughing and throwing ants all over the place. They settled back down and reconsolidated the deck.

"Do you want to cast another one?" Ikasa asked.

"No," Mary said. "I'm so bad at that game, I was getting crushed until your pop showed up. Hey, Mr. Spider, are you going to tell anybody where I am?"

He kept walking, carrying a cardboard box, but turned around briefly.

"It is not in the nature of the Garden Spider clan to tell the truth," he said, disappearing into the back.

"He means he's not going to answer that question," Ikasa grumbled. "He does that when he thinks you won't like the answer. Better escape back to your fort."

They grabbed up all their things and rushed north around the backside of the town, through discarded plywood and sheet metal and the pieces of larger buildings, through the destroyed rubble of the outskirts of town, and through little green-dappled paths full of lizards that ran at their approach. They jogged all the way up to Oksachee and Mary's second-floor fort. She gave Mary a boost and waited patiently for the ladder, which wasn't as forthcoming as she thought it should be.

Instead, Mary kicked a pot over the edge and scowled down.

"Did you tell the cops where I was?" she asked.

"No," Ikasa said.

"Yeah, well!" Mary screamed.

There was a sound not unlike a foot on metal and the splintering of wood, and Mary dropped down on top of Ikasa, confusing her enough that she didn't understand what was happening until she felt her lip split open on her teeth under Mary's fist.

"You did call the cops, didn't you?" Mary shouted, kicking Ikasa in the stomach.

Ikasa coughed and rolled, then stood and grabbed at Mary's waist. Mary rained her fists down on Ikasa's back.

"I did not!" Ikasa said.

"Your pop said Spider clan always lies! All of the stories about Spider clan are about them lying and lying and lying and being assfucks!" Mary said.

Ikasa ran and carried Mary with her, but Mary was strong. She grabbed Ikasa by the shoulders and threw her off into the ankle deep water in the causeway north of the atrium. Ikasa grabbed moss and mud with her hands and turned, throwing them in Mary's face, before lashing out to grab one of the girl's ankles and yanking back. Mary hit the water and screeched.

"They're just," Ikasa panted. "Stories."

She struck Mary in the face. Mary grabbed her nose and frowned.

"Let's see if I can make a black eye that actually stands out on you," she said, falling on Ikasa, holding her down with her knees, and pulled her fist back.

Ikasa felt her lungs light up with fire, and she coughed as water leaked in through her nose and the corner of her mouth. She thrashed about uncontrollably, and she gurgled. Mary stood up and backed away in a panic. Ikasa sat up on all fours and coughed until she could breathe normally again, albeit with a slow wheeze. She felt like a burning ember had been touched to the back of her throat.

"I think I puked a little," Spider said.

Mary laughed.

"Okay, okay," Ikasa said, slowly standing up. "I think I'm ready to-"

The entire left side of her face turned insensate. A slow heat crawled back into it, and she saw Mary's fist coming back again.

"Ready to go!" Ikasa said.

She swung at Mary, and found her hands swatted away like they were nothing more than particularly annoying mosquitoes.

"You fucking after school martial arts shit-hole!"

"Greasy dick eater!" Mary said.

"Do not start this game with me, you maggot-infested slime-dribbling vaginal shit taco!" Ikasa said.

Mary stopped and blinked.

"Where did that come from?"

"Gramma," Ikasa said.

"Yeah, well," Mary said, and punched Spider in the stomach. "Once more, for having an actual family."

"Fair," Ikasa groaned, and dropped to the ground.

Mary sat down in the water and watched some minnows swim by.

"I believe you about the cops," she said. "I'm not sorry, though."

"That's fair," Ikasa said. "We know which of us wins with fists."

"That's because I'm tough and wiry," Mary said. "And you're like, made of dry twigs, I keep being afraid I'm going to break one of your bones."

"Gramma says it's from her side of the family," Ikasa said, stretching out her arms and wiggling her fingers.

"And your hands are enormous."

"And you have a government haircut," Ikasa said.

Mary kicked some of the flowing water around.

"Is it okay if I go back, dry off, and stay by myself today?"

"Yeah," Ikasa said, standing and shaking water off. "Chicomay, come."

He pulled his head out of the nearby bushes and followed

along, chirping and stumbling. Ikasa waved a goodbye and headed back to the storefront. Mr. Armadillo crushed boxes out back of the store, packing them and throwing them in the dumpster while grackles crowded around and yelled at him. She gave him a wave and went inside. Pop was knocking over stacks of newspaper around a set of rusted metal and hoses.

"And what the fuck is this?" he screamed. "An oil barrel? Why is this even here? It's the fucking drifters come through here and don't care what kind of trash they leave around!"

He knocked over the barrel and saw Ikasa in the back door.

"Oh, hey," he said. "Sorry. We're just. Going through some difficulty."

"It's a spaceman," Mr. Armadillo said.

"What?" Pop asked.

"A spaceman, look," Mr. Armadillo moved some more papers out of the way.

Pop wiped grit off a broken glass dome and pulled a few sheets of scrap metal off.

"Did this used to be a mechanic shop?" Pop asked.

"Spaceman looks broken," Mr. Armadillo said.

"It's not a spaceman!" Pop and Ikasa said in unison.

"It's a golem," Pop said.

There was a big round chest with a mess of exposed buttons and switches and a little awning over the top to keep rain from drizzling down into the dials. The whole thing was slumped in the middle of the floor next to a pair of legs stacked neatly to the side and wrapped in a big blue tarp spotted with mold. Ikasa fiddled with some of the switches.

"What's the diagnosis?" Pop asked.

Ikasa looked at the five huge vacuum tubes in the big dome head - one of them cracked deeply - and checked the shoulders where the arms were missing, following a line of confluence to one metal limb buried under more newspapers. The forearm was one big cylinder, and there was a massive set of four pincer-like fingers with one joint each set on the end. The shoulder socket was rusted out.

"It needs new shoulders," Ikasa said. "Only one arm is here. Do you want me to fix it?"

"If we fix it, we own it," Pop said. "Can you fix it?"

"Of course I can fix it-" Ikasa said, and yanked the hatch on the backpack open. "Okay, maybe not."

"What's wrong with it?" Pop asked.

Ikasa reached into the back and felt around in the dirt and leaves.

"It's all dead," she said, and tore out great heaping handfuls of dry leaves and twigs. "Would have to re-bind all the spirits individually."

"We got the parts we need at the house?"

"We haven't done a full inventory of Gramma's collection," Ikasa said. "But I bet if we assembled everything we have here, I can call Jerry and he can send us what we don't have."

"For how much?"

"Postage," Ikasa said. "Some of the stuff in here looks good, though. Seems like they used a turtle."

She sat down on the concrete floor.

"Hey, we haven't washed that floor yet!" Pop yelled. He picked her up by the wrist before helping her up with her shoulders.

"For storage. They used a turtle for memory storage."

"You okay?" Pop asked.

Mr. Armadillo came over and looked into the back.

"Turtles are gatekeepers," he said. "They hold keys to things, protect wisdom inside their bodies, and things like that. Box turtles especially."

Ikasa tore her wrist free of Pop's grip and went back to the golem.

"Sorry," she said. "I got lost in something. Box turtle for memory storage, it's intact. There's a few things intact in here, we'd have to re-plant all that stuffing. We can use potting soil if you want to."

"How about just dirt?"

"If it's from the river," she said. "So we can keep it?"

"If you can fix it, you can have it," Pop said. "Add it to the stack of shit we're taking home in the car. Brad, you and me can move this. 'Kasa, keep cleaning, okay?"

She nodded.

"And sweep up all that dirt!"

Ikasa grabbed a broom off the wall and started sweeping shattered glass, leaves, dirt, little screws and the like out the back door. She focused on the hiss of the bristles over the floor and wondered more about the turtle in her pocket. The mana beat once like her brother bringing a drumstick down on a truck hood. The weight pulled her down against a wall, and she felt burning limbs crackling over her leg. She reached a hand down into the pocket, feeling the white-hot turtle, and then threw the rattle into the bushes.

As she finished her sweeping, she kept looking back at the bushes, expecting the rattle to come crawling out of there at any moment and leap upon her face like an alien monster from a pulp magazine. When no terror was forthcoming, she dug through the grass again and put the turtle back in her pocket. She thought briefly about trying to hook up the golem and seeing if she could wire Ikasa's old memories into the machinery, perhaps to hold a conversation with the old woman, but she thought she might have to be the focus herself. Mr. Armadillo came back, sans golem, and nodded at Ikasa. He started moving a few more pieces of sheet metal around. Ikasa jumped when a buzzing hiss echoed through the building.

"Oh! You're okay there, buddy!" Mr. Armadillo said.

"What is it?" Ikasa said, trying to look around him.

She recognized the yellow-on-black hatch mark pattern almost instantly.

"A rattlesnake!"

"Tiny dragon," Mr. Armadillo said. "Ikasa, go get me a leafy branch."

She ran outside and fetched one covered in little oak leaves. Mr. Armadillo put it down on the rattlesnake, letting the hay-colored coils wrap around the branches.

"One time, there was a boy who was out hunting, and he came across a rattlesnake at the edge of a thick wet swamp," Mr. Armadillo said. "Now there was a big rope bridge across this swamp, but there were lots of little pieces of wood missing." He picked up the snake, slowly, holding the tail while the head slithered around in the leaves. The rattle stopped, and Mr. Armadillo started to walk outside.

"The snake stops the boy and says 'hey, there, you! Carry me across!' and the boy answers, 'no, sir, Mr. Rattlesnake, you'll bite me!'" Mr. Armadillo said, and put the snake down in the bushes. "And the snake says 'oh, no, I promise!' and there's a little more convincing to be had with both parties, and eventually, the boy nods and picks up the snake, and they start going across. They get not three steps off the side of the shore and the snake bites the boy hard on the wrist."

Mr. Armadillo pointed with his lips and knocked his head at

the snake, which slid away into the bushes.

"And as they're drowning in the muck, the boy says 'why did you bite me?' and the snake says 'you knew what I was!'"

He dusted off his hands and looked at Ikasa.

"You get it?"

"Yeah, I think so," Ikasa said.

"You know something's going to bite you, don't pick it up."

Ikasa nodded.

"Yeah," she said. "Thanks."

She felt the turtle in her pocket and tapped it with her finger, hearing the hollow sound.

Chapter 24
Rough Start

A Nuwep woman went out to gather food. She took her child with her, and while she worked, she stuck the points of her cradleboard in the ground and left the child alone near the river, for only a moment, she thought.

A large King-in-Yellow butterfly flew past, and she started after it and chased it for a long time. She would almost catch it, and then just miss.

"Perhaps I can't run fast enough because of this heavy thing," she thought, and she threw away her robe.

But, still, she never could quite overtake the fluttering creature. Finally she threw away her apron, too, and hurried on, chasing the butterfly until night came. Then, her child forgotten, she lay down under a tree and went to sleep.

When she awoke in the morning, she found a man lying beside her.

"You have followed me this far; perhaps you would like to follow me always. If so, you must go through a lot of my people," he said.

Without thinking of her child at all, the woman rose and followed the butterfly man. By and by they came to a large valley, whose southern side was full of butterflies.

When the two reached the edge of the valley, the man said, "No one has ever come through this valley alive. But you'll be safe if you don't lose sight of me. Follow closely."

They traveled for a long time.

"Keep tight hold of me! Don't let go," the King-in-Yellow man *said again and again.*

When they had come half way through the valley, other butterflies swarmed about them in great numbers. They flew every way, all around the couple's heads and in their faces, for they wanted to get the Nuwep woman for themselves.

She watched them for a long time, holding tightly to her new husband. But, at last, unable to resist, she let go of him and reached out to seize one of the others. She missed that one and she tried to grab now one, now the other, but always failed, and so she wandered in the valley forever, dazed and lost.

She died there, and the butterfly man she had lost went on through the valley to his home.

And now when people speak of the olden times they say that this woman lost her lover, and tried to get others but lost them, and went crazy and died. The child grew up and became a butterfly, too, and they say he is still out there, looking for his own wife.

"You don't have a fucking inventory, Daniel!" Mom screamed. "You don't have a fucking anything! You never discuss this shit with anyone and then you're in it and you're wallowing around and you drag us all the fuck down with you!"

"I don't need one, I can just do spirit summoning until we get some inventory," he said.

"And then what? All of our fucking margins will go right to Nihpej-Wodara!" she threw a box of newspapers on the floor. "And Mom! Clean up your damn shit!"

Gramma opened a new beer and kept listening to the radio. She turned it up a little.

"Mother of shit," Mom said. "We have to open the store. Or work somewhere. Or do something. I don't want the kids weighed down with that money forever. I know it's the right thing, you just don't have any kind of penetration in town."

"I know," Pop said. "I wish we could have gotten something in Shimookooah, but we got the Fort Hammock storefront for free. It's not a great location, but it's something. Ikasa's going to fix that golem, then we'll have an employee we can pay at the BIA wages."

Mom punched the wall lightly.

"Got it. If you're going to do this shit, you'll do it right. Where's the papers?"

Pop sat down at the kitchen table.

"Ikasa, go get that file folder I gave you the other day."

She went upstairs to her room and took the over-stuffed file with "new store" written on the cardboard surface in marker out of her nightstand. She went back down, handed it off to Pop, and left out the side door. More screaming followed. Ikasa stopped listening to the words and went around back into the junk piles. She approached the golem, sitting under a tarp next to the old icebox. She kicked over marble tiles until she found the box of car batteries, taking the few that looked the least corroded back to the golem.

The back panel came off just as easy, and the breadboards inside, while they were largely intact, were saturated with rust from broken wires. She started pulling, and when she had a pile of tangled short wire, she started separating out the corrosion. When she had a big handful, she buried the green chunks in a tree just inside the woods. She picked up her pack and threw a tarp over the batteries.

"What's up, shithead?" Eddie asked, grabbing her by the head.

"Let me go, I need copper for wires!" she said.

"I'll go with you, man," he said.

"I'm going down into a cave!" she said.

"You don't have to do that," he said, grabbing some bolt cutters from the carport. "We can go out to the fences to the power-poles they're not using. Bet there's lots of wires in the bunkers out there."

"Oh, that's true," she said, and then went back to the golem.

She shined her flashlight around inside the back, tore the wiring diagram out from inside the maintenance panel, and hopped back to Eddie.

"Oh, hey, this is even better," he said. "Let's go. I don't want to be home while mom and Pop are going at it."

Something solid and heavy ejected itself out of the kitchen window, scattering glass everywhere.

"Tell me about it," Ikasa said.

"Okay. They'll get to a point where they realize they've both been agreeing with each other this whole time, just using different words," Eddie said. "Then they'll fuck, then they'll figure out how they're going to open a new store without going even deeper into debt, argue again, fuck again, then they'll open the store. It's a cycle."

"The world works in cycles," Ikasa nodded.

"Eating," Eddie said.

"Sleeping," Ikasa said.

"Fucking," Eddie said.

"Getting high," Ikasa said, nodding.

"So fucking high," Eddie said.

Chicomay hopped up on an overgrown car and barked. He was starting to get adult feathers, and the end of his fishing-pole tail was starting to grow a sort of feathery flag on the end.

"Oh, yeah, I forgot," Eddie said. "Quality of life shit, art and pets and crap. Did you name that thing?"

"Chicomay!" Ikasa shouted, and he jumped off the car, ran over, and started sniffing her fingers and gnawing on the fringe on her poncho.

"Number seven?" Eddie asked.

"Umpoh-something on chicome," Ikasa said. "Forty-seven flavor sauce."

"Oh, ha!" Eddie said. "I get it, that's funny. Ompohualli. Ompohualchicome. Gramma uses Alhacuan numbers when she's speaking Xiuteotl and it's so fucking annoying."

"Would you say she's a mean bitch?"

"Not to her face, she might hurt me!"

"She already hurt me," Ikasa said.

"Wisdom," Eddie said.

They crunched up the bank along the railroad and to the poles on the other side of the rise. Ikasa could see the tweaker hideout with her circle still intact just down the way. The tracks cut through the forest on either side, forming a line through the scrub, hidden by trees until someone walked straight up onto the gravel. Ikasa poked through rocks for ones that were cold or hot or that thrummed beneath her fingers like beating hearts. She stuffed a few trilobites into her pockets. Eddie looked up the nearest pole and shook his head.

"Huh, it looks like someone stole all the salamanders out of this one," he said, moving down the line. "Can you go up about a hundred feet and see if there's a line of poles through the woods north?"

Ikasa saluted and jogged up the line. She looked and saw where two poles seemed a little closer to each other than they were along the track and stood beneath them, not able to see anything through the trees other than unclouded sky. She squinted and looked up, following a pine tree to the ground, and looked beyond the fence. Something felt a bit odd about the white sand between a set of scrub oak growth. She clambered over the simple wire barrier.

"Found something!" she called out, digging her fingers into the sand.

"What is it?" Eddie said, shielding his eyes with one hand.

"Human mana touched it," she said. "Like it's scattered on the ground like glass."

She felt what she thought might have been a root at first and yanked. A long power line came up out of the sand.

"All right!" Eddie said. He started following the black cable, pulling it up hand over hand.

They walked down the forgotten sinew up to a little plaster dome set in the sandhill. The remains of a watchtower lay crumpled up in a corner, and what may have once been a tall fence had fallen down into a pile of low growth shrubs, and served as a city wall for ant hills. Thick concrete walls formed a narrow path down which they had to walk to enter the main building, as well as a pair of metal doors with heavy bolts that could slide into place in case of large animals. Inside, the bare room smelled like mold and reeked of paint. Ikasa kicked over a nearly empty bucket; water and wrigglers went everywhere, as did the stink of sulfur.

A few typewriters sat under dirt and cypress leaves, which seemed a bit odd at first, but the maps everywhere were mostly of the area south of Shimookooah. She recognized what had been the mack fields they had driven by coming into town among them, and started sweeping off large boxes full of tape and glass.

"Are these computators?" she asked.

"Yeah, looks like it's war-era," Eddie said. "You found your golem parts."

She opened up the side of one.

"Cool! It's all reel tape and microfiche, two oscilloscopes, no ticker or anything, it really is war-period!" she said, crawling inside one of the large boxes.

Softly glowing quartz bricks sat inside, and their interior gave off a gentle violet light.

"There's still working core stacks in here," she said.

"What, really?" Eddie said. "We have to mail those back to the government if they're still on."

"Aw," Ikasa said, already unhooking the blocks and kicking them out. "They're heavy."

"Yeah, well, the spirits in them might still remember parts of old programs, so we have to," Eddie said. "There any copper in there?"

Ikasa pulled out a ball of wires.

"Copper, gold, you name it, we got it," she said, grinning. "Lots of glass and other junk. I need a screwdriver. A really tiny flat head. I'm going to start sliding parts out, you strip, okay?"

She heard him digging around in her pack, and a flat head slid up next to her. She grabbed the handle and started working on screws.

"Strip? No problem," he said. She heard his belt buckle snap.

"You know what I meant!"

"I don't know, do I?"

"You're so gross," she said, and yanked a sheet of vacuum tubes free. "Core memory unit exterior panel, coming through."

She slid it out, and was able to pull herself up further inside. There was a nest of little clamps with shining heads mostly untouched clipped onto a pile of fish spines glued to a breadboard.

"There's an 8-bit parallel serial bus in here, holy shit," she said. "It's connected to-"

Ikasa followed the lines back up and down into another box turtle shell. She sneered and kicked it, caving in the shell, and watched tobacco fall out onto the floor.

"You okay? I heard you scream," Eddie said. "It was kind of a rage scream."

"I'm okay," Ikasa said. "Hey, Eddie."

"What's up?"

She saw his face looking down at her through the holes where there had once been switches. Moving so she could look into his eyes, she let out a breath.

"If you could become a super-powerful magician overnight, would you?"

"Oh, fuck yeah," he said.

"I'm serious!"

He moved back out of sight.

"Is this about that turtle?"

"I think the old Ikasa from the world before is inside it," she said. "She whispers to me to open up the turtle and sit in the cot in the underground world. To put the little battery inside my head. To become her."

"Well, I think that's the sort of thing you have to figure out by yourself."

"Yeah, but that's hard," she said, kicking the inside of the computator again.

"Everything's hard. Life's hard. Not getting in trouble's hard. Getting a good job's hard."

He sat quiet for a moment.

"My abs are hard," he said, standing up and flexing.

"Everything about me is hard!"

"You are no help," she said.

She started unscrewing more panels. The smell of dry tobacco got stuck in her nose.

Chapter 25

Mr. Blue Crab

One day Johnny Lee was out picking fruit from the frost-vines when he heard a cry for help. He followed it to a find a small clearing where there was a woman sitting there with a scowl on her face and her arms crossed. She huffed at him when he entered the clearing, and he looked at the pile of sticks by her feet.

"So, what is the matter?" he asked.

"Wood is hiding the fire from me again," the woman grumbled, and Johnny Lee nodded in understanding.

"Wood hides fire from me quite a lot," he said. "But sometimes I can get it to give it up."

She looked at him and nodded.

"That is all well and good, but how does it help me?" she asked.

"Very simply," he said, and clapped his hands together. "I will make the fire come out."

He scowled at the fire, screaming in rage and anger, then struck his fist into the ground.

"Wood!" he shouted, "give up your fire or I will come in there myself and get it!"

No sooner had he shouted this than all the sticks in the clearing burst into flame. Startled, he quickly dumped all his water out on all the flames except the one at the woman's feet. Now the woman was smiling in excitement.

"Can you teach me to do that?" she asked.

Johnny Lee was a friendly sort, so he nodded and patted the

woman on the shoulder.

"Certainly," he said, and sat down to cook his dinner at the newly-made fire. "Tomorrow we will begin."

The next morning, the woman and Johnny Lee started looking for a rock, a big one like a cliff, and when they found one, they stood side by side looking at the rock. He pointed up one side.

"Climb this rock," he said. "And you'll see how it's done."

She tried to climb the rock, falling each time she tried, breaking her wrist once and forcing them to sit and wait for many days until she could try again.

"Can't you tell me how?" she asked.

"I can't tell you how," Johnny Lee said. "You got to see it. You got to know it."

So it went, and eventually she managed to climb all the way up the cliff. She leaned over the edge and watched Johnny Lee scowl at the cliff, and handholds appeared wherever he reached, and he quickly and easily pulled his way up.

"How about now?"

"I told you already, you got to see it."

They looked at what was on top and saw nothing but more jungle. Johnny Lee started walking again, and the woman complained that her feet hurt. He said nothing, and had her make a fire and cook food when it came time to camp and carry his pack when it came time to leave in the morning. She was inconvenienced by this, but being an honorable sort, said nothing.

Eventually, however, it started to rain. Johnny Lee scowled at the sky, and the rain went away.

"Can you tell me how it's done now?" she asked.

He scowled at her this time, and she put up her hands in defense.

"It's not far now, I'll show you in a minute."

He came to a big herd of uchgrunchucks, and waved to her.

"It's almost here," he said. "Come out into the field."

So they went, and they waited for several days until the herd was suddenly spooked and the ground thundered.

"It's coming!" he shouted. "The way is coming!"

And he quickly hid, not telling the woman to do so.

Suddenly, a great big gariax burst out of the trees, and the woman screamed and ran, being chased by the terrible beast. She felt the hot breath on her neck and heard the roar of the monster just behind her. She ran over fields and through forests and over *rivers, but it never gave up. She could see Johnny Lee out of the corner of her eye, laughing and howling while riding a stormcloud.*

By now she was running out of energy, for she had run almost all the way to the sunset, and could take no more. She was so angry with Johnny Lee for lying to her, angry at the sky, angry at the gariax for not giving up, and so ticked off she just stopped and turned around. The woman shouted as loud as she could and struck her fist into the ground, making the gariax stop in its tracks. She narrowed her eyes and stuck out the side of her lip, and the gariax walked away. Suddenly, her eyes went wide, and she started to smile.

"That's how it's done," said Johnny Lee, who walked off waving goodbye..

Ikasa sat out back partially inside an old chicken coop stripping electric wires, braiding the copper by hand, and rolling them in wax before attaching them to transistors and vacuum tubes installed on the interior of the golem's thick frame. She tried to achieve as close a duplicate as possible to the diagrams inside, but she had to make a few adjustments along the line. She spot-soldered a few things in place, and affixed the old turtle shell to the center of the inside of the box. With ease, she slid the switchbox into the receptacle on the chest, bolted the four corners, and folded down the entire assembly into the main trunk. The dome was still cracked, and one big vacuum tube in the head was still shattered, but she thought that might be perfectly fine for the moment.

She wriggled around front of the metal man on her butt. He still had no arms or legs, but everything in the center should be ready to work well enough. She cranked the primer handle until it clicked and pressed the button to close the connection. Sparks went flying. Lights and light bulbs went up and all over the place, and the front panel flickered, highlighting buttons and switches.

"Good-goo-good. Good. Morning, each morning, a magazine his wife concealed, explained how people who are civilized. In THIS great nation, we arrive every morning to our houses, schools, jobs, and even to the very borders of our perfect country, wondering what possible thing could disrupt so beautiful a picture!" it said, voice radiating outward like a man on a radio. "Country. Country."

"What country is this?" Ikasa asked.

"OCTOBER COUNTRY." The speaker belted out. "Beautiful day! Let's! Let's! Let's. We all should go to the park."

She pulled the main power. The whole thing slumped over like an old man tired of living.

"What's the news, cuz?" Pop said, scratching his stomach through his undershirt.

"It's really fucked up," she said. "I might have to ask you to rebuild the whole main board."

"Yeah?" he asked, crouching down to her level. "Is that even worth it?"

"It would be. We have all the parts, it's just labor at this point," Ikasa said.

"All the parts?" Pop lifted up the nearby tarps. "Holy shit, you do have all the parts. Think you can build me a rocket belt with this, too?"

She gave him a flat look.

"Father, you are not being funny right now. If I am going to build a rocket belt it will be for me. To get off this rock."

The leaves started to hiss, and then droplets of rain began to fall, small ones, barely registering as a prickle on her skin, but enough to make working slightly greasier. Pop stepped a little closer in to the awning as the rain hammered out tiny railroad spikes in the roof. He sat down on the coop bench and sighed. Ikasa held part of a spirit trap transistor to her lips and blew. She felt dirt scatter, and plugged the three little legs back in place.

"Still haven't found a job, nobody in town will hire me," Pop said. "Turns out that Spider reputation proceeds us."

"Precedes."

"What?"

"It comes in front of us. Precedes," Ikasa said, and then punched the golem's glass head-dome.

"Oh. Well, I can never figure out that shit," Pop said. "You're the genus in this family."

He leaned in and squinted at the control box on the front of the big round chest.

"What are you using for memory storage?" he asked.

"The same stupid turtle that was in here before!" she said.

She hooked up the power again, and the wires hummed. The little valves inside lit up and flickered before all the coupling rods and wheels in the base of the head started spinning up again, clicking like a ticker-tape machine.

"Good morning everyone! And it is with this fine day, I greet you, as always, with a hand raised in salute, to show to our brothers and sisters of every clan and tribe the spirit of this great nation!"

Something in the arm sockets moved. Ikasa pulled the power again.

"Same shit," she said.

"You know, if it's military, we have to send it back to the government," Pop said.

"Seems like it's more just shouting mindless propaganda, like it's not a war machine. Like a gizmo supposed to talk about how awesome our side is. Don't worry, I'll take care of it," Ikasa said. "I can't do anything else right now, I need some spirits bound before I can go forward. Fire stuff."

Pop nodded, and they headed back inside.

"You talk to her?" Mom said.

"Yeah, sure," Pop said, grabbing a six pack out of the fridge. "I'm going over to Andy's."

Mom watched him go with a scowl, but smiled at Ikasa.

"Are you okay?" Mom asked, giving Ikasa a hug.

"You know what? No," Ikasa said.

"What's wrong?"

"Everything happens around me," she said. "It's like everything happens, and then I get told that it happened. The shop disappears. I get told we're moving out here. We get out here, and it's stupid. Everyone is stupid and crazy here. Then, Pop doesn't have a job, and he gets drunk with Gramma and Mr. Blue Crab, and stupid shit that I can't control happens all the time and I'm just trying to push and push back and nothing happens except I get slapped for it!"

Ikasa shoved a chair.

"And I can't fucking do anything right! And everyone thinks I'm fucking stupid," she said, stomping upstairs.

She slammed the door to her room and sank down under the knob. Chicomay sat up and chirped a mild warning before settling back down again, hips wobbling like a hen. Ikasa heard a knock on the door. She ignored the sound and picked up Hornhead instead. Someone tried to open the door, and she leaned back hard against the peeling paint.

"We don't shut you out, we just take care of you," her mom said. "You're still a kid."

227

"And if you don't talk to me about shit, I'll never get an adulthood anything," Ikasa growled back. "I'll just be a fucking kid forever, keep failing all my shit. Then grow up and live in a tiny box in the middle of the woods just like you!"

She continued to scowl at the door until she heard Mom walk away. Her face burned and she felt stupid and useless. She crawled over to Chicomay and grabbed him probably harder than she should and heard him squeal in alarm, but try to clean her hair anyway. She fell back into her clothes-pile bed and let tears escape for what felt like the first real time in ages. Trying to fight the rising tide, she rolled over on her side and curled up; that didn't help, and she just felt like she was choking. Chicomay was like a big ball of spikes, with feather shafts sticking into her sides. When she finally did manage to stop blubbering on the floor, she crawled to her agayateni box.

Unfolding the Hornhead where she'd crumpled the woman in her hand, Ikasa got out one of the house foldouts from a nearby magazine and pinned it to the wall. She drew a line for a yard just underneath, and put Hornhead up on the landscape by the front door. Ikasa sat, cross-legged, and put her hands on the drywall. With one pulse, the woman fell to the earth. She stood up, brushed herself off, and looked in both directions before heading to the door.

"I have a piece of my shame. Spider's greatest shame, which is mine. Inside, I could become an all-powerful magician, the equal of the ancient Ikasa, but I might get lost inside her. I can feel it every time she rumbles in my pocket. At night when the box turtle sits on my desk."

Hornhead went inside her house; the place was laid out in two dimensions, with stairs or ladders going up to other rooms. She climbed the stairs up to the living room and stood across the floor from a glowing cutout of a small crystal, radiating concentric circles of magical power. Hornhead put up her hands, as if she were unsure of touching the hexagonal diamond. Ikasa clenched her teeth, and the waves expanded out, knocking Hornhead to the floor.

"I can feel it in everything I do!" Ikasa said. "Who's really in control of my life?"

She leaned on her hands, feeling them burn and freeze in equal measure. The tips of her fingers were indistinguishable from the drywall that felt as though the plaster might buckle at any moment. The diamond began to make sounds, a low squealing roar like electricity escaping into the air.

"What do I really control?" Ikasa said. "This stupid shit? Or does it just happen. Does shit just happen, or is somebody there? It's not like it's just one person, is it?"

"I don't know," Hornhead answered, her voice deep as an empty chasm. Something old was crept up behind her visage.

Ikasa let go of the wall. Everything held still. She stood up, grabbing her knife quickly, and kicked open her door just in time to see Mom walking down the hall with a pair of sandwiches. Ikasa grabbed one off the plate and looked up at her.

"I got to go meet somebody, I'll be back," Ikasa shouted, running down the stairs and out the back door.

She ran, and that was why Chicomay chased her. She ran all the way to the river, then got too tired and had to walk. Wishing she had a bike, she made her way back up to the ruins and down into the hole, right back to the dark room.

"Hey!" Ikasa said. "Wing monster!"

Staring off into the dark, she turned on her flashlight.

"I know you sent me a message! The mana behind the Hornhead was old. Old and dusty and gross like you!"

A tall figure with a bald head and big round yellow eyes streaked with black slits emerged from the shadows. It wore a thick robe and coat, and its lipless mouth was curled back in either a snarl or a smile. It blinked with all three eyelids. The olive skin shone with flecks of mica when she passed the light over it. A crawling, clutching dread crossed over her own skin for a moment, but she just gripped the flashlight tighter.

"I figured out what you are. The earth-angels, the voices in the ground, the people who steal milk by taking human shape. What were you trying to say to me?" she asked.

"That, I don't know," it said. "I don't know if the events you speak of were engineered, or if they are simply occurring. But I know that you are capable of following lines of confluence, you followed them here in the first place. You haven't been looking recently."

"That's just because so much shit's been going on."

"Well, I can tell you what the big angry Deathwalker believes."

"What's that?"

"Adahi'i, the poison monster, calls 'destiny' the Lair of the Irresponsible. Destiny is an excuse for people to be lazy, to claim they have a destiny, to think the world is prepared just for them. Well, if it happened, it's just destiny, the prophecy says. It's an excuse to poison everything and claim that they must do so, out of respect for their destiny. Then, when they pull out the guts and eat the fat and spoil the meat, they can claim they're no longer hungry because that was their destiny, and they can write whatever prophecy they like and point to it and say that's how it always was. No, not destiny at all. If it's destiny, why even do anything at all? Destiny is just the claim of absolution of the greedy and the lazy alike. This is what Adahi'i says. There might be truth in it."

"But Adahi'i is the power behind black magicians," Ikasa said.

"No one ever said that wisdom cannot be held in darkness. Remember, a black magician is not corrupted by magic. They corrupt the magic."

"Gramma said that to me once, too. You don't become corrupted, you corrupt," Ikasa said. "I get it, then. You're implying that lines of confluence aren't like anything that's required, they're just a sort of feeling you get when you walk by a poorly stacked pile of junk. If you push it over, stuff will fall over, it'll form new piles of junk. It's not destiny, but it looks like it, is that it?"

"I think that is what I'm trying to say. You're good. Of course, I expect this sort of understanding of the movement of a web from a Spider."

Ikasa nodded.

"Yeah, thanks," she said, starting to head out. "Don't go anywhere. I might need your help later."

"Not a problem." it said, disappearing into the depths again.

Ikasa ran all the way back home, so much that when she got back to the front door with Chicomay, she had to run the hose on her face until she could breathe again. After a moment to catch up to herself, she saw Andy running up the road. She handed him the hose when he got up to the house.

"It's that kind of day," she said. "I thought my Pop was with you."

"Nope."

"Where's Ronnie?"

"Doesn't matter. Where's your pop?" he asked.

He stepped past her.

"Hey, Danny Spider!" Andy shouted from the front door. "I got you a job!"

"You got who what?" Mom said.

"Wilmer says Danny Spider can work floor at the store until you get your shop squared away."

"Let me get the car," Mom said, and they all drove up the road until they found Pop sitting under a tree and Andy gave him the good news.

He seemed excited by it, and they drove up to Wilmer's. The old man was out front, sweeping away when they pulled up.

"Oh, good," Wilmer said. "Andy says you're a good worker, and you was going to open a shop for wonder-working once you have some cash."

"That's right, sir," Pop said, shaking the man's hand nervously.

"Well, welcome aboard," Wilmer said. "Andy, you're fired."

"You are one fucked-up mother fucker," Pop said.

Chapter 26
All They Want is to Sing

In the beginning there was only the forest. Three voice-men emerged from the forest, long and thin, with gourds for faces and hollow, black eyes. Their limbs were made of sticks bound together by cloth rope. The gods spoke to them and through them, and with this power, they created creatures out of the forest, animals and plants to work the will of the gods outside the between-leaves.

When they had done, the gods called them back to the mountains of Ruakulu, deep in the between-leaves of the undergrowth. Knowing that the world needed stewards to guard it, they came together and began to make people out of mud and stone, with leaves from the trees. They split the forest into parts, and then climbed to the top of Ruakulu, the mountain in the undergrowth. The gods agreed, and called the beast they made the beast of knowledge.

They told the beasts of knowledge where each sacred site was, and where a limitless supply of the other beasts dwelled, and they would continue to be placed into the world, so long as the beasts of knowledge sang the songs and performed the rites of the three voice-men. These were the rites of Looking After Country, and the beasts wrote them down in their dreams.

The people they made were fifty strong, and before long, began to get hungry. They made weapons out of the forest to catch food, and bowls to capture water so they would not be thirsty. Since there were as many animals as they wanted using the Looking After Country songs, they did not curb themselves and ate their fill.

They built a few villages in the trees, and for a time lived in peace and harmony. Ilahai of the gods decreed that no spirit or god associate with the beast of knowledge, for to make it able to perform the rites of Looking After Country, it had to be able to invent new things and slay animals. Granting it the knowledge of spirits would only be asking for trouble.

However, all was not well in the between-leaves, for Bidjuju the black shadow, the shortest and slimmest voice-man, did not like beasts getting the knowledge of making beasts. He gathered together all his own beasts and gave them the knowledge too, specifically, he gave the wasps and bees the power to make their own kind out of mud and wax. He sent them off into the jungle, and was satisfied with his work.

It soon became apparent that this was a mistake. The wasps and bees, without knowledge of excess, soon became too numerous, forcing the people to hunt them. This caused a great war, which lasted many years, and the people dwindled in number until Ilahai was convinced to make a move. He told Bidjuju the black shadow to do something, and so, unable to steal the knowledge back, he simply made wasps and bees ever so much smaller. Still jealous, he stole away some of the original giant insects and hid them.

The beasts of knowledge, however, had shrunk in number by only half, so many of them having been dead and gone. There were so few of them, so they begged the gods in the between-leaves knowledge of the sacred places where the beasts of knowledge could be sung, and they refused. They instead sought out the beasts and gathered them together. They explained the situation, and the beasts could not think of any way to help, which made them upset because without the beasts of knowledge, all beasts of the forest were doomed.

That was when Abir-Akkai the bird spoke up. He knew of the caves in Ruakulu, but to get to them, they would have to ask permission of Gudjhara the lizard. So the beasts went, and asked the lizard for his help. He happily directed them to the caves, from which lights and whispers ushered.

"You will find two caves," he said. "One whispers and is warm, but filled with the sounds of creation, and one howls and is cold, but is filled also with the sounds of destruction. Half of you must go inside one cave, and the other half go inside the other."

So the beasts went up the mountain to find the caves, and

after many days of deliberation, they decided who was to go into which cave. As they came out on the other side of the mountain, they found themselves changed; those who entered the cave of whispers became women, and those who entered the cave of howls became men.

"Now you are part of each other," Gudjhara said. "You can make more of yourselves, but only through cooperation."

They returned to their villages, but they were not yet people. How they became people is not important right now. All that must be known is that the beasts of knowledge were created to sing, and all they wished to do is sing.

Ehano clenched his fist with joy when the ball split into three, and Ronnie became even more unstoppable with the flippers. They were playing on Ikasa's last dime; she'd felt a power in it, and decided it was better served in the pinball table than in the phone this time. Ronnie shook the table to shove one of the balls into a scoring pit. Ikasa grinned as thunder rumbled outside.

"You had pinball back in the big city, right?" Ehano said.

"Yeah, sometimes they were metal or plastic, too. Not awesome and wood," she said.

"That sounds cool, though," Ehano said. "Oh, shit, Leech said you got a golem. She says she buys her shit from Armadillo, and last time she was there, he said you guys found a golem in the old storefront."

"Yeah, that's true."

"Man, I must've fucked at least three girls in there and never saw it. So weird."

"Ha, I saw one of your shirts in there under the mattress in the back corner. It was dark green, I think. Had a really fake jacket look to it. Big Limpkin patch on the right shoulder with your style."

"With the brown sleeves? Oh, man. I wondered where that went. You guys still have it?"

"Yup, I took it back and ran it through the washer, it smelled awful."

"Badass," Ehano said.

Ronnie shoved the machine again; the orange crate under the back left leg almost came dislodged. Ehano went over to fix it.

"Don't be too rough on that!" Wilmer shouted at them. "You

kids steal enough comics from here already, don't break my pinball machine, too. That's a fucking collector's item."

Ikasa thought about telling him that a machine with a broken leg wasn't a collector's anything, but leaned against the wall instead.

"I got money, old man!" Ikasa said. "Bring me a mango parfait."

"I want my thirty five cents up front," he said.

She walked over, pulled herself up on a stool, and slapped a dollar on the counter.

"I need dimes for change because we want to use your machine more."

"Ain't complaining that you're using it," Wilmer said, walking up to the front door of the shop.

He let Chicomay in, who rushed up to Ikasa's stool and started gnawing on her socks, until she pulled them up out of reach. He settled down, shook water off himself, and started preening.

"Rain's bad, you're all stuck here for at least another hour," Wilmer said. "You just keep him off the counters and out of my shelves, you clean up his shits, and he can hide in here. Could never stand to see a wet hopper in the rain."

"Thanks," Ikasa said.

"Your pop was supposed to be here ten minutes ago," Wilmer said, a pair of headlights washing over him. "Can you call him?"

Ikasa pointed past the old man at her pop, busy trying to get through the front door. Pop slipped inside and threw a wet newspaper into the trash.

"Ten cents," Wilmer said, holding out his hand.

"I got that," Ikasa said, reaching into her pockets.

"Oh, I was joking, they're all soaked, and they're all from two days ago, anyhow," the old man said, nodding. "Boy, you look rattled as a possum got its smoke stash taken."

"Andy stole my shit," Pop said. "All my shit."

"What'd he steal, Pop?"

"He came over to do a little bit of drinking with me and your gramma before work, we went out to the river, Gramma took off back to the house, and he beat the shit out of me and ran off with all my shit, not like twenty minutes ago. Then I realized the fucking fight made me late for work," he said. "So I drove right up here."

He nodded at Wilmer.

"What am I doing today?" he asked.

"Andy said you used to work at a wonder-business," Wilmer said. "You know how to butcher a hog?"

"Sure do, I ran that business. I can do your blocking, inventory, books, cleaning, scraping, sweeping, sewer handling, and hazardous disposal," Pop said. "Not sure if I could cook anything."

"Well, first off, get this little shit a mango parfait," Wilmer said. "Instructions are in the folder behind the counter. Then get to the meat counter and dress those two omitl heads I got in this morning before they go bad."

He gave a little salute, got behind the counter, and started peeling and chopping a mango. Ikasa thought about making it rough for him, but she didn't like the idea of someone, especially Pop, handling her food while upset with her. He kept checking the paper folder full of recipes while he was working, and he narrowed his eyes at the black-and-white picture.

"This is only thirty five cents?" he said. "I got to talk to this man about profit margins."

"For what? Seven cents of fruit, three cents of ice cream?" Ikasa asked.

"Oh, I'm only supposed to use half the mango," Pop said. "Whatever. Told you I was no good with cooking, man!"

"You get better by doing. Already a sight better than that Blue Crab fellow!"

Pop shrugged and slid Ikasa some ice cream, yogurt, and mango all stacked up in a mason jar and handed her a spoon.

"Don't ruin your dinner," he said.

Pop went into the back and Ikasa heard the sound of a cleaver in meat and the solid impact of bone on metal. After a moment she smelled rotten grass and leaned into the scent. She wondered what the organs might be saying before she recalled the earth-angel's statement, then wondered what many interpretations might be found among them. She recalled the argument about the divinations done when she was born and started to wonder how much of it was useful information or just people finding what they wanted to find.

The turtle in her pocket made the sound of a single heartbeat. Someone reminded her that all the knowledge she sought was within her grasp. She clenched her teeth and gripped the mason jar so hard she thought the handle might break off in her palm. Taking in a long breath, she ignored the turtle's cries. She heard instead the echoing rings of bells from the pinball machine and the rain lashing at the roof in sheets.

"Avos!" Ehano shouted.

Ikasa turned back to the machine to see the score placard flopping around like a dying fish. The little silver balls inside reached a peak, slowed, and all lines were yanked away to the door. She felt her entire back grow warm as her skin in the day, and the rain flew into the building. She knew she'd see Andy in the doorway when she turned.

He stood in the door, breathing slowly, rain falling onto him and rolling around in the wrinkles and streaks on his face, through the scar on his lip, down along his chin and into a dark mat over his shirt. His hair hung ragged, unkempt, and streaked with clay hastily torn out. He curled up his nose in disgust, and Ikasa felt it roll over her like a sickening wave. Andy had a few fresh cuts on him and a bruise like an open hand across his cheek; it looked like Pop had run him through a ringer.

"What are you doing back here?" Wilmer said. "I already told you I don't want you hanging around this store anymore."

He pulled something metal out of his belt.

"Where the fuck did you get a gun?" Danny Spider asked.

"It's mine," Ikasa whispered. "It's my gun."

She cast her look over to Pop.

"It's mine! It's my gun! It's the one I lent to Ronnie!"

"What?" Pop howled, more in anger than anything else.

That, too, boiled in the room. Andy pointed the barrel of the .22 at Wilmer, looking like a toy in Blue Crab's enormous hands.

"Shut up, Danny, you did this! And you, old man! You don't talk to me any way I don't want to be talked to!" Andy screamed in a panic. "You got to give me my job back!"

Wilmer put up his hands.

"Now, come on, let's put the gun down," he said.

"You fucking give me my job back, you old shit!" Andy shouted, stepping forward like he was invincible.

He probably was. Ikasa curled her fingers. Pop had his hands in the air, but he glanced quickly at Ikasa.

"Tocalt cihuapilli, cuica," Pop said.

Ikasa nodded and closed her eyes, drifting side to side. She began to sing. Low at first, but slowly rising for a couple of bars.

"Hey-a, hey-yo. Ain't no problems in my eyes," she croaked.

"No problems in my ears," Pop said.

"Got no problems in my bones," Ikasa sang.

Andy cast a glance at her, and that was all it took. Pop took two steps and grabbed Andy's wrist with both his palms, twisting it to Andy's left side. The wrong side. All the lines went away. She felt nothing, a moment in which anything meant everything, and nothing meant anything. Andy lunged forward. The two of them fell back into a soup display and Ikasa heard a horrible crash coupled with a chemical smell that stung the inside of her nose, and all at the same time she heard a scream. Back over at the pinball table, Ronnie was bleeding. He clutched his elbows and sat down on the ground. Ikasa screamed.

"My stomach feels like a pinch," he said, calm enough to be scary.

"You shot him!" she shouted.

Andy dropped the gun and Pop took the moment to deck Andy across the face before rushing over to Ronnie.

"Oh, shit," Andy said, wiping his face with his hands. "Wilmer, you get on the horn right now, call somebody! Call somebody right now!"

Wilmer picked up the phone. Andy continued to mutter to himself and pace. Pop tried to wrangle a handkerchief out of his pocket while he held Ronnie.

"Andy, get over here," he said. "Come over here to your boy."

Andy crouched down, tears in his eyes and the smell of liquor heavy on his hair.

"What? What do I got to do?"

Pop handed Ronnie over to him and gave him the handkerchief.

"Just hold that there, just over the hole," Pop said. "It looks like a gut shot."

"They're on their way, but they're driving all the way from Shimookooah, gonna be about twenty minutes, maybe a bit longer in the rain," Wilmer said. "Cops is on their way, too."

Andy looked up, hurt in every way, forehead scrunched up in a shape that said he'd accept everything that happened without question or complaint. He had control once, he was in charge of the entire situation just a few moments ago and now it was gone, poured out into the floor and mixed with Ronnie's blood. She looked down at her hands. The turtle shell rumbled again like the thunder in her heart, her body. Control was something she'd had all along, in little bits and pieces, scattered around the landscape like fulgurites burned into the sand. By trying to protect Ronnie she'd set in motion the events that led to his injury. Each one, from lending him the gun to telling Pop where the abandoned store sat amid the ribcages of old buildings.

She saw now that the turtle's thundering beats from within her pocket were all her own; she had assigned mana to that which had given up all mana long ago. The only meaning the shell held now was that which those who held the dead animal projected upon the scrimshawed carcass. The Ikasa inside never should, never would, be again, and the illusion of external command over events faded away like the last dream of the night.

"Looks like he passed out," Pop said.

She stood up, face on fire, eyes blurred. She punched the wall. She ran out into the rain, hot like tears rolling down from an ashy cloud. She collided full force with the elephant ears that leaned with conspiratorial glares into the parking lot, and she heard her father behind her.

"Ikasa! Where you going, girl?" he shouted.

She kept running, all the way up to the train tracks, and she stood, straddling the center of the track, holding her turtle rattle up into the sky. Absolute control. Sadie Kaw had given her the clues to having that power, and she hadn't paid attention to them at all. Everything she did drove everything that happened. The dark and intelligent design that had emerged from her thoughts and fears was a beast of her own making. Humans aren't corrupted by magic. Magic is corrupted by humans. She held up the turtle and screeched like a train's whistle.

Pop tackled her to the side and rolled down the thick gravel, both of them gathering up little cuts and bruises as they went. A train rocketed by.

"Why are you calling for Death? That boy ain't going to die!" Pop shouted.

"I got to sing this death song, I got to call her up!" Ikasa said, crawling back up to the tracks. Rain lashed her sides like maddened laughter. "I got to send it away!

"What? Ain't nobody's dead! That boy just got a gut shot, a ricochet gut shot, it bounced up from the concrete to hit him!" Pop said.

Ikasa stood up and held her arms out.

"Mother of Maize! Grandmother of us all!" she shouted, and the storm whirled around her. The rain changed direction, rushing sideways now to land on tree bark, pounding like the drums at a mound sing. She put the turtle down, right on top of a dark brown railroad tie.

She ducked down low as if she were a vulture pecking at a corpse. She spread out her arms, and thus her shawl, as if she were a hunched bird, and did a half circle dance around the turtle, up until tapping on the hard shell with her finger.

"You show a particularly grown-up prowess with what those dances mean," Sadie Kaw said through the rain.

"The white bird in four! I couldn't figure it out before," Ikasa said. "White bird is the eye of death, looking for things that slipped through death's grasp. But White Bird usually appears as a man!"

Sadie Kaw walked up and shrugged.

"Sometimes the magic works, sometimes it doesn't," she said.

Her normally dingy cossie looked almost clean. Shining. Bone-white, and dangling braids of hair tied off with ribs, shells, leaves, and skulls. She was followed by a flock of grackles, and the rain refused to touch any part of her. She wore a skin cloak that was black, but mottled with the shining stars above.

"Sadie Kaw!" Ikasa said. "I did everything you asked! But I need a favor from you!"

"What's that?" the woman asked.

"Take this turtle?" Ikasa said. She picked up the mummy, and there was a moment where the power it held over her made her hesitate for one more moment before she dumped it into Sadie Kaw's waiting hands. "It's the orgus and memories of Ikasa Spider, the one from the previous world."

"I've been looking for this for nearly, oh, I've forgotten how long. A sore spot on my record," she said.

"White Bird is the messenger for death. Sees all the little critters and people she missed, makes sure they get where they're going," Ikasa said. "On my first day I saw five blackbirds, and one of them was a big white crow. I wondered what it meant, because it meant something."

She looked at the ground, all worn from foot traffic up and down the bridge.

"Up until now, I thought maybe I couldn't control anything, but now I've seen that just touching the water makes the whole lake ripple," Ikasa said to her father. "I lent Ronnie my gun. Everything changes, the potential for Andy getting a weapon increases. Andy gets fired because you're looking for a job to help get ready for the store, Wilmer's looking for an excuse to fire Andy because he's a lazy klutz, and Wilmer's is right across from the store where you're getting set up. It's all because of me, you get it?"

"But calling Death up to come take you away isn't the answer!" Pop said, panting.

"You don't get it, do you?" Sadie Kaw said. "I bet he doesn't talk to you nearly as much as he ought to."

Ikasa nodded.

"Yeah."

"Your family's Maize, isn't it?" she asked Danny. "Before you got married."

"Yeah," he said. "Maize."

She took off the burlap shawl covered in stars that she wore about her neck and tossed it to him.

"Take that shit," she said. "Family treasures and all. I hid a boy under it once. He destroyed the world even after I warned him about it. Think of it like. Well, it's giving you a family treasure back. It's a piece of the cloak of night Spider's husband uses to drape over the world so he can take a break."

He nodded. She looked down at Ikasa.

"You know what?" Sadie Kaw said, shaking the box turtle at her. "You're a good kid! A bad Spider, but a good kid. Danny Spider! You have a good kid. Tell her mom that, too."

"I will," he said.

Sadie Kaw disappeared into the forest, followed by bones and dead leaves. Ikasa frowned as she walked away. Rain clouded her escape into the darkness.

"What was that?" Pop asked.

"Just me being allowed to take charge of a situation for once," Ikasa said. She breathed heavily, lungs hot and rebelling at her demands.

He took her hand, and they started to walk back to the Wilmer's. She stopped and looked back into the dark of the night through the rain.

"Shit!"

"What?" Pop asked.

"She still didn't declare me an adult," Ikasa said.

ABOUT THE AUTHOR

Adam Thaxton, 6th generation Floridian, is an artist and writer. He is the author of *Ten Ghost: A Novel.* This novel, *Spider & Turtle,* is the first in a series of novels set in the swamps and pine barrens of a strangely familiar landscape to those who know Florida well. Adam lives in the Orlando area.